Also by Taran Denner

The Defectors
Enemy Inside
The Last Uprising
Exposure

Recon

Book One of The Fringe

By Tarah Benner

To Andrew and Nicole — my best friends and favorite critics.

The atomic bomb made the prospect of future
war unendurable.
It has led us up those last few steps to the mountain pass, and beyond there
is a different country.

— J. Robert Oppenheimer

one

Eli

It always goes quiet during a fight.

They tell you everything slows down. Your heart rate speeds up. Your muscles tense, and your vision zeros in on the threat. That's all true.

What they don't tell you is how the fight makes you nothing and everything all at once.

They hang a bright florescent light over the ring so you can't forget you're under a microscope. You can't see them, but they're watching you.

If you get greedy or try to take something for yourself, they'll send you out to remind you that you're only alive because they allow you to be. They own you, but ultimately, you're expendable.

The crowd sees none of this. To them, you're fascinating and powerful: the man who beat the machine, the fastest race horse.

That's enough to make anyone drunk on their own ego, except you don't see the crowd. You don't even hear them shouting.

Tonight, it's just me and him.

Miles is six feet four inches of pure muscle hulking in the corner, his dark skin glistening with sweat. I'm only a couple inches shorter but much leaner. This is an illegal fight — he's not even in my weight class.

I don't know how he got so big. He must be stealing rations again. In Recon, they give you just enough to stay strong, but not strong enough to run very far.

He's tatted up from hip to shoulder, and I'm probably the only one who notices the solid "B" stamped over his heart in the stormy haze of ink.

This isn't just a fight. Miles is my only friend. He fights as a big "fuck you" to the board, which is funny, considering it's only at their whim that these fights take place. We have to pay off the controllers with a cut of the bets, but underground fights among tier-three workers are an open secret.

Miles fights in the hope that he'll be injured badly enough to be excused from duty for a month. One month isn't a lot, but it can mean a lifetime in Recon. A month off duty means one less deployment.

It's the final round, which means I have to make it count to get him roughed up bad enough. My left eye is starting to swell, and he's got a fat lip, but those hits were just to get the crowd warmed up.

I regulate my breathing, waiting for the bell. Down here, I don't have to pretend to be grateful or functional. I don't have to think; I can just fight. I don't have to be the good soldier. I can be ruthless, angry, off the leash.

That's why you're everything in a fight.

When that bell rings, I become the man they made me — the one whose only purpose is to kill. That's how they make you nothing.

The ref steps out of the way, and Miles comes at me. He's all offense, and for good reason. He's the killer whale in the ring — the top of the food chain — whereas I'm the great white shark that stalks its prey with patience.

He's not as slow as the other sluggers, but all I have to do is dodge Miles's brick-wall punches and wait for him to tire himself out. I can't lose focus for even a second, because one well-placed hit from him, and it's lights out — see you tomorrow.

As we circle, I try to forget his laundry list of weaknesses. When you train together every day and fight at night, it's not fair to take that cheap shot to his bruised rib or target his weak left knee. He knows I won't hurt him. I don't fight dirty against other Recon.

Miles lunges; I dodge. He delivers a cross. I block it and aim a jab. He's undefended, but he barely feels it. I throw a round kick. His knee buckles, but he recovers and swipes at me again. I duck and deliver two punches to his side.

I can tell when he's had enough. He's just fast enough to aim an uppercut that I can't avoid completely. It glances off my chin, but it still sends me flying back against the ropes.

Miles punches again, but this time I block his hit and strike my elbow across his face, meeting him halfway with a punch to the gut. I grab his shoulders, pushing him down so I can jab the back of his neck with my elbow. He falls to one knee, and I get him with a right hook.

A slightly better friend would give him a second to recover, but I want this to end. I bring my elbow down on his spine again, and he crumples onto the mat. He taps out, and the crowd goes wild.

The sounds all flood in at once: the cheers, the boos, the drunken insults from the Exterior Maintenance and Construction guys. My arm is yanked into the air, and I try to keep my expression neutral so no one can see me coming down from the adrenalin high.

"Aww. Fuck you, man," Miles groans.

"You wanted me to drag it out?" I murmur, not making eye contact with the expired slab of meat on the mat.

"You could at least . . . let me get one good hit in . . . so I don't look like . . . a pussy."

I grin despite my best efforts and reach down to pull Miles to his feet. He spits out his mouth guard, and one of our guys in the corner yanks off his gloves.

As if anyone could mistake Miles for a pussy. He's the scariest guy here.

"One good hit is too many," I say.

He rolls his eyes, and a line of blood dribbles from his nose. "Is Brooke here?"

"Why would she be?"

He nods once and looks at the mat. Brooke is tier two. They shouldn't even be seeing each other anymore, and Miles knows it.

I climb down, and people are slapping my shoulders and pumping my arm. I resist the urge to swat them like flies. It's mostly burnout chicks with vacant eyes and tier-three workers looking for a little distraction. Most of them are just trying to forget they're serving a life sentence at the bottom of the ladder.

I know I should be grateful. The compound saved me from a slow, hard death on the Fringe — or at least it made my death a little slower and easier.

Once a month, I'm sent out under the pretense of gathering data on radiation levels, air quality, and wildlife. But in reality, Recon's job is to defend the compound against some of the same thugs I used to run with on the Fringe.

Miles drags himself over to the ropes, and I help him down. If it were me, I'd just go home and ice my face, but you don't get exempt from deployment without recommendation from the medical ward.

The clean, smart doctors up there will patch him up, shake their heads, and go home to their families, feeling oh so lucky and fulfilled. They escaped this life.

The crowd clears away, and I sink down on the rickety bench outside the ring to mop the sweat off my face. The referee appears with a battered credit transfer device. He's probably pissed he has to work late. EnComm merchants have lives and families — not just a job. They sell their wares and then close up shop and go home.

Numbers flash on the screen as he adds fifty credits to my account. When he walks away, I put on my interface and automatically transfer twenty-five to Miles's account.

We always split the winnings, no matter who ends up a drooling pile of garbage on the mat. Not that the ref would care. All he wants is a good fight. That's what everybody wants.

Now that it's almost midnight, the pounding of the bass from Neverland has reached a teeth-rattling decibel. It shakes the grimy walls around the ring and climbs up the foundation to meld with the beats emanating from the levels above.

I hate the wary looks the tier-two people give us when I drag Miles onto the megalift. EnComm, Manufacturing, Operations, Control — they're comfortably middle of the pack. Their lives are good enough that they don't go making trouble, but they try to ignore people like us because they know it could just as easily have been them. Every time the lift stops on the way to the upper tunnels, the people who get on are cleaner and more domesticated.

Tier-one people take one look at us and avert their eyes. They know who we are, but they don't like to think about it. Systems, Information, and Health and Rehab workers are as privileged as it gets in the compound. They don't want to have to look at the people whose job it is to die slowly of radiation poisoning on their behalf.

The megalift stops on one of the dorm levels, and the loud,

upbeat music rattles the lift shaft. Everyone's partying tonight because tomorrow is Bid Day, a sick tradition that makes my stomach clench with dread.

The doors open, and two girls stumble in giggling. They're covered in glitter and wearing short red nurses' dresses. Their laughter stops when they see Miles hanging off my shoulder, and the blond one hiccups loudly.

I see it in their eyes; they can't wait until tomorrow. All the higher-ed kids are living it up in anticipation of their bright futures in a tier-one section. They think their future is set.

I was that certain once. I'd gone to my Bid Day Eve party wearing blue. But nothing ever shakes out the way you think it will.

Right now, they're still friends — equals — but that's all about to change.

Tomorrow, each section will place their bids based on recruits' Vocational Aptitude scores. Most higher-ed kids take classes geared toward a tier-one or tier-two section, but the kids who score low on their VocAps usually end up in tier three — Recon, ExCon, or Waste Management.

After the bidding ceremony, I'll get seven shiny new twenty-one-year-olds. It's the third class I'll be tasked with training, but it's futile, really. Most of the kids from my first year as a lieutenant are already dead.

I made a mistake with that first class — I let myself get attached. I told myself I would train them *better* so they could live longer, but the numbers don't lie.

Early death is a statistical certainty in Recon.

We go out into the Fringe so the rest of the compound can sleep soundly at night. We tell them the outside will be inhabitable soon, even though none of them will leave the compound in their lifetime. We *don't* tell them who we're chasing away — what they should really be afraid of.

When we reach the medical ward, I'm relieved to see there are still some real nurses on duty. They rush out when they hear the lift, but the urgency leaves their eyes the second they realize we're just Recon. We're always in the medical ward for something.

A woman in red scrubs comes over with an automatic wheel-chair trailing behind her. She helps me lower Miles into it, and he zooms off behind her to an exam room.

He doesn't expect me to wait for him, but I'm always wound up after a fight — too high on adrenalin to stop moving.

It's late, and the ward is mostly deserted. It's clean and bright, just like all the upper levels. I can see blurred outlines of people in red moving behind the frosted glass walls like colorful ghosts. This is their life: bright and clean and organized.

The automatic lights flicker on as I walk down the empty tunnel. I've been here too many times to count, and I know where every door goes. My body is tired, and my feet carry me to my usual destination without consulting my brain.

I pass the intensive-care unit and an entire tunnel of closed doors to the only part of the medical ward where people are living instead of dying.

I rest my head against the glass and feel the smile tugging at the corners of my mouth. Sometimes I like to come here when I'm admitted postexposure just to remind myself that there's still goodness in the world.

Three perfect bundles are lying in identical white boxes. They don't know they're already marked by their sections instead of their names. They don't understand that hours after their birth, they already have their place in the world. It may change slightly when they receive their bid, but not significantly.

They're Fourth Gen. They won't remember the barrage of nuclear attacks that leveled most of the country during Death Storm or the years the compound was on the verge of collapse.

Two of them have their little eyes squeezed shut, but one is staring up at me. Just out of the womb, he knows I don't belong here. There are no Recon babies — no tier-three babies at all. That's no accident.

There's a second room with a window like this one, but I've never seen it occupied. It's separated from the main nursery by six inches of glass, and the incubator is covered in a big plastic bubble.

It's where Fringe babies are monitored before they're sent to the Institute to integrate with the others, but we haven't had a Fringe baby in two decades. I was fourteen when they brought me in. Harper Riley was probably the last one, but she's not a baby anymore.

two

Harper

I hate the trip down to the lower levels almost more than I hate Neverland. It feels like descending into Hell.

Sawyer and I are alone in the megalift, watching the white number over the doors tick down as we descend into the bowels of the compound.

She's unusually quiet tonight, and I know her nerves are as frayed as mine — maybe even more.

We've both been on edge all week because everything we've done for the past three years has been leading up to tomorrow. Well, technically, today. It's oh-five hundred, and I still haven't slept.

All the late nights studying and years of putting up with Systems-track douchebags who were raised in tier one will be worth it when I receive my bid.

Systems *has* to bid on me. I'm the best developer in our year. Writing code is all I know how to do. There is no plan B.

I wipe my sweaty palms on my pants and give Sawyer a strained smile. I know she's still thinking about her VocAps score — wondering if she did well enough to attract the attention of Health and Rehab. She has no reason to worry, though; she studied her ass off for that test, and she's first in our class.

The megalift stops on the ground level, and I glance over my shoulder to check for controllers before hopping the scuffed silver turnstile in front of the frozen escalator.

We reach the Underground platform, and our footsteps echo loudly in the black abyss. The faint blue light of my interface illuminates the long dark tunnel, and I get a shiver, as I always do staring into the emptiness.

Only Operations workers are allowed to be here. If you take the stairs down from the ground level, you'll reach tier-three living quarters. But on this side, you can see the supply train roll out, carrying goods to neighboring compounds in Nevada, Arizona, and New Mexico. It's also the fastest way to Neverland.

The door to the emergency stairwell groans loudly as I yank the sticky handle, and I have the immediate urge to disinfect my hands.

I take the steps quickly, not pausing to notice the way the temperature drops the farther we go or the distant vibrations beneath my feet. As the beam of my interface bounces off the dirty walls, the faded layers of spray-painted swear words leer at me in warning.

They never closed off the old Underground tunnels after one collapsed, which allowed a whole new world to take root in the compound: a den of drugs and sex and an endless parade of people trying to numb themselves to reality.

By the time we reach the bottom, the vibrations are rattling my teeth through the heavy steel door. I drag in a shallow breath. I don't know how people enjoy this. The loud music, the darkness, the flashing party lights — it makes me feel panicked, aggressive, and a little bit sick.

Sawyer shrinks back against the bottom step automatically. If I'm out of my element down here, for her it's like taking a spacewalk without a suit.

Neither of us is much of a partier, but I practically had to drag her out of our dorm to go find Celdon.

He's already on thin ice with Systems. Celdon is a year older than us, which means he's being sworn in tomorrow. He should have spent his gap year learning everything he could about network security, but he chose to spend it partying.

That all ends tomorrow. He'll start his job as a penetration tester — an ethical hacker, as he calls it — or risk not getting paid.

Before we go in, I double-check to make sure Sawyer's right behind me and almost laugh at her appearance: blue Oxford shirt, neat black bob, thick nerd glasses. My tall boots and fake leather jacket are a little edgier, but anyone with eyes will be able to tell we don't belong here.

As I pull the door open, the wave of music and body odor almost knocks me over.

Bodies — bodies everywhere. That's always what shocks me about Neverland.

There are so many people crammed together down below that it's a miracle anything ever gets done in the upper tunnels. More overwhelming than the sheer number of people is the conspicuous lack of clothing. Most of the men are shirtless, and women are draped over their laps and shoulders wearing nothing but underwear, microskirts, or — as I've seen once or twice — body paint.

It isn't just burnouts who hang out down here, though. Celdon swears he once saw the Secretary of Security, but you can never really be sure with Celdon. He was probably burned out of his mind at the time.

I let my long dark hair form a curtain over my face so I can avoid the gaze of a few sleazy guys leaning against the wall. Pushing my way through the crowd, I cringe as I brush up against strange, sweaty bodies.

My chest tightens at the thought of being so far underground packed together with all these people. I don't know how the tunnels haven't collapsed, but I don't want to be down here when the train comes rattling through the new tunnels.

Every few seconds, a flash of silvery light punctuates the disorienting darkness, and I fight the urge to throw up. The crowd is too dense to see if Celdon is among the mass of gyrating bodies, but I know where he likes to hang out.

I trip down the empty train tunnel, eyes raking the shadows for a flash of blond hair. The pounding of the bass echoing off the concrete is already giving me a splitting headache.

We need to find him *now*.

Broken plastic and stray pills crunch underfoot — cheap uppers, by the looks of it. As we walk deeper into the tunnel, I switch on my interface again, and Sawyer does the same. The lights from the main dance floor don't reach this far, and it's nearly pitch black. A few people slumped against the walls have had the same idea, but most of them are paired off in the shadows, making out and passing pills.

Sawyer moves her head, and the light from her interface catches a flash of gold down under the platform.

"Celdon!" I yell, relief pouring through me.

"Hey!" slurs a guy several yards down the tunnel. "I'll be Celdon, sweetheart!"

"Fuck off!"

I jump down from the platform and feel my boot squash real flesh and bone.

"Oaff!"

I've landed on some random guy passed out in the gravel.

"Sorry," I mutter, nudging the stranger out of the way with

my boot. "Celdon!"

The beam of my interface hits the blond guy's face, and I realize it *is* him, though he doesn't look good. His messy hair is plastered to his forehead with sweat, and his heavily lidded eyes are half-closed.

"Harper . . ." He flashes the shadow of a grin, and his pale chest heaves through his orange mesh shirt.

"Celdon. Come on," I groan, trying to pull him into a seated position.

I turn to Sawyer, but she's already crouched on his other side, his wrist in her hands. She's taking his pulse.

"He's messed up, but he'll live."

"Huh-hey, Sawyer," Celdon chortles, his eyes rolling over to her. "You're looking *super* Asian today."

"You're looking like a super fucking waste of space today," she says, punctuating her last words with a good-natured kick to his leg.

"Come on," I choke, my back aching as I pull him up from under his shoulders. He's all skin and bones with an enviable washboard stomach, but he towers over me by several inches. Even with Sawyer supporting his weight on the other side, he's heavy.

I half prop him against the concrete platform and drag him up the rest of the way.

"I'm comin' back for *you*, sex-ay," he slurs to the guy I accidentally landed on.

"Ugh," Sawyer groans. "Seriously? You could do so much better."

With Celdon draped between us, we drag him down the tunnel back toward the main dance floor, moving like a couple of drunks.

When we reach the crowd, I try to hold my breath as my senses are overwhelmed by the mix of cheap perfume, sweat, urine, and booze. The bodies press closer to us, and I almost lose Celdon as he stiffens and tries to pull out of my grip. He's still burned, and he wants to party.

"Nope!" Sawyer snaps, pushing against his side with an impressive amount of force. Celdon staggers back into me, and I make a mental note to slam his head into a door when we reach the upper tunnels.

We finally get him to the stairwell, and I toss him onto the filthy steps to give my back a break. He falls over onto his elbows, grinning stupidly. Now I can see just how burned he is.

"Come on, Harper," he slurs. "You really gotta loosen up. It's your last hoorah before Bid Day. Pretty soon, you'll be like me."

He holds out his wrists, locked in imaginary handcuffs, and I do a quick scan for track marks. "A fucking *slave* to Systems."

"Lucky you," I mutter.

If he keeps talking, I'm going to kick him. Celdon is effortlessly smart and obscenely talented, and he wastes it. I would *kill* to be in Systems. Hell, everyone wants to get a tier-one bid, and no one who does wastes their gap year partying.

Most Systems recruits are too busy trying to get up to speed, Health and Rehab recruits have to intern in the medical ward, and the Information kids usually get started on their first research project. But playing by the rules just isn't Celdon's style.

"They bought me," he mumbles. "They *own* me."

"Yeah . . . a year ago. Most people have been working since then."

At first I think he's going into one of his drug-induced fits of rage, but then his serious mask slips, and he smiles.

At the sight of his stupid lopsided grin, all my anger fizzles out. He's an idiot for wasting away his gap year, but he is my oldest friend.

We grew up in the Institute together because we were both wards of the compound. Celdon gets me better than anyone because only he knows what it's like to try to claw your way out of that place and make something of yourself. Unfortunately, his self-worth is sometimes overrun by his childhood demons.

Somehow, we manage to yank him up three flights of stairs and get him onto the megalift without running into a controller.

When the lift opens onto Celdon's level, it takes my eyes a moment to adjust to the bright, clean aesthetic of Systems. The upper tunnels are a labyrinth of pristine white walls and frosted glass, and my heart beats a little faster as I take it all in.

In a few hours, this could be my home.

A handful of early risers throw us wary looks as we shove Celdon down the tunnel toward his compartment. I'm sure they're used to him stumbling up here at all hours in various stages of undress, but the mesh shirt still attracts a lot of attention.

Celdon's studio is twice the size of the dorm room I share with Sawyer, with a window looking out on the Fringe. It came pre-furnished and painstakingly decorated in a minimalist style, but you'd never be able to tell. Empty Energelz tubes lie everywhere, scattered among the empty canteen takeout containers and wads of dirty clothing.

I fish out a fairly unwrinkled white shirt from Celdon's closet and grab his favorite pair of pants. I drape the clean clothes over the bathroom door and shove him fully clothed into the shower.

Celdon swears loudly as the cold water pelts him clean in fifteen seconds flat, and I throw a towel straight at his face and slam the door shut.

He emerges a few minutes later, clearly exhausted. But at least now he's clean, dressed, and body glitter–free.

"What's with the attitude, Riles?" he slurs, toweling his hair dry and grinning lethargically.

I square my shoulders, unwilling to be worn down by his pet names and bullshit. "Do you know what day it is?"

He rolls his eyes. "*Yes.* Call the media. It's Bid Day!" he says with a burst of fake enthusiasm. He holds out an imaginary microphone. "Har-per Ri-ley — you just got a bid from Systems. What are you gonna do next?"

I bite back a laugh. "It's not funny. This is a big day for you, too. You have to be there."

He lets out a heavy whole-body sigh. "Yes, I know. I'm being sworn in. Logic . . . service . . . strength . . . all that jazz. Not all of us are so excited to sign our lives away."

"Screw you."

I glare at Celdon, but an unexpected pang of nostalgia hits me in the gut. This could be the last time the three of us are together.

After the bidding ceremony, we'll each go our separate ways. If I get into Systems, I'll see Celdon every day, but Sawyer will be ushered into the medical community and have little time to hang out with us. Being separated from the rest of our classmates doesn't bother me, but Sawyer has been by my side for the last three years.

Celdon can sense an onslaught of emotions coming on and clears his throat loudly.

"What?" snaps Sawyer, completely lost in thought. She's been pacing by the door for the last several minutes. "We should go. If we hurry, we can hit the canteen before the ceremony."

I grin. She's even more nervous than I am. But then *everything* makes Sawyer nervous.

Celdon tosses the towel onto the floor and grabs the rumpled white blazer lying over the back of a chair. "Amen. Let's roll."

three

Harper

W hen we emerge from Celdon's compartment, the tunnel is already crammed with people scurrying toward the canteen. We stand out in the sea of white pants and jackets, and I feel a swell of envy.

The Systems workers carry themselves with a quiet dignity, exuding confidence and intelligence. They have it all: a large stipend, better food, beautiful living quarters, respect.

When they walk, they nod politely at each other in greeting, but they aren't boisterous or overly friendly. That suits me. I'm not known for my friendliness.

It's a long wait for the megalift, and I spend that time scoping out the Systems people, wondering if my direct command is among them. One woman with her hair pulled back in a tight bun eyes Celdon ruefully, and her ID badge says she's supposed to be *his* direct command in penetration testing. Celdon is oblivious as usual, but at least he looks sober.

When we reach the canteen, the line of white polyester is quickly engulfed by a mishmash of other colors: red and black, green and yellow, blue, orange, and gray. It's a little less luxurious down here, and all the furnishings are designed to be functional rather than beautiful.

I stop in line in front of the scanner, waiting for the machine to read my ID. My name and picture flash up on the computer screen, and an Operations woman in light blue serves up my morning bowl of mush. It's a basic higher-ed meal: rice, a protein cube, and half a bowl of green algae. All the calories we need — no more, no less.

"Hey," says Celdon, flashing a smile at the burly bearded man behind the counter. "Didn't see you last night."

The man shifts uncomfortably, and I roll my eyes. Celdon always confronts people from Neverland up above when they clearly want to forget they were ever there in the first place.

He upends the ladle in Celdon's bowl again, and I see the flash of blue-green algae I don't recognize.

People move through the food line and split off to sit with their sections. Sawyer and I sit with the other higher-eds, and Celdon plops down next to us.

No one pays him any attention. Most recruits align themselves with their sections during gap year, but not him. And though Celdon rarely makes an appearance at mealtimes, everyone knows he's in limbo.

"What's that?" I ask, pointing at the slimy bluish stuff in his bowl.

"It's good for hangovers," he says, shoveling it into his mouth. "Tastes like shit, though."

I shake my head. People are always doing Celdon favors — myself included. There's just something about him that makes you want to strangle him one second and take care of him the next.

I eat my food slowly and deliberately, fighting the nausea creeping up from nerves and a lack of sleep. The higher-ed table is buzzing with anxious chatter, and Sawyer is rattling off the names of other people pursuing Health and Rehab and Systems, weighing the odds that they scored higher than us under her breath.

I try to ignore her. When Sawyer goes into panic mode, she reverts to calculating her odds of failure and laying out all the possibilities, whereas I just want everybody to leave me alone.

I stab my fork into my protein cube, and Celdon's elbow pokes me in the ribs. When I make eye contact, I can tell he's been staring at me for several minutes. He's wearing this look of pure understanding that so few people get to see.

"Hey, don't worry," he says quietly. "You'll get a good bid. Systems would be idiotic not to snap you up."

I drag in a deep breath, which is a mistake. I'm teetering on the verge of a total meltdown.

"You don't know what my score was," I remind him through clenched teeth.

He rolls his eyes and fixes me with that megawatt smile. "I know it was off the charts."

"No, you don't."

Celdon smacks a hand to his chest violently enough to make a few antsy higher-eds look over at us. "Of *course* I do." He looks genuinely offended. "I taught you everything you know, didn't I?"

I let out a choked laugh and shove him away — hard — trying to rein in my reluctant smile. He catches himself gracefully and spins around to harass Sawyer about her calculations so I can finish my breakfast in peace.

Once he's got her worked up to the point that she's about to start pulling her hair out, we join the crowd jostling toward the main hall.

The Entertainment and Commerce people are practically bouncing off the walls in their colorful clothing — all high fives and bright smiles that look out of place next to a swarm of grungy tier-three workers shuffling along in front of us.

Tier three encompasses the worst sections in the compound: Waste Management, Reconnaissance, and Exterior Maintenance and Construction. Even though today is considered a compound holiday, Bid Day isn't a celebration to them. They don't view recruitment as an opportunity the way tier-one workers do. To them, it's a life sentence.

Excited voices bounce off the frosted glass ceiling in the entryway, and bodies push together as though we're down in Neverland.

Beads of sweat spring up all over my forehead, and I can feel the heat rising up my chest. I tug my hair into a ponytail and concentrate on holding down the breakfast that's threatening to make an appearance.

We push our way into the hall, and I'm immediately blinded by the natural light spilling in through the full-length windows. We're surrounded by a panoramic view of the rugged, burnt-orange terrain of the Fringe — frightening in its severe beauty and vast open spaces.

Celdon gives me a two-finger salute as he sidles off to sit with Systems. Sawyer and I take our seats in the front rows among the other higher-eds, not saying a word.

By oh-nine hundred, the hall is standing-room only. A few thousand people are packed into the stadium-style benches — proud parents, friends, last year's recruits, and old people who have nothing better to do. The board members are seated behind the raised platform, dressed in their crisp taupe suits, and the ten senior leaders are in the very middle of the room with white paddles resting on their laps.

They're not talking — just staring straight ahead at the stage. A few consult their interfaces to review the recruits their section wants to bid on. Interface communication will not be allowed once the ceremony starts.

President Ferguson is the first of the compound leaders to speak — a long-winded rant about tradition and duty and the values of the compound.

He's pandering to the tier-two sections, yammering on about all the value Entertainment and Commerce businesses provide the compound, the goods Manufacturing produces, how Control works tirelessly to keep us safe, and the importance of Operations' work within the compound.

What a load of bull. He'll spend the year leading up to election courting the tier-one sections, but no board member is stupid enough to neglect tier two. Their votes are weighted less than tier one, but they're overwhelming in their numbers. Tier three can't even make a dent in the polls with their votes. I can't say it's completely fair, but it makes sense. Tier one and tier two have always had the most influence because they're the smartest.

After a few minutes, I start tuning out the president's voice. I just want to hear my bids and get on with my life.

Systems *has* to bid on me. I'm one of the few who've taken all the classes. I'm better than anyone in our year.

Shooting for Systems is the riskiest choice, but at worst, I should receive a good bid from Control. A lot of the classes on emergency protocol and intracompound law overlap.

Sure, Control is a tier-two section and controllers are terrible people, but it's a good stepping stone to a position on the board, if I wanted.

By the end of Ferguson's speech, my nerves are stretched so far they're threatening to snap.

Even if I bombed the test, Entertainment and Commerce wouldn't be terrible. At least I wouldn't get stuck ladling slop in the canteen as an Operations lackey.

Now Sullivan Taylor, Undersecretary of Vocational Placement, is delivering his speech about the solemn duty entrusted to each section. He's a pale, slight man with a thin mustache and surprisingly kind eyes. He's the only board member who doesn't look like a khaki-clad robot, even if he still sounds like one.

I zone out again after the bit about the complexity of data, information technology, and network security. I don't care much about the rest of the sections.

What is taking so long? Bid Day ceremonies already push five hours — five hours of sweaty palms, tedious bidding procedures, and frayed nerves.

Finally, he begins calling names in alphabetical order.

There's nothing like Bid Day. Each round of bidding lasts no more than two minutes — two minutes of the most intense scrutiny, where a person's future is decided based on a single number.

Some recruits try to stand with confidence to show the senior leaders they're a worthy investment. But as the bidding drags on and a group of strangers vies for their future, their faces get paler, and their shoulders sag lower. When the gavel hits the table to end the bids, some people cheer, and some people cry. So undignified.

I hear "Lyang, Sawyer" and see Sawyer's shiny black bob bouncing up the aisle. She looks *terrified* — more scared than I've ever seen her.

"Sawyer Lyang has been pursuing the Health and Rehabilitation track, with a score of . . . ninety-four."

I jump to my feet and whoop loudly. A few new Health and Rehab recruits nearby join in, but Sawyer zeroes in on my face. She looks ecstatic. A ninety-four is fantastic. She's a lock.

"Let's start the bidding at . . . sixty-five thousand."

I cheer again. Sixty-five thousand is an *unheard of* starting bid for a new recruit.

"Sixty-five thousand," says the woman from Health and Rehab.

"Seventy." It's the man from Information.

"Seventy-five."

"Eighty."

Of course Information would want Sawyer for the research branch, but the Health and Rehab woman is undeterred. "Ninety-five."

I can't stop the grin that's spreading across my face. Even if Information has the funding to bid more than ninety-five thousand on one recruit, there's no way Health and Rehab is letting her slip away.

"Ninety-five going once . . . twice . . . Sawyer Lyang has officially been recruited for Health and Rehabilitation."

I scream and stomp my feet, attracting a few irritated looks from the end half of the alphabet still stewing in their own misery. Sawyer is glowing with pride as the undersecretary lowers the blood-red silk cord over her head. I'm smiling so hard my mouth hurts.

She walks down the side of the stage to shake hands with the woman who just bid on her, and when she sits down between two men in red scrubs, my heart swells.

Half the battle is over. We can still both get what we want.

The undersecretary blazes through the Ms and Ns. The longer the ceremony goes on, the faster the bids move. People shuffle in and out, bored by the lack of crying recruits and surprise upsets in the bidding.

One guy I know scores a sixty-two. He only receives one bid.

Soon there are just two people left to go before me.

I'm gripping the edge of my chair so tightly that angry red

indentations are carved into my palms.

"Riley, Harper."

I jump to my feet, nearly flipping my chair over in the process. My legs are asleep from sitting for three and a half hours. Despite my shaky legs, I reach the stage in seconds.

Did I run up here? The hall is quiet and still. Half the crowd has already dispersed. I glance around hoping to see Celdon, but he's just a single particle in a cluster of white-clad bodies.

The metal steps groan a little as I step up. The platform feels impossibly high. I glance over at the senior leaders, my eyes settling on a dark-skinned man in a white suit with a severe goatee.

"Harper Riley has been pursuing Systems, with a score of . . . forty-six."

Hushed whispers fill the hall, then silence.

I wait.

Nobody cheers or claps.

I'm sure I've heard it wrong. It sounded as though he said forty-six, when I know it had to be ninety-six.

Then the man in the white suit lifts the corners of his mouth in a short chuckle. He doesn't move his paddle.

"Let's start the bidding at . . . twenty-two thousand."

My stomach hits the floor. I'm going to vomit.

Twenty-two thousand? I've never heard such a ridiculously low starting bid. It's insulting. It has to be a joke.

"Twenty-two thousand," says the scruffy man from ExCon.

My face burns with shame. A few snickers erupt from the pool of waiting recruits. There's no way I'm going to spend my life doing manual labor outside the compound.

I glance at the man from Systems, but he doesn't even blink. He's lost interest and seems to be peeling the white backing off his paddle.

"Thirty thousand," says a sharp female voice. I look over. It's the woman from Recon.

This can't be happening. I want to flee the stage.

"Thirty-five thousand," says the ExCon man. It's almost the end of the bidding ceremony. He has money to burn.

"Sixty thousand," snaps the Recon woman.

My limbs are so hot, I'm sure I'm going to burst into flames. The murmurs are growing louder.

"Sixty thousand going once . . . going twice . . . Harper Riley has officially been recruited for Reconnaissance."

The gavel hits the table, and suddenly the lights are much too bright. I don't feel hot with nerves anymore. I feel cold and clammy. It's as though someone has sucked all the oxygen out of the room.

Someone clears his throat across the platform. The undersecretary is standing at the other end, holding up a silvery-gray cord.

No. This isn't right. I'm supposed to be in Systems. I killed that test. And even if I hadn't killed it, I couldn't have scored lower than a fifty. I don't know anyone who's ever scored that low. I didn't even know that was possible.

My feet are moving somehow, and still no one has clapped for me. The twisted silk cord falls heavily onto my shoulders, and I stumble toward the opposite end of the stage.

As I step down from the platform, I catch a glimpse of blond hair off to my right. Celdon is standing in the crowd. He meets my gaze and shakes his head once as if to say, "What the hell happened?"

It's customary to shake hands with the leader who places the winning bid, so I shuffle over to the cluster of chairs, trying to avoid the smug grin of the Systems leader.

The woman who bid on me is in her late twenties — the

youngest one there, but old by Recon standards. When she stands, she's so slight that she only comes up to my nose.

She has dark hair pulled back into a tight bun and severe, predatory eyes. The patches on her uniform tell me she's achieved the highest rank in Recon. My brain supplies a name: Commander Jayden Pierce.

She thrusts out her hand, and I take it reluctantly. She crushes my knuckles.

I hate her immediately.

The undersecretary has already called another girl's name, and I realize I have no clue where to sit.

I can't go back to sit with the other higher-eds. I have to sit with my section. Out of the corner of my eye, I see a cluster of guys in gray outfits sitting near the back. Before I even make a decision, my feet are carrying me over there.

There are a few girls in the mix, but they're all built like lacrosse players with a good twenty pounds of muscle on me. They give me an appraising look, and I take a seat next to a well-built guy with short dark hair.

He's sitting with his long legs spread wide and his arms folded across his chest, as though he's fed up with the ceremony. He has sharp cheekbones and a mouth that's set in a permanent scowl. Not friendly.

When I settle back against the chair, I feel his eyes on me. He can't be more than a few years older, but the patches on his uniform indicate he's a lieutenant.

I glance at him out of the corner of my eye. He looks angry and slightly curious, but then he shifts his body away from me.

I ignore this obvious slight and stare straight ahead, trying not to cry. I drag in a deep breath to steady myself and focus on the last stragglers walking across the stage to receive their bids.

But no matter how hard I try, I can't shake the horrible mantra playing in my head: Forty-six. Failure.

A forty-six? How is that even possible? You'd have to be brain-dead to score that low.

As the last new recruit crosses the stage and takes the white cord — my white cord — the lieutenant leans over and mutters just loud enough for me to hear, "Welcome to hell, Cadet."

four

Eli

After Systems plucks the last shaking, pitiful recruit, the undersecretary explains the rules of gap year: The recruits can take the time to prepare themselves for the section they've been placed in, begin training, or leave within thirty-six hours to try their luck at another compound.

I roll my eyes. Gap year is really a tier-two holiday. Tier-one kids have to start training immediately, and tier-three recruits are put to work.

He doesn't spell out the implications of leaving the compound, but the message is clear: Once you leave, you can never come back.

I'll be damned if any of *my* recruits spend gap year partying in Neverland. If Recon did that, we'd all be dead. There's never enough time to train these kids as it is.

I get up to leave the crowded hall, and I realize several of the new recruits are trailing behind me like a brood of sad baby ducklings. They can't know I'm overseeing training, but I'm the only commanding officer besides Jayden who attends these sick ceremonies.

I groan and lengthen my stride. Maybe I can lose them in the crowd.

The doors to the megalift don't close fast enough. New recruits bounce into the corners of the lift like pinballs, and I spot seven of the dingy-looking gray cords.

Jayden snapped up at least thirty kids — way more than previous years — but they're probably still wandering around the main hall, completely shell-shocked. They'll meet their commanding officers later.

In my pitiful group, there's a short girl with curly red hair and a shocking dash of freckles across the bridge of her nose, a dumb-looking boy the size of a linebacker, and a skinny burnout with copper hair dyed green sticking up in all directions.

A frail-looking girl with mocha skin is already crying silently behind the football player, and there's a pale, flabby vampire kid with jet-black hair.

Next to him is the tiniest human being I've ever seen with a white-blond bob and a pale, heart-shaped face. Her clothes hang off her tiny frame, and her eyes are the size of doorknobs.

What a crew.

Then the linebacker shifts, and I see lucky number seven. It's the girl who sat down next to me at the ceremony — the girl with long raven hair who was going for Systems but received a forty-six.

She's leaning against the side of the lift with her arms crossed over her chest, holding me in place with fierce gray eyes framed by sooty lashes.

What's the expression? *If looks could kill.*

And Harper Riley definitely wants me dead. I try to pull my eyes away, but her behavior just baffles me. I've punched cadets in the face for doing less than she's doing now. It's as though she's silently daring me to tell her to drop and give me twenty.

She doesn't look dumb — at least not a lethal forty-six-caliber dumb. Miles would say she's hot.

But right now, all I see is arrogance, which is dangerous. They should really put that in the cadets' permanent files.

The megalift dings, and I get out as fast as I can. I take a left, and the new recruits practically trip over their own feet to follow me to the stairs and down into the bowels of the compound.

The temperature drops almost instantly when we reach the Underground, and I turn down the tunnel to Recon. The motion-activated overhead lighting sputters and then dims. Sometimes I think Manufacturing produces a special brand of flickering yellow lightbulbs just for Recon.

Our footsteps echo down the deserted main tunnel, and I gesture to where it branches off to the rows of compartments.

"Welcome to Recon City," I say. "Cadet living quarters are here. Lucky you. There's another stairwell that's a straight shot to Neverland. I suggest you lock your doors."

It sounds like I'm joking, but I hope they know I'm serious. When I was a recruit, I went out one night and came back to find two guys shooting up in my room.

The tunnel widens, and the smell of bleach, sweat, and old mats drifts through the double doors. It smells like home.

"This is the training center. This is where you'll report every day at oh-eight hundred. I do not tolerate lateness, and I do not train recruits who spend their gap year getting burned in Neverland."

I eye Harper Riley. She's giving me that look again.

I scowl. "You need to *show up* if you want to live. At the end of training, we *will* shove you out of those pretty airlock doors, and you will have to survive. I suggest — you pay — attention."

They're all looking at me in shock, as if this is all one big prank — as though this can't possibly be their life.

Only Harper Riley and the redhead seem aware of what's really going on. The redhead is wearing a sassy look that tells me she is not accustomed to taking orders.

Then she does something she shouldn't. She lets out a nervous little snicker.

"What's your name, Cadet?" I ask, stepping toward her so I tower above her slight frame.

The redhead swallows. Her peaches-and-cream complexion loses some color, and suddenly, she's not so sassy. She looks caught between laughing and throwing up. Mission accomplished.

"Lenny Horwitz."

"Something funny, Horwitz?"

"No."

"O-*kay*." I step over to the huge football player guy with the buzz cut and beady eyes. He's already sweating and panting.

"And your name?"

"Bernard Kelso. But everyone calls me Bear."

And then I hear it, though Lenny's low whisper is barely audible: "*What's* your *name? Lieutenant Thunderdouche?*"

I close my eyes. This can't happen. I don't care about being liked or respected, but they have to take this seriously.

I draw in a deep breath, preparing to unleash that part of myself I hate — the part of me that kicks fighters when they're down and beats the shit out of people.

"My name is SHUT THE FUCK UP WHEN I'M TALKING, HORWITZ! I'm trying to SAVE YOUR FUCKING LIVES. If you don't LISTEN . . . if you don't TRAIN . . . you will DIE!"

I wheel around, and her pale face bleeds into such a deep crimson, I'm pretty sure she's going to combust or have a heart attack.

"Is that fucking IMPORTANT ENOUGH for you?" I yell.

I lower my voice. "You don't need to know my name. The ONLY thing I want to hear from you, cadets, is YES — SIR! Is that understood?"

"Yes, sir!" the other cadets parrot. All except for Harper Riley. I've lost my patience.

"Think you're too good for us, Harvard?" I hear myself say. What is *wrong* with me? I'm an asshole. That's what.

For a second, I wonder if she'll even understand the pre–Death Storm reference, but then her face glows red as six pairs of eyes snap onto her.

"No."

"No?"

I take a step toward her. She's at least five inches shorter than me, but it doesn't feel that way as she stiffens her spine and levels my gaze. Either this girl is crazy, or I'm starting to lose my touch at intimidation.

"No."

"No, what?" I growl.

"No . . . *sir*." She elongates the last syllable with so much contempt I'm actually impressed. "And the name's *Harper*. Harper Riley . . . *sir*."

I grin before I can stop myself, but I twist it into a sneer. "Right. Harvard Riley. It's that or 'forty-six.' Your choice."

She glares at me and tosses her long ebony ponytail over her shoulder. That gesture almost unravels me. It's so cocky and self-important that I can see she genuinely believes she's been placed here by mistake. I drag in a deep breath, willing myself not to scream at her.

"Harvard, I know you took the Systems exam, so you probably think you're above all this. You probably don't even know what Recon does. Let me enlighten you."

I step away to get some distance and address all seven of my scared, green little ducklings.

"Forget everything you *think* you know about Recon. Two of

you will not make it through training. By this time two years from now, at least three of you will be dead. Four years from now, all but one of you will be dead.

"If you're very lucky, you *might* have a shot at retiring out. This year, Commander Pierce will be the first to retire out of Recon in *five years.*"

The big one called Bear looks as though he's about to wet himself, so I try to soften my tone a little.

"I don't tell you this to scare you. I tell you so you'll train hard. You need to know the odds are against you. And radiation poisoning is the absolute last thing you should be worried about."

I realize I'm pacing and stop, turning to look at them. "If you're planning to transfer, leave now. I'll see the rest of you at oh-eight hundred."

All the cadets scatter, and for a few minutes, I wonder if I've overdone it. I give the same speech Jayden gave when I was a cadet, but if I scare them so much that they all transfer to the next compound, she's going to kill me.

Once the tunnel is deserted, I let myself into Miles's compartment and flop down next to him on the sagging couch. Miles doesn't like heavy talks, and he *always* says the wrong thing, but when things get shitty, he's the only one who can talk me down.

Miles's eyes are fixated on the wall screen, where he's playing one of those battlefield video games. His face is screwed up in concentration. As he shoots an invisible rifle, the virtual Miles fires on-screen, and the real Miles lets out a disturbing laugh.

Between the black eye and the swollen nose, he looks like a zombie. I'm sure Brooke wants me dead, but Miles won't say anything about it. The two of us frequently got our asses handed to us in the Institute, and we're so used to nursing a collection of cuts, bruises, and broken bones that battle scars barely register with us anymore.

"Well, that could have gone better," I say to announce my presence. I close my eyes and squeeze the bridge of my nose to alleviate the headache I feel coming.

"You meet your fresh meat?"

Miles shoots again, and one of the other virtual players groans and dies on-screen. I look away, trying to hide how twitchy the sounds of his game make me. Most of us who spend our lives dodging death on the Fringe don't need to rehash it in a game, but I guess it helps Miles downplay the real danger.

"Yeah, I met them. And let me tell you, it does *not* look good."

"Ug-os or walking body bags?"

I cringe, but I'm not sure which bothers me more: him thinking of my recruits as pieces of ass or insinuating that they're all going to be dead soon — which they will be.

"They're just so . . . green. They're either terrified or cocky."

"Hey. You need some help scaring the little shits, you just let me know."

I laugh when I think about Miles teaching my last class how to fight. He was really just a prop in there — I wouldn't actually let him beat any of them up — but his tree trunk–sized arms and menacing glare were enough to make even the toughest recruits piss their pants.

But the thought of bringing Miles in to cut Harper Riley down to size doesn't cheer me up.

"I don't think they need to be scared straight," I say, thinking about that defiant look in her eyes that reminded me so much of myself.

"Then what's your plan? Positive reinforcement? Sharing time? Building up their self-esteem?"

I laugh even though I don't want to. Miles is joking, but he's right. Nothing I do can guarantee their safety. I feel restless and defeated.

I need to train, but Miles is in no shape to go another round. He needs to let his nose heal before he's deployed again. I could ask Lopez, but he hates me, and I don't like sparring with people who can't keep their emotions in check. It's a good way to get injured.

Miles can sense I'm itching for a fight. He's got a sixth sense for stupidity. "Listen. I know you hate this, but you just have to do what you can. After they're trained, they're not your responsibility."

Something stirs in the pit of my stomach, but I shove it down farther. I hate how well Miles knows me. That's the risk you take when you come up in the Institute with someone. They know you better than you know yourself.

"Yeah, I know."

He stops playing and rounds on me. "No, you don't. You look like you're about to have a meltdown."

I shrug. "I'm fine."

He gives me a look of disbelief. "You think the other lieutenants care? They don't give two shits."

"Well, I'm not like them," I say through gritted teeth.

"I know you aren't. That's the problem. This is the third time I've had to watch you go through this, and it's depressing as hell."

"Sorry if my conscience depresses you," I snarl.

"Screw your conscience. Just do your job. Jayden didn't promote you to be a whiny little bitch about it. She hired you to do the best you can with what you've got."

"What I've got is seven soft cadets and not enough time to keep them alive," I say. "You think the other lieutenants are doing the best they can? Their cadets are lucky if they show up for training!"

Miles levels me with a sympathetic stare. "Yeah, yeah. I know. They're a bunch of lazy assholes. But . . ."

"But *what?*"

He cracks his neck, and his eyes shift from side to side. Miles isn't scared of anything, but for some reason, he's treading lightly now. "Maybe they have the right idea."

I open my mouth to rip him a new one, but Miles sees my rage coming and keeps going.

"All I'm sayin' is you can't let yourself get attached. Some of them aren't going to make it, and there's nothing you can do about it."

Miles's indifference bothers me, but he's right.

I can't afford to care about these cadets. It doesn't help keep them safe. In fact, it's more dangerous for them if I'm personally invested.

Friends make you do stupid things. Friends make you lose your edge.

five

Harper

I pack slowly as Sawyer paces back and forth in our compartment. I can feel the stress coming off her in waves, and it's just piling onto the panic welling up inside me.

"How in the *hell* did you score a forty-six?" she asks.

"Obviously something's wrong with the test," Celdon snaps.

She shoots him a death glare. The idea that the test could have messed up is too much for her to handle. Sawyer's faith in the system is absolute.

"Maybe your scores got switched with someone else's," she suggests.

Celdon lets out a derisive laugh. "Are you serious? You think a multimillion-credit program just accidentally swapped two people's scores?"

"Unless you're suggesting that she somehow *lost her mind* and screwed up half the test!"

Sawyer's voice is getting higher and higher, and Celdon is exuding pure smugness to cover up his frustration.

Sometimes I forget that just because Sawyer and Celdon are *my* best friends doesn't mean they're each other's best friends. Sawyer has always been disgusted by Celdon's partying, and because she grew up in a tier-one section, Celdon has always thought Sawyer was a little bit snotty. They push each other's buttons as if it's their job, and right now, they're little more than reluctant allies.

"Maybe I did," I sigh. "People choke under pressure all the time."

"But you don't," says Celdon firmly. He isn't just reassuring me to be a good friend. His voice says he's certain.

I wish I were.

Sawyer helps me load my clothes and computer onto a cart in silence while Celdon sits on my old bed, staring at the wall.

I know Sawyer feels guilty for being happy about her bid, but I don't want her to. It only makes me feel worse. Sawyer deserves to be in Health and Rehab more than anyone. I just don't know what I did to deserve Recon.

I ride the megalift down to my new compartment alone. They don't say it, but I know neither one of them wants to be seen slumming in Recon territory. Plus, Sawyer probably has a penthouse compartment in the upper tunnels with her name on it.

It's a torturously long descent to the lower tunnels all by myself. When the megalift stops at the ground level, I wheel the cart over to the emergency stairwell and peer down the treacherous dark corners. I didn't think about the stairs when I packed up the cart.

Fighting the impulse to shove the whole thing off the landing, I unload my computer to carry it down to safety first.

"Hey! Let me help you!" says a voice over my shoulder.

I whip around and almost bang foreheads with the short red-headed recruit the lieutenant yelled at.

Up close, her huge green eyes and pale, milky skin have a startling effect. She could almost be beautiful, but there's an impish quality to her features that's a little off-putting.

"Uh . . . thanks," I mutter.

I set my computer back down, and she grabs the front end of the cart. She's much stronger than she looks.

Together, we manage to carry the cart down the stairs without incident, and I sigh with relief that my computer didn't slip off and shatter into a million pieces.

Now that the shock of the bidding ceremony has worn off, I notice the damp smell that lingers in the Recon tunnels and the permanent-looking grime coating the cinderblock walls. It's more echoey than in the upper tunnels, and I can hear voices and laughter drifting from the long row of compartments.

"I know . . . it's super shitty," says the redhead, following my gaze. "I'm Lenny Horwitz, by the way."

She sticks out a tiny hand, and I take it. "Harper Riley."

Lenny returns the squeeze with bone-crushing pressure, and I cringe in surprise.

"I'm from EnComm," she says, confirming my suspicions. The merchants and showbiz people in Entertainment and Commerce all share Lenny's ballsiness.

"What about you?" she asks.

I know she's just being polite, but it's a loaded question for someone like me. I clear my throat. "I grew up in the Institute."

"Oh," she says. She's all red again, and I swear I can feel the heat coming off her.

That's a conversation stopper if I ever heard one. I know how people who grew up with actual parents view kids who grew up in the Institute.

I push the cart ahead of me, hoping we reach my assigned compartment soon so I can get rid of her. I don't want her pity.

"This is you," she says quickly, stopping behind me at a dented metal door. "Sorry. I'm nosy. I already scoped it out." She wrinkles her nose. "It's kind of a dump."

I back up, dragging the cart with me. Sure enough, there's a tiny piece of paper shoved in the door jamb with my name scrawled in sloppy cursive handwriting.

I punch in four zeros — the default code — and all the numbers on the battered keypad blink haphazardly. There's a sickly *beep*, as though its batteries are about to die, and I hear the door unlock. I throw my shoulder into the door. It bounces open and ricochets off the adjacent wall, and a single strip of florescent lighting flickers on.

Lenny was right. This place is a dump.

As soon as I step inside, the smell of stale air hits my nostrils. The room looks like a steel box with a thin layer of stained carpet on the floor for warmth. It's about the size of the dorm room I shared with Sawyer, but instead of an extra twin bunk mounted on the far wall, there's a cramped living area with a saggy black couch and a table that folds out from the wall.

"They really go all out for new recruits, huh?"

"They call us cadets. But at least you have a window."

She's right. I jump up onto the lumpy mattress and draw up the shade. It's not a window to the outside world — just a streaky glass partition overlooking the dark Underground platform.

"That's handy," I mutter.

Sitting on the shelf next to the bed is a small stack of gray fatigues: seven pairs of gray cargo trousers made out of some thin synthetic material, seven black tank tops, and seven lightweight gray overshirts. I touch the tiny cadet patch on the shoulder, and my eyes wander down to the outline of a hawk embroidered in dark gray thread over the heart.

"It's weird, isn't it?" Lenny murmurs. "That we're actually here."

I nod, feeling the tears burning in my throat. I swallow them down. I will not cry in front of this girl.

I don't want to be here. I don't want any part of it. I was supposed to be wearing white by now. I belong in Systems.

Lenny leaves to go try to bring some charm to her lunchbox of a compartment, and I lie down on my bare, smelly mattress, staring at the line of rust where the ceiling meets the walls.

In the upper tunnels, new tier-one recruits are busy socializing and meeting the recruits who just aged out of gap year. Sawyer is shy, but she's probably already making friends with some nerdy new Health and Rehab girl, and I'd bet money that Celdon is getting burned in Neverland with the Systems kids.

Here, the shame and collective sense of failure outweigh our need to make friends. Somewhere down the tunnel, a new recruit is crying, and it echoes through the vents.

That's a mistake. In tier three, they'll eat you alive if you show weakness. I need to cry, too, but instead I smash the musty pillow over my head and sleep for the first time in two days.

six

Harper

Standing in line in the canteen the next morning, I can't help but feel as though everyone is watching me. It isn't true, but the gray fatigues feel heavy and foreign.

The canteen is already packed for breakfast, with a mess of different-colored uniforms crammed in at long rows of tables. The lighting is bright this time of day, meant to maintain our correct circadian rhythm despite being in the windowless interior of the compound.

Across the room, Sawyer is sitting with her recruit class. She's wearing bright red scrubs and already looks as though she belongs.

The Operations man who was on the line yesterday is here today, too, but he looks right through me as he hands me a bowl of boiled sweet potatoes, beans, and green algae. No protein cube. No flavor. It's worse than the food I got yesterday.

I watch the credits disappear from my account on the screen and scowl as the man serves the Systems recruit behind me one perfect white hardboiled egg with his sweet potatoes. I feel a surge of jealousy. That egg would cost a week's worth of my Recon stipend.

I stand self-consciously at the end of the line, fighting the urge to grab Sawyer and drag her off to our usual table. Celdon didn't merge with Systems during his gap year, but he'd had us to fall back on. Now our old table is filled with strange kids, and

Celdon is eating his egg with the Systems recruits.

"Hey! Riley!"

I recognize that voice instantly, and hate spills into my gut like toxic sludge.

Looking around, I see Paxton Dellwood waving boisterously from a table full of Control recruits. He's wearing his navy blue slacks and jacket like a second skin and swinging his new electric nightstick under the table. The sneer plastered across his face makes me sick to my stomach.

Of course Control bid on him. Paxton is the biggest asshole in our year. He'll feel right at home with all the other sociopaths, which is probably why he isn't taking a gap year.

I have no choice but to walk right past him on the way to my table, and I bite back the urge to hit him.

"Hey, Riley! Nice outfit." He whips back his slick blond waves and lowers his voice so only I can hear. "I suppose a congratulations is in order."

His sharp eyes rake up my body in an intrusive way.

"Congratulations, Paxton," I mutter. "They finally gave you a stick to put up your ass."

He smirks, flipping the nightstick in his hand. "I meant you, Riley. You broke all the records. I don't think anyone's ever scored a forty-six before . . . and I don't think a Systems wannabe has ever fallen so far down the ladder."

"Eat shit, Dellwood," snaps a voice behind me.

I turn. Lenny is standing near my left shoulder, wearing her new fatigues. Her hair is pulled back in a tight French braid, and she's managed to stuff the excess material of her too-long trousers into her combat boots. I don't like our uniforms, but even I have to admit she looks tough.

"Hey, gimp. How's it hanging?" Paxton turns to me and whispers, "She's a cripple."

Lenny's face goes scarlet, and she turns to walk away. But just as Paxton's mouth lifts into his trademark sneer, Lenny's elbow shoots out to the side, striking him across the nose.

"Fucking hell!"

As I stare, a triumphant swell of respect for Lenny blossoms in my chest. Maybe I'm going to like Recon after all.

"I could arrest you for that!" Paxton gurgles. He moves his hand, and a dribble of blood escapes from between his fingers.

A few controllers look up from their meals to see what all the commotion is about, but they can't be bothered to write Lenny a citation while they're trying to eat their breakfast.

"Go ahead," Lenny snarls. "Then you'd have to tell everyone you got beat up by a girl who's a gimp." She sticks her middle finger in his face and cocks her head for me to follow her.

As we walk between the tables, I watch her neck burn scarlet. I know she's thinking about me watching her walk. She does favor her left leg, but it's barely noticeable if you aren't looking for it.

Paxton being recruited by Control fills me with a sense of dread. He already walks around as though he owns the place. He's Third Gen, and as he likes to remind everyone, his grandparents were among the first wave of humans who settled in the compound. If you ask me, they had to be the creepy cultish type to shut themselves up in this place at the first whisper of nuclear warfare. Most people didn't come to the compound until after the first wave of attacks.

Lenny slams her tray down at a Recon table and swings her legs over the bench. "I hate that guy."

"You shouldn't have done that," I say, though I'm glad she did. "You can get away with mouthing off to Paxton, but humiliating him is going to cost you."

Lenny shrugs and starts shoveling sweet potatoes into her mouth. "Like I give a shit. What's gonna happen to me? It's not as if they can put me in Recon *again*."

I laugh without meaning to because she's right. We really don't have anything to lose.

While Lenny's busy shoveling food into her mouth, I look up and down the table at the other people in gray. Most of them have the hardened look of people who've been at war. Their skin is darker than everyone else's — tan and leathery from time spent in the sun — and there's a strange, permanent grunge to it, as though the dirt and polluted air from the Fringe have stained the palms of their hands and the beds of their fingernails.

"You should put your hair up," Lenny muses. "That's how they all wear it."

I glance down at a cluster of female cadets and see that she's right. Then my gaze lands on Bear. He's already demolished his bowl of food, but his eyes are still hungry. Packing over two hundred and fifty pounds of muscle and blubber, I don't know how he plans to survive on the Recon meal plan.

A few of the other recruits sitting nearby get up to leave, so Lenny and I dump our trays and follow them out of the canteen.

We take the stairs back down to the lower level, and my dread compounds with every step. We wind our way through the dimly lit tunnels to the training center, where several groups of older Recon are already working out. I see three clusters of nervous-looking cadets across the room, but their commanding officers haven't arrived yet.

"Harvard! Horwitz!" yells a voice. "On the mat."

The angry lieutenant from the Recon welcome wagon is standing off to the side, arms folded across his chest. He isn't wearing his full fatigues — just the gray pants and a tight black

T-shirt that shows off his chiseled arms.

"His name's Eli Parker," Lenny whispers. "A friend of mine was in his recruit class. He's the youngest lieutenant in Recon. He's only like . . . twenty-four."

"He's an ass."

Lenny makes a low sound in her throat that I think is a growl. "A sexy ass."

I stifle my laughter and follow her over to where the tiny blond girl and the weird-looking burnout kid with the spiky hair are already standing in line.

Before we reach them, Eli points to a line of peeling tape on the mat. I roll my eyes and put my heels on the tape, feeling like an idiot.

I didn't study three years for Systems so I could stand on a line like a kid in gym class.

Up close, I can see that Eli's sharp features are actually handsome. And Lenny's right — he has an okay ass. But with that permanent scowl on his face, he's way too sour to qualify as hot. His intense blue eyes scrape over us, scanning for weakness, and I feel the hatred bubbling in my gut.

"You got any lip for me today, Horwitz?" he asks.

"No," says Lenny.

"No, *what?*"

"No, sir."

Eli just stands there, eyes boring into her. Finally Bear arrives, slightly out of breath from power walking down here. He lines up on the tape on my other side, and Eli claps his hands together.

"All right. Day one." He pauses for effect. "Cadets! Look around you."

I glance at Bear and Lenny, who both look as nervous as I feel.

"What do you see?"

Nobody says anything.

"Harvard!"

I'm going to punch him. I'm going to punch him in his handsome face.

"Yes, sir," I say through gritted teeth.

Eli's sizing me up, baiting me. "What do you see?"

"I see there's only five of us."

"Right!" He smacks his hands together again. "Two of your little friends already punched their one-way tickets out of here." His eyes dart down the line, lingering for a second on each of us. "This is your last chance to crawl away and join them."

He waits.

"No? No takers?"

Silence.

"Great. You belong to me now. Every moment you are in this room, from oh-eight hundred until twelve hundred and thirteen hundred until seventeen hundred, you do as I say. If you train hard and *listen*, you may live longer."

"Sir?"

I glance to my left, where Bear is still standing with both his heels touching the piece of tape on the floor. He looks terrified, and I'm actually amazed that Recon found fatigues big enough to fit his bulk.

Eli whips around as though seeing him for the first time. "What is it, Kelso?"

Bear's huge round face grows a little paler, and a line of perspiration forms above his lip. He swallows and speaks again in a strained voice.

"Could you be more specific? Only . . . only you haven't really told us why we're going to die."

Eli smirks, which is a little off-putting, and he nods in approval.

"Good question. I told you all to forget everything you think you know about Recon. I'm sure you all learned about our efforts to gauge the relative 'livability' of the outside world in school. They tell you it's our job to keep an accurate estimate on the Habitation Clock, counting down the days until we can crawl out of this glass box and run free in the wild."

He rolls his eyes, as though he thinks this is a waste of time.

"That's all true, but gathering information about radiation levels, soil composition, and air quality are just a small part of what you'll actually be doing." He frowns. "Your main task is defending this compound."

"Defending the compound against *what*?" I blurt before I can stop myself.

Eli shifts his attention to me, rooting me where I stand with a piercing stare, as though he's deciding whether my outburst constitutes curiosity or insubordination.

He seems to make a decision and takes two long strides toward me. When he speaks, his voice is a cold whisper. "You're First Gen, Harvard. I'm surprised you haven't asked before."

All the blood rushes to my head and inflames my face. I can feel it pounding in my ears. The fury is too strong — stronger than I've ever felt. I clench my fists until my nails dig into my palms so I don't deck him across the face.

"I'm sorry," he says, clearly not sorry at all. "Did I strike a nerve?"

I don't say anything, but I can feel myself shaking.

He turns to the rest of the group. "What do you all think happened to the people who were left out there?" His voice is deadly quiet. "The people they didn't let in?"

"Th-They went to the other compounds," stammers Bear.

"All of them?" Eli pauses for a beat, standing completely still. "No. Saving everyone wasn't an option."

"They all died," says Lenny in a quiet voice. "Eventually."

"You would think so, wouldn't you? Anyone still alive out there when Death Storm hit should have died. Recon operatives who have prolonged exposure to the outside environment often develop radiation poisoning or cancer. A few early operatives who stumbled into red zones got exposed to such a high dose of radiation that they died within days. So how are they doing it?"

"Who?"

"The drifters — the people who are still alive out there."

"I've never seen anyone out there," says Lenny, a note of challenge and desperation in her voice. "There's nothing out there on the Fringe."

"You've never seen anyone out there because of Recon. We patrol the perimeter to keep anyone from getting too close. Gangs of drifters have attempted to sabotage the compound in the past, and once, they almost succeeded." He raises an eyebrow. "Defending this compound is your job."

"Parker!" snaps a voice from behind us.

We all turn, and I see the same diminutive woman who bid on me at the ceremony.

"Commander," says Eli with a quick nod.

"Is it story time, or are these cadets here to train?"

"I'm just bringing them up to speed."

"Please save your excuses for someone else, Parker. Are they soldiers, or are they as useless as they look?"

"They're new recruits, Commander. I'm just —"

"Stop wasting my investment," she snaps. "Show me I got my money's worth."

I feel the commander's eyes boring into my forehead, and I look up, forcing myself to meet her sharp gaze.

"This one cost a fortune. And for what? A forty-six?" She shakes her head. "I don't think so. There must be *some* reason she appeared at the top of my list."

My face is burning, but I'm too curious to care. *What list is she talking about?*

Eli claps his hands together. "Right. Your training starts now." He turns to me. "Riley! Front and center."

When he says my name, the anger roars low in my stomach. Of course he would drop the "Harvard" bullshit to look good in front of Jayden.

I step forward and turn to face him. As he towers over me with that smug look on his face, I wonder if Recon always singles out a recruit just to instill fear in the others.

He takes a step to the side and circles me, looking me up and down as though searching for weakness.

"Well?" snaps the commander. "Are you going to fight or ask her to dance?"

Eli sighs. I hear the mat give behind me, and suddenly he has his arm around my neck, choking off my airway.

I gag and stagger backward, flailing around, but his grip doesn't loosen.

"The element of surprise . . . is what will kill you ninety percent of the time," says Eli. He squeezes harder, and I feel my eyes watering. "Don't let this happen again."

I force myself to focus through the panic and tap his arm, hoping he just grabbed me as a scare tactic. But he doesn't let go. All my muscles seize in response, and I feel the fear shooting up my chest.

"Come on, Harvard," he growls into my ear. "Figure it out."

I struggle, but the lack of oxygen is making my brain fuzzy. Out of the corner of my eye, I see Lenny staring at me, her mouth hanging open. The commander has her arms folded across her chest. She looks pleased.

All my limbs jerk haphazardly as Eli drags me around the mat like a rag doll. With a huge amount of effort, I swing my elbow back as hard as I can. I feel it connect with Eli's abdomen, but it might as well be a brick wall. He doesn't budge.

"Never took you for a sweetheart, Harvard." He leans back, lifting my feet off the ground.

A horrible sound escapes my throat. My entire upper body is burning. I jab my elbow back again, trying to shake loose of his grip. I feel his whole body behind me, supporting my weight, but he is unshakeable.

I kick a leg back, but it just grazes his knee. There is no oxygen in my body. I feel my brain shutting down.

Suddenly I'm on the ground, choking and retching on all fours.

"Pathetic," the commander snarls. "You're dead, Riley. Parker just killed you."

I glare up at her, still unable to suck in enough air to form a response.

Eli's eyes are locked on mine, but they're no longer gleaming with satisfaction. What *is* that look?

"You want another go?" he snaps.

I really don't, but my body is moving without any direction from my brain. I'm on my feet, striding toward him and preparing to strike.

Eli smirks, backing up just fast enough to stay out of my reach. Then he stops, and without thinking — without considering the fact that he's my commanding officer — I swing out a balled fist, aiming for his jaw.

Eli slips sideways to avoid the brunt of my hit, and I feel my hand glance off the side of his face.

Before I can prepare myself, Eli's leg shoots out. He kicks me just above the kneecap, and I collapse. His foot comes at me again, but I roll away on the filthy mat, panting and heaving like crazy.

I stagger to my feet, but I haven't even regained my balance when his leg comes from behind me, sweeping me off my feet again. I hit the ground on my side, and the pain reverberates up my ribcage.

I roll onto my stomach in silent agony, trying to regain my breath.

Eli's face appears above me. "You had enough, Cadet?"

I won't look at him. I'm still summoning the strength to get to my feet, and then Eli is gone. He isn't talking to me anymore, but I hear the hum of his voice nearby. He's addressing the others. Something about surprise. *This is what you're up against.*

Tears burn my cheeks, and I wipe them away furiously. My skin feels too hot, and I'm shaking uncontrollably.

I can't believe what just happened.

"You're going to have to be tougher than that, Riley," says the commander from somewhere off to the side.

White-hot anger surges through me. She's the reason I'm here, and she's taunting me. But before I can retort, she's gone. I hear the other cadets' anxious voices, but then they start to trickle out, too.

Eli is back. He's kneeling in front of me, looking at me with those sharp eyes. He looks . . . worried?

"Harvard!"

With all the energy I have left, I swing my fist out and collide with the side of his face harder than I'd ever thought possible.

"Don't call me Harvard."

seven

Eli

I'm not surprised when Harper doesn't return to training after lunch. I try to ignore her absence, but the other cadets don't say a word for the rest of the day.

Even though Jayden's appearance should have spurred me to train them more ruthlessly, I just can't summon my harsh, cold alter ego after knocking Harper on her ass.

I knew she was crazy and aggressive enough to take the bait, and part of me was curious to see how the legendary Institute shit-starter fared on her first day in a fight. But I scared the crap out of her, and the memory of it fills me with a sick sense of shame. I should never have let Jayden goad me into it.

I'm relieved and a little impressed that Harper hit me. It shows she has a spine.

The rest of the cadets . . . I'm not so sure. I work them until they're bone tired, and they all disperse at the sound of the quitting bell before I formally dismiss them.

That isn't good. I can't let a little remorse destroy my authority.

I work out through the dinner bell and prowl the training center like a caged animal. I'm not hungry. There's no room for hunger with this sick feeling in the pit of my stomach.

Finally, the desperation gets the better of me. I grab my bag and head toward the maintenance tunnel that runs adjacent to the Underground. The stench of sweat, blood, and old mats hits my nostrils, and the sides of the tunnel press in closer on either side.

When the tunnel opens up and the dimly lit room comes into focus, the sick feeling in my gut gets a little bit stronger. Two Recon guys are squaring off in the ring, one looking a little worse for the wear. Lopez has his shiny bald head between the ropes, shouting directions at his guy in the ring. But when I walk in, Lopez meets my gaze and sneers.

The room isn't as packed as it was on Bid Day Eve, but they've attracted a decent-sized crowd of lower-ranked Recon operatives. A few turn around to stare at me when I walk in. I know how I must look: drenched with sweat, pissed off, that crazy gleam in my eyes.

I don't recall asking Lopez to fight. You don't really ask Lopez anything. But when his guy finally hits the mat, the drunken spectators shove me toward the ring, and Lopez throws me a glare that says he's looking for payback.

The last time we fought, I laid him out for a week. But I wasn't looking to lose that time. Tonight, I'm not so sure.

Lopez is one mean son of a bitch, which makes him lethal in a fight. He's short and stocky, but he's as strong as an ox. He doesn't drop his gaze as I yank off my shirt and pull on some gloves. He's watching me like a predator as I climb into the ring, and a tiny voice in the back of my head urges me to walk away.

But then somebody hits the bell, and I lunge at him as if my life depends on it.

I'm drunk on my own self-pity, and I barely block his wild haymaker. Lopez isn't as strong as Miles, but he's much more scrappy. His swings are random, hard, and fueled by rage.

One of his punches connects with the side of my jaw, and I grin hazily at what Harper will think when she sees that bruise tomorrow. It's the same place she hit me earlier.

She hates me and she doesn't even know me, but I know everything about her. I read her permanent file. Talk about the poster child for charm school. Lots of fighting in the Institute. Lots of hair pulling.

It's not surprising. The Institute is for Fringe kids and any tier-three children who are conceived by accident or stupidity. The compound doesn't need any laws to keep tier-three workers from starting families, though Recon and ExCon expressly forbid it. No tier-three workers can afford to support a child on what they make. What you get is a bunch of unsupervised, parentless little thugs. Most of them self-destruct, either with drugs or by failing out of their classes and ending up in the same sections their parents were in.

But Harper is smart as hell. She desperately wanted to escape that place, just as I had.

Lopez swings out wildly, and I block his hit and counter with a fierce jab cross of my own. He isn't as fast as me, and I nail him right in the side of the face.

The crowd lets out an angry jeer. Lopez staggers backward, and I aim a kick above the knee. He buckles but doesn't go down.

Harper probably doesn't remember, but I met her once about six years ago. I was just weeks from aging out of the Institute, and she was probably fifteen. Worlds collide in the headmaster's office.

I was nursing a black eye, about to be issued yet another demerit for fighting. She was sitting in the chair next to me with her tangled dark hair spilling everywhere, knees scuffed under her skirt, looking as though she didn't give a shit.

She knew I was staring at her. Even then she was hot. She looked over, cool as can be, and spit blood into a napkin.

Harper walked out of the headmaster's office that day with a black mark on her record, but I heard the other kid spent a week in the medical ward. I all but forgot about Harper Riley after that — until she appeared on a list of recommended recruits for Recon.

She fascinated me because she and I are the same: Both of us came into the compound with nothing, and both of us desperately wanted to achieve something.

When that Recon worker brought me into the compound, I thought I'd been given a gift — a chance to live life on my own terms. That was before I encountered the meat grinder of Bid Day.

I didn't get a bid from Control, but I swore to myself I'd be good at something — even if that something was killing drifters and teaching cadets to do it.

But the meat grinder doesn't stop when you're recruited. It keeps tearing you apart until the day you die.

Lost in thought, I let my glove slip down. Lopez sees his opening and lands one hell of a punch. But there's so much adrenalin coursing through my veins that the pain barely registers.

I lunge forward and manage to get him in a headlock, but his right elbow is vicious. I groan and let go of him, planting an uppercut in his abdomen as he slithers away.

Lopez is on the ropes, but I don't stop. I keep pummeling him in the gut and then strike an elbow across his face. His head swings to the side, and a few beads of sweat slide off his polished bald head. He has a hawk tattooed down the middle of his skull. Suddenly that hawk is flying at me, and I yell as he headbutts me in the chin.

My neck snaps back, and the jarring sensation is enough to shake me out of my stupor. As I stagger backward, he throws out his right foot and connects with my leg. It folds under me, useless and weak.

Time slows down as I hit the mat, and he comes down swinging.

I manage to block the worst of his hits, but I can't get enough leverage to buck him off. Lopez knows this. He's built like a tank.

This time, I feel every one of his hits to the bone. I don't even try to block the pain. It's strong enough to make me forget. It feels like penance.

Somewhere in the back of my mind, I know I need to end this fight. He's landing too many punches.

But then the pain dissipates. All I feel is the blood rushing to the surface. Lopez isn't hitting me anymore.

"What the hell?" somebody yells.

I open my eyes and peer through the cage I've made around my face with my arms. Miles is towering over me, holding Lopez in a headlock. The noise from the crowd rushes back to me. They're angry he stopped the fight, but one of his menacing looks is enough to make them back off.

"It was just a friendly match," I mumble, feeling like an idiot. I'm sure whatever Miles saw looked anything but friendly.

"Are you out of your mind?"

"It's fine." Miles rolls his eyes and lets Lopez go.

Lopez staggers away, clutching his abdomen, and throws me a look that says this isn't over. He'll probably ambush me in a dark tunnel one day, but even he won't try to take on Miles.

I pull myself into an upright position, ignoring Miles's concerned gaze. The crowd is still a little agitated, but they're not about to start anything with both of us in the ring. He jerks his head toward the tunnel, and shame spills into my gut.

I slide between the ropes and follow him out, trying not to

look as though I just got my ass handed to me. It's not the beating that's embarrassing — it's the loss of self-control. It's bad enough that Lopez's crew got to witness it; they don't know just how fucked in the head I am.

As soon as we're out of earshot in the dark tunnel, Miles rounds on me. He's trying out a look of uncharacteristic disapproval, and I know he's gearing up for a lecture.

"Man, what were you thinking?"

"I wasn't," I pant, wiping the blood from my upper lip.

"I *know*. But Lopez? I thought you were smarter than that."

I shrug, but Miles isn't about to let this go.

"You have got to stop doing this," he says in his best tough-love voice.

"Doing what?"

"This self-destructive bullshit you put yourself through every time you get a new recruit class. A fight here and there for kicks is one thing, but Lopez will lay your ass out. If Jayden thinks she might lose her best lieutenant to an illegal fight because he's depressed —"

"I'm not depressed," I snap, shoving past him.

"— she'll find someone else to beat up on your cadets."

I freeze. "You heard about that?"

"I heard you went easy on her. Too easy."

I wheel around and glare at him. "You weren't there."

"You know you didn't do that girl any favors by holding back, right?"

"It was day one," I snarl.

Miles is right up in my face, his mouth twisted into a scowl. "That hasn't stopped you before. What *is* it with this girl?"

"Nothing."

"It's not nothing. What the hell is going on with you?" he

yells. The darkness is throwing shadows on his already severe face, and the close proximity to such rage would be enough to make anybody else lose their shit.

I step back and square my shoulders, and his face falls out of its hardened expression. I know that feeling. Sometimes the aggression is so automatic that you have to remind yourself who you're talking to.

The worst thing is that he's right. I've changed a lot since the Institute. Hell, I've changed a lot since our cadet year. Back then, I was a mean little shit, but Miles and I could always find something to laugh about. These days, it's a struggle just to get out of bed, and he can tell.

"Listen," says Miles, regaining his composure. "Jayden's on the warpath. She thinks you're going soft. What's your problem?"

"I scared her, Miles. I really scared her."

"That's your job."

"She'll never come back now."

"The hell she won't. What's she gonna do? She has nowhere else to go."

"She could still leave the compound."

Miles sighs. "You know she won't."

"She might. She has no family here."

"Is that what this is about?" he asks incredulously. "She reminds you of you? Jesus." Miles rolls his eyes. "Every Institute brat isn't yours to save."

"It's not that."

He raises an eyebrow. "Trust me, she'll get over it and be mouthing off to you by Friday."

I take a deep breath and look around to make sure there's no one who could possibly overhear. "What am I going to do with them?"

"Your little grasshoppers?"

I nod. "They aren't going to make it, Miles. Jayden's just going to draft again."

He lets out an uncomfortable chortle. "She keeps that up and ExCon won't have anyone left."

"Yeah, well, after a few deployments, neither will we."

eight

Harper

It's nearly midnight when I hear a heavy knock on the metal door of my compartment. It's probably a controller coming to arrest me for striking my commanding officer.

But when I peer through the peephole, I'm shocked to see a familiar face plastered with a shit-eating grin. He tousles his blond hair in a half-flirty, half-oblivious way, and I groan. If Celdon is here, he's probably coming from Neverland, burned out of his mind.

I open the door and he bounds in, looking amused by the relative shabbiness of my living arrangements. His eyes dart from the dented metal walls to the suspicious stain on the carpet.

He snaps the door closed. "Nice digs, Riles."

I open my mouth to let out some snarky reply, but when I turn my head, his jaw hits the floor.

"What the hell happened to you?" he splutters.

"My commanding officer wanted to make an example of me."

"Holy shit."

Celdon reaches out and lifts my chin so he can see the bruise forming along my neck where Eli choked me.

"Who . . .?"

"Eli Parker."

His eyebrows shoot up. "I remember that guy. He was three years above us in the Institute. I can't believe he did this!"

"Believe it. This is Recon. They take shit seriously."

Celdon levels me with his gaze. "What did you do to piss him off?"

I shake my head. Truthfully, I'm not sure *what* I did to make Eli single me out like that, apart from exuding clear disdain for Recon.

But thinking back to what happened when the commander entered the training center, I realize he probably had to choose someone to bully.

"I hit him."

"*What?*"

"I punched him in the face," I say, still a little shocked myself.

"You can't punch your direct command," Celdon says incredulously. "Especially Eli Parker. He's a poster boy for Recon *and* their best fighter. You know that, right?"

I nod, and Celdon chuckles.

"Jesus. You really *aren't* going to survive here."

I shove his shoulder lightly, which sends a shooting pain up my wrist. I'd forgotten how hard I hit Eli.

I stare into Celdon's eyes. They're clear and bright. He's sober, which fills me with a sense of relief. As useless as it is to cling to old friends now that we're all in different sections, I'm so freaking glad to see him.

"Why are you here?" I ask quietly. "You can't keep blowing off Systems."

He holds up a hand, and I'm surprised to see a wry smile playing on his lips. "Save the lecture, Riles. Sawyer already beat you to it."

He glances at the closed door and pulls me closer to the window, as though he doesn't want to take the chance of being overheard by someone passing in the tunnel.

He takes a deep breath, and I'm startled by the serious look on his face. "I have to show you something."

I hesitate, but Celdon isn't going to take no for an answer. Before I can even ask where we're going, he's dragging me out of my compartment, down the tunnel, up the stairs, and onto the megalift.

I've never seen him so anxious before, and I know whatever he found has to be big.

We're alone in the lift, but I can't shake the feeling that we're being watched.

"Does this have anything to do with my VocAps score?" I ask in a low voice.

He nods.

I don't dare say anything more as we shoot up through the center of the compound to the upper tunnels. It's ridiculous, but even talking about it makes me feel as though I'm doing something illegal.

The megalift dings, and I follow Celdon out into the main tunnel in the uppermost level that leads to Systems headquarters. It's completely deserted, and our footsteps echo off the white tile floor as we pass a row of offices and restricted access rooms.

There are no adornments along the walls, but every Systems tunnel is gorgeous in its starkness. It's like being in an art gallery with no art.

As we walk, I can't help staring up at the geometric skylights placed between the cross braces in the ceiling. The velvety black sky is dotted with stars. It's so beautiful after spending such a long time underground that I can almost forget how dangerous the Fringe is.

Finally, we reach the end of the tunnel, where a heavy steel door stands between us and Systems headquarters.

Celdon produces his access card, and I swallow down my envy

as he swipes his way in and leads me inside the room.

The door slams shut, and for a moment, it's pitch black except for the stars twinkling through the skylights. Celdon moves, and the motion-activated lights flicker on at all the workstations.

I've never been inside Systems, and I'm immediately shocked by its sheer size. Dozens of rounded workstations hemmed in by frosted glass are nestled in a honeycomb configuration around an enormous bank of servers.

There's a hiss behind me, and a stream of cold air shoots through the vent on the adjacent wall. I can only imagine how hard the air conditioning has to work to keep this room at a crisp sixty-eight degrees.

Celdon strides purposefully toward the row closest to the servers and disappears into one of the half-moon cubicles. I follow him in and touch the desk reverently as he punches in a user name and password.

It's cramped inside, but the gentle hum of the computer in the small space makes me feel right at home. I try not to stare too hungrily at the razor-thin twenty-seven-inch monitor or the ultra-compact CPU.

"Who's Jacob Morsey?" I ask, reading over his shoulder.

"A moronic new recruit," says Celdon, cracking a grin. "I helped him set up his account today."

"This isn't your computer?"

"I'm not an idiot. Do you think I want someone to see that I logged in at midnight and accessed files I have no business snooping in?"

He laughs as though *I'm* the crazy one and pulls up a folder labeled "Vocational Aptitude Results."

I feel guilty and want to punch Jacob Morsey in the face all at the same time. This could have been my desk.

The folder is password protected, but Celdon's fingers fly across the keyboard and produce nine identical black dots in the field.

"Sullivan Taylor oversees the VocAps test and allocates each section's recruitment budget. He sends the test results to Systems every year so our computers can perform the algorithm that ranks each recruit's aptitude for every section. Then the board sends a list of the best matches to each section's leaders."

Celdon breezes through the files and pulls up a spreadsheet. Before I have a chance to see the data, he swivels around and looks up at me with an uncharacteristically serious expression.

"I debated whether or not I should show you this." He swallows and looks away. "It isn't good. If you'd rather not know, we can turn around and never talk about it again."

The look on his face is making my breath get stuck in my chest. You'd think someone died.

"I need to know."

He nods. "I figured."

Turning back toward the computer, he swivels the monitor so it's right in front of me. Down the left-hand column is an alphabetical list of recruits, and across the top is a row of more than a hundred categories.

Celdon scrolls down to the Rs and finds my name.

"These are the results for every category of your VocAps test," he says, dragging his finger down the row.

My eyes flicker down the numbers for "Operating Systems," "Computer Architecture," "Programming," "Software Design," "Discreet Structures," and "Mathematics." All my scores are high — even higher than I scored on my practice exams.

"Look," says Celdon. "You scored a ninety-eight overall. That's the highest I've ever seen."

"What did you score?"

He shrugs, trying to look indifferent. "Ninety-five."

A slow grin spreads across my face, and Celdon concedes with a chuckle. "Shut up."

I elbow him in the ribs, and my eyes shift to the other cells to the right of my VocAps score. "So what are these numbers?"

"These categories factor in your health history, your immune system, and your genetic predisposition to about a hundred different diseases."

"What?"

My heart is racing. I remember taking the physical exam, of course, but that was just standard procedure to make sure I was fit for duty.

"It took me a while to work out their formula, but they score you based on how likely they think you are to kick the bucket — your risk for everything from heart disease to cancer to Alzheimer's," says Celdon.

"They can't know that . . ."

"They can. Genome mapping. It's very speculative, but they view it as your odds. They're betting on the people with the best chance of survival." He stops, running a hand through his crazy locks. "They call it your viability score."

"What was my score?" I ask, not sure I even want to know.

Celdon grimaces, and for a moment, I wonder if he's even going to tell me. "Thirty-three."

"Thirty-three *what?*"

His eyes crinkle in pain. "Thirty-three percent chance of living to the age of thirty."

It feels as though the floor has dropped out from under me. The cubicle is suddenly too small, and my entire body goes numb with shock.

"What am I going to die from?"

Celdon lets out a humorless laugh. His face is deadly serious and full of regret. "I don't know, Riles. But by the looks of it . . . I'd say some type of cancer."

I feel the tears burning in my throat. Celdon can see I'm on the verge of breaking down, so he presses on. "It's not a sure thing. Your genes don't seal your fate. There are environmental factors and your behavior . . . but this is what dragged down your score."

"But if my aptitude score —"

"It's weighted, Riles. Aptitude is only about twenty percent of your total score."

"What's the other eighty percent?"

"How likely you are to survive and pass on your wonderful — or not-so-wonderful — genetic traits."

"*Eighty percent?* That's ridiculous. People's scores would be so low!"

He shakes his head slowly. "Your risk factors are way outside the normal range. You have a pretty nasty health history score because of the radiation from the Fringe."

"How did you score?" I ask, my voice hoarse and scratchy. "You're First Gen, too."

He shrugs. "An unbelievable eighty percent, though they did deduct points for my 'risky lifestyle.'" He puts an admirable amount of contempt on the last two words, and I feel a little sick.

"This is so wrong. If people knew —"

"But people *don't* know. And you can't tell anyone."

I stare at him in disbelief. Celdon — the burnout who refused to be grateful that the most prestigious section bid on him — is scared. Though whether he's scared of Systems or the board, I can't quite tell.

I feel numb all over, but something is still nagging at me. "It still doesn't explain why Recon bid so high on me."

"I know. I'm working on that part. But guess who was ranked at the top of Recon's recruitment list."

"Me?" I shake my head. "But why?"

"Probably because you're too smart to be in ExCon and you're going to die young anyway."

I roll my eyes. "Thanks."

"They also increased recruitment to Recon," he says quietly. "Do you have any idea why?"

I shake my head. Frankly, that feels like the least of my problems.

Feeling nosy, I scroll up to Sawyer's scores. She scored high in aptitude and viability, which makes sense. She's Second Gen. Her parents both work in Health and Rehab.

"They can't do this," I say.

"But they have."

"What about you? How are you okay with this?"

Celdon's eyes harden. "I'm not, but there's nothing I can do."

He logs out of Jacob Morsey's account and turns off the monitor. I listen to the gentle hum of the system shutting down and the hiss of the air conditioner.

All I wanted was to earn a spot in this room. Now I'm here, yet I couldn't be farther away.

"Why did you show me this?" I ask finally.

Celdon looks surprised. "You're my best friend, Riles. I figure you deserved to know — even if there's nothing you can do about it."

In that moment, I have the strange urge to hug Celdon. He may be a pain in the ass sometimes, but he's always looked out for me. He's the closest thing I have to family.

My parents brought me here before our region was hit during Death Storm, but they died a few weeks later. Celdon was found alone near the compound by a Recon worker when he was just a toddler. Nobody knows what happened to his parents.

"We should tell Sawyer," I say. "She won't believe this."

"You can't tell Sawyer," snaps Celdon, clear panic in his voice. "She's one of them now."

I stare at him. The three of us spent all of higher ed together, and now Celdon's acting as though she's a completely different person.

"One of them?" I say incredulously. "One of *you*, you mean. You're tier one."

"That's different. I'm in Systems."

"How is that different?"

"Health and Rehab is supposed to put ethics above all else. If Sawyer knew, she'd have to say something."

"And you don't care about ethics?"

"It doesn't matter what I care about. All that matters is what you're willing to do. Systems is about pragmatism. If that means burying this deep just so the lights come on and people get fed, I'm willing to do that."

"What are you *talking* about?"

"What good would it do? If we told everyone the bidding was rigged? What if we told everyone that what they did didn't make any difference — that they had no control over their lives?"

He lowers his voice. "This is how it works. This is how it *has* to work."

I shake my head, but he keeps going. It sounds as though he's trying to convince himself, not me.

"People have to do their jobs. If they knew, the compound would collapse."

"It's easy for you to say!" I snarl. "They aren't sending you out there to die."

"It's not just about you, Riles," he says in a strained voice. "It's about everybody."

I stare at him in disbelief. I've never seen this side of Celdon. All he's done for the past year is resist recruitment, and now that Systems has their hooks in him, he's willing to fall in line as though nothing is wrong.

He takes a deep breath. "If the compounds collapsed, we'd die out. *Humans* would die out. We're the last survivors."

I shake my head, looking up at the inky patch of sky visible through the ceiling. I know I shouldn't tell him, but I can't hold it in anymore. "No, we're not."

nine

Eli

The dream always starts the same, always just as vivid. You never forget the first time you're pushed out of those airlock doors, but you *especially* don't forget the first time you force someone else out.

It's the heat that hits you first — a blistering, dry heat that makes you think the sun is exploding, that it's cooking you alive on the dry, cracked earth. A lifetime, a decade, or even just three weeks between deployments will make you forget how hot it can get.

I'm sweating so much I think I'm going to die. That's when the panic hits. You're no longer protected by thick lead-coated glass walls, and you think you feel the radiation leeching into your system.

You don't. At least not yet.

It might take days, weeks, or years of exposure for the radiation to kill you, and even then, half the cadets die before the radiation can make them sick.

Even behind their masks, I see my own fear reflected in their faces. The airlock doors have closed. The first time you're shoved out there, the sheer size of the compound is staggering. It's a smooth glass box stretching up as far as you can see.

You wonder if anyone is watching in the upper tunnels. You wonder if anyone even cares.

With nowhere else to go, you start the trek across the wide

expanse of Utah desert. There is no air. It's so dry your pores are sucking dust rather than moisture as your feet stir up the cracked dirt.

I hear two pairs of feet shuffling behind me. The girl, Kara, lets out a little whimper and sniffs. I might as well leave her here, because she's not going to make it out there beyond the cleared zone.

There's the soft, friendly note of an interface turning on. The other kid called Juan is consulting the interactive map of the area, but it will only be useful in the cleared zone.

Once we pass the solar fields and the two-mile radius of safe, drifter-free desert, all bets are off. It's a war zone. You're more likely to run into a drifter because you're not paying attention than wander twenty miles off course into the nearest red zone.

When we reach the border, I finally turn on my interface to scan for land mines. They light up like angry red boils in front of my eyes, and we navigate around them in silence.

Once Juan and Kara clear the mines, I let out a breath of relief I didn't realize I'd been holding.

They've had training, I tell myself. *I trained them. They know what to do.*

But they've only had three months of training. They were supposed to have a year.

I'm on high alert now. They are, too. It's not as though anyone can sneak up on us in the huge expanse of nothing, but a good sniper could take us out from the dunes if he had the right weapon.

Still, there's an itch on the back of my neck that has nothing to do with the two terrified kids trailing behind me. Their steady breathing tells me they've recovered from the initial shock of the Fringe and have begun to calm down, but that's a mistake.

The danger only increases the farther you get from the compound.

We reach the first abandoned town after twenty minutes of unnerving silence. It was a shitty place before Death Storm — one of those pit-stop towns you think people can't possibly live in — but now it looks like a ghost town.

I jerk my head over my shoulder to tell them to look alive. Towns are always the most dangerous, which is why I hate patrolling them. But we can't allow settlements to take hold this close to the cleared zone.

When drifters gather, they get greedy. They get aggressive. The last surge into the cleared zone happened years ago, and Recon was cleaning up body parts around the perimeter for weeks.

We make our way in silence from one building to another. I secretly hope we don't find any squatters, because I don't want to traumatize these kids any more than I have to. As it is, they'll probably need a few days of sedation and weeks of psychotherapy before they're fit enough for active duty.

I can hear Kara's ragged breathing again. I'm pretty sure she's just dehydrated, but then she touches my arm, and I almost jump out of my skin.

I turn quickly enough to catch a flash of red near a scuzzy old restaurant with a faded yellow sign. That's not good. I signal Juan to approach quietly, and his round face goes pale. He's not checking his interface anymore.

We flatten ourselves against the nearest building — a Laundromat — and inch toward the restaurant. We haven't even reached the corner when I hear the yell.

A bullet whizzes past my face.

They're shooting at us. I can't tell how many.

I don't even bother to check if the coast is clear. I grab the two cadets and yank them around the corner out of the line of fire. They're completely numb with shock.

I hunker down behind a rusted-out car and search desperately for the source of the shots. Now I know the other guy was just bait. They knew we were here all along.

Juan is shifting around behind me, trying to line up his shot, but he knocks over a trashcan, and a volley of gunshots follows the source of the noise.

I see two of them hiding behind another parked car and shoot at their feet. One of them yells out and stumbles to the side, and I get a clear shot at his head.

The other one is well hidden, but he's too cowardly to pursue us knowing he's outnumbered.

"Go!" I croak, and Juan and Kara take off between the buildings. Juan flies out first, and a shot echoes through the alley. He yelps and falls backward, and everything slows down.

I yank Kara behind me and aim at the man in the red shirt who shot Juan. He's got a dusty black bandana wrapped around his head, and his brown skin is so filthy he practically blends in with the desert. I hit him in the head.

Juan has collapsed on the ground, and I take the chance of darting out into the road to get him.

As soon as I look down at him, I know it's too late. There's a gaping, bloody wound in his chest, and he's sweating and whimpering as he bleeds out. I kneel down beside him and yank off his mask.

"It's okay," I tell him, trying to keep my voice steady as I apply pressure to the wound.

"It hurts," he blubbers. "Can you take the bullet out?"

"It wouldn't matter."

I shouldn't have said that. I don't even know why I'm trying to stop the bleeding. It's just causing him pain in his last few minutes on earth.

He nods a little, and I see tears in his soft brown eyes.

"It's going to be quick," I murmur.

"How quick?"

"I . . . don't know. A couple minutes at most."

I glance up the street, but the other man has disappeared. We don't have much time.

"I'm s-sorry," Juan whimpers.

I shake my head. "Don't be." I want to make a joke — tell him I got shot my first time out, too, but that doesn't seem like the right thing to say.

"Tell my dad I'm sorry."

I nod, though I don't know Juan well enough to know what he's apologizing for.

Then he dies. There's no warning. I don't even have time to think of what else I should tell him.

What a failure. I killed my first recruit, and I didn't even have the decency to give him a proper sendoff.

I hear a gurgle behind me and turn. Kara's hunkered down against a dented trashcan, hugging herself and sobbing like a moron. *What is she thinking? We're in a war zone.*

I close Juan's eyes with my fingers — something I've never had to do before — and jerk my head at her to tell her to follow me.

I don't even bother to check the rest of the buildings. I'm pretty sure those men were the only squatters here, and even if there were more, I don't think I'd be able to get us out alive with Kara the way she is. Her sobs have escalated to full-body spasms so violent I'm surprised she's still walking.

"You'll be okay," I say to her. My voice sounds oddly distant coming through the mask. "You're fine."

I don't know what I'm saying. I keep turning around to check on her, feeling really scared for some reason.

I get her out of the town, but she isn't growing quiet. If anything, she's getting worse. I turn to face her and see she's covered in blood. But it isn't Juan's blood. She never touched him. It's her own blood — a slow leak from her abdomen.

"You're hit," I say. My voice sounds very far away.

Her glassy eyes focus on me, but they aren't pale blue as Kara's were. They're stormy gray.

I don't see dirty-blond hair rippling in the desert wind. It's dark and shiny, and it's Harper who's shot — Harper who's folding in on herself over the dry, cracked earth.

This can't be happening. I can't lose another one.

I stumble toward her, but I hit a wall. It's six inches of lead-coated glass, and she's dying on the other side.

She pulls her hands away from her uniform, and they're wet and shiny with blood.

I gasp and then jerk awake, sitting bolt upright.

I'm covered in cold sweat, and the covers are twisted around my legs like a straightjacket. I rest my head in my hands, trying to catch my breath as my heart rate returns to normal.

Get a grip, I tell myself. *That's not what happened.*

You'd think after having that dream a hundred times, it wouldn't bother me as much, but you'd be wrong. It doesn't even make sense. Kara wasn't there the day Juan was killed. That happened weeks later. Back-to-back missions — back-to-back failures.

What's worse, my brain has added another sick layer of torture: Kara turning into Harper.

I know it doesn't mean anything because I don't believe in

premonitions, but I can't shake the gnawing dread. These cadets aren't as soft as Juan and Kara were, but it doesn't matter. The Fringe will take them anyway.

When I lie back on my pillows, I don't see their faces anymore. Harper's face is superimposed against my eyelids, staring up at me in horror with those gray eyes. I pushed her too far today. She'll never listen to me now.

Harper doesn't fear me; she hates me, and she should. She just doesn't know why.

ten

Harper

I wake up at oh-six hundred to the deafening rumble of the approaching train. A small earthquake rattles my flimsy compartment walls and nearly shakes me out of my bunk.

I squeeze my eyes shut. I have this horrible, sick feeling brewing in the pit of my stomach. It reminds me of mornings when I've woken up after getting completely wasted and wondered what I did the night before.

Unfortunately, I remember everything.

Part of me wishes Celdon would never have shown me what he had. The other part — egomaniac Harper — is relieved that I didn't actually fail my VocAps test.

Then there's the fact that I hit Eli in the face yesterday. He deserved it, but I have no idea how he'll act today.

How did my life get so messed up in a matter of days?

As I examine the ugly bruise around my neck, I think about the fact that my window of opportunity to leave the compound has closed for good. I could have gone to another compound in hopes of a better bid, but leaving would have felt like the ultimate failure. And with a forty-six, I'd most likely end up in Ex-Con and spend the rest of my twenties repairing the compound and maintaining the solar fields.

A loud banging on my door shakes me out of my moment of self-pity.

"Harvard!" yells a familiar voice. "Get out here!"

I groan loudly enough for him to hear and take my time answering the door.

Eli is leaning against my doorframe, his crisp gray uniform straining against his well-muscled shoulders. When I meet his gaze, my jaw drops, and I take an automatic step back. He's sporting a huge bruise on his jaw and one hell of a black eye. I know he didn't get that from me.

"What happened to you?" I blurt out.

He fixes me with a sharp gaze. "I walked into a door."

I raise an eyebrow, wondering who in the compound could get the jump on Eli. I glance behind him and am surprised to see a very unhappy Bear. His shoulders are sagged in defeat, and there are dark purplish shadows rimming his eyes. He looks as though he hasn't slept since Bid Day.

"You going to hit me again, Harvard?" asks Eli, a smirk cracking the sharp lines of his face.

"No, sir," I groan.

His smile widens — a startling contrast to all the bruises — and I'm surprised how much it adds to his looks. "Good. There's only so much my face can take."

There's a brief, awkward pause, and Bear lets out a sigh that seems to deflate his oversized body.

"I have to say . . . I thought you'd take the ticket out of here." I shake my head. I can't bring myself to talk to him about it.

"Well . . . since you're still here, training starts now."

"You said it starts at oh-eight —"

"I changed my mind. We're getting an early start. Now move it!"

I groan again and gather my hair into a ponytail. When I pull the dark strands off my neck, Eli's eyes land on my bruise. His mouth hardens into a thin line, but he doesn't say anything —

just clears his throat and takes off at a jog.

He pounds on Lenny's door next, and she takes several minutes to answer. When she finally stumbles out into the tunnel, her bright curls are tumbling out of a disheveled braid, and her face is pale under all those freckles.

She glares at Eli and falls in behind me, muttering under her breath about the odds of getting away with murdering your commanding officer.

Eli bangs on two more doors, and when the other cadets emerge, he takes off down the tunnel again. My feet scuff along behind him until I realize he's taking us up the stairs.

Lenny lets out a note of exasperation and stops dead. Eli bounds up the steps two at a time without looking back. I follow slowly, still in a haze of sleep, and I hear Bear whimper a little as he pulls his weight forward to regain momentum.

The spiky-haired kid is surprisingly fast, considering he just woke up. His long spidery legs clear the first set of stairs before Lenny is halfway up, and the petite blond girl huffs along behind her with a determined look on her face.

Eli leads us around the ground level and up several more flights of stairs.

There's an angry stitch in my side, but I ignore it and focus on moving my feet. Spiky Hair is keeping a good pace drafting just behind Eli, and I manage to stay a few yards behind them, my eyes fixed on Eli's shoulder blades. The other three quickly fall behind.

By the time we reach the mid-levels, the tunnels are bustling with EnComm merchants heading to their shops in the commissary. They avoid eye contact as we jog past. Tier-two workers don't regard us with open distain the way Systems and Information do; they look at us as though they dodged a bullet.

Around the commissary, news bulletins snake along the walls in bright plasma ribbons, throwing flashes of neon light off the spotless store windows. The results of Bid Day are all over the news, along with the names of tier-three recruits who took the train to another compound.

Staring up into their enlarged digitized faces, I wonder how many of the recruits who left received poor bids because of some genetic deficiency. Two hundred miles away in the nearest compound, there's talk of closing admission to outside recruits due to overcrowding.

We run a loop around the tunnels and up three levels. Eli has picked up speed, and I'm struggling to keep pace. My legs feel as though they're made of lead, and I'm gasping for air. Lenny, Bear, and the blonde are nowhere in sight.

Eli leads us around the narrow tunnel skirting one of the glass-enclosed ag labs, where hundreds of plants stretch toward the artificial light in their hydroponic tanks — a scenic route by compound standards.

Food engineers drift between the rows in their neon yellow suits, carefully adjusting the plastic tubes carrying water and fertilizer to the plants.

It's an intricate system: Manufacturing grows, cleans, and processes the food that's sent to the canteen, and Waste Management rejuvenates any unused organic material for fertilizer. They're used to having an audience of lower-ed children and early risers out for their morning walk, so they don't pay us any attention as we huff past.

When Eli doubles back toward the stairs, I seriously consider pushing him down a few flights. But then he heads back toward the lower levels on his own.

He stops on the ground level and waits for the rest of us to catch up. Bear looks like a hot mess with sweat rolling down his temples, and Lenny's face is the same color as her hair. The other girl looks like a paper doll that could blow away any second, but she's wearing a faraway look — so different from Lenny's contemptuous scowl.

"Get some breakfast," says Eli in a clipped voice. He's not even breathing hard. "I still expect you at oh-eight hundred."

He stalks off toward the canteen, and Lenny limps up behind me, singing a murderous tune under her breath.

"I don't know but I've been told; Eli Parker is mighty cold."

Her angry expression makes me let out a snort of laughter. Spiky Hair breaks into a hazy grin, and even Bear smiles. The other girl is still lost in her own world.

As the five of us shuffle toward the canteen, I can't help wonder what's wrong with each of them. They didn't score a forty-six, but there has to be some genetic defect that landed them in here. That knowledge causes an uncomfortable pang in my gut, and I feel a little guilty for knowing what I know and not being able to tell them the truth.

I catch Sawyer leaving the to-go line, and she waves shyly, eyeing the sweaty horde of cadets around me. My heart contracts a little at the sight of her, and I desperately want to catch up to her and spill about what an ass Eli is. It's so strange to be eating breakfast without her, but I know she must be busy now with the long hours med interns work.

The food today is even more disappointing than yesterday. It's the grossest kind of algae, beets, and a cold block of protein. The blonde finds us an empty table, and when I join her, she's engrossed in an image on her interface.

At first, I'm not sure she notices me, so I clear my throat and clank my silverware to announce my arrival.

"I'm Kindra, by the way," she says, still not making eye contact through the shield of blue light around her face.

"Harper."

"I know," she says dreamily. "Harper Riley, Systems track."

"Not anymore," I mutter.

She frowns. "You shouldn't give up what you love just because you're here now."

I raise an eyebrow, utterly bewildered by this strange girl.

"Haven't you?"

She lets out a soft, musical laugh and shakes her head. "No. I don't think I could if I wanted to." She sighs. "Say . . . when were you born?"

"Sorry?"

Kindra moves her hand, and I see the reverse image on her interface rotate. "What day were you born?"

"April second."

"What time?"

"Uh . . . I don't know."

"Find out for me."

That strikes me as odd. "Why?"

"She's reading your birth chart," sighs Lenny, sliding onto the bench beside me and digging into her beets.

"My what?"

"It's an astrological picture of the day you were born," says Kindra, the image reflecting off her wide, orb-like eyes.

"Oh," I say, trying not to be rude. "I'm an orphan. I don't know my time of birth." I exchange an awkward glance with Lenny. "I never asked."

"Lucky you," Lenny murmurs. "She, uh, read my chart yesterday."

I nod slowly, a little weirded out.

"Won't the medical ward have your birth records?"

I shift uncomfortably, wishing I could extract myself from this conversation. "I wasn't born in the compound."

"It's all right," says Kindra, switching off her interface. "I can still get some insights from the date." She gives me a small smile. "We'll talk later."

Lenny makes a little choking noise around her food, and I realize she's trying not to laugh.

"Where did you learn to do this?" I ask. I've never heard of anyone practicing astrology in the compound. Most people are empiricists to the core.

"My grandmother. She does some readings and palmistry in the commissary, but most of that stuff is only for show."

"Good to know," mutters Lenny under her breath.

"So your family is EnComm?"

Kindra nods, not seeming at all put out by the fact that she was bumped down to tier three.

"What did they say about . . . you know . . . your bid?"

"Oh, they were expecting some kind of upset," she says in a bright voice. "We weren't sure what, but it was in the stars."

"I think that's nice," says Bear, his voice barely audible. His head is bent low over his bowl, glaring at the meager portion, but I can see the dark look in his eyes.

Kindra smiles at him, and Lenny's eyebrows are so high they're in danger of disappearing into her hairline.

The rest of them nod and respond politely as Kindra babbles about their birth charts, and I can't help thinking that I couldn't have picked a more absurd group of people if I tried.

Kindra is soft-spoken and serene, and the spiky-haired boy named Blaze laughs and jokes easily, completely unruffled by Eli's morning power trip. Bear is sad and broody, and Lenny is a snarky little firecracker. I like her the best.

I finish my food quickly, and Lenny and I head back down to the training center. I'm not looking forward to seeing Eli again so soon, but I really want to get away from Kindra and her birth charts.

"That one's got a few screws loose, doesn't she?" says Lenny as we head down the stairs.

"Yeah. You could say that."

Though I know she meant well, I'm a little unnerved by Kindra asking about my birth. Most days, I can avoid any mention of the bizarre way I came into this world. Celdon's the only other Fringe baby I know, and I don't broadcast the fact that I'm First Gen.

According to my guardian in the Institute, I spent my first two weeks in the compound under a plastic bubble in the medical ward for observation. I wasn't even with my parents when they died. Even though I can't remember them, the thought of being alone while they were getting sicker and sicker makes me sad.

Most of the time, I like to pretend that my life began the day Celdon and I met in the Institute. At least that way, I can pretend I know who my family is.

When we reach the training center, it's already buzzing with other new recruits. They look lost like us — desperately striking up conversations and trying to make friends. The only difference is that they're still fresh and full of energy. They didn't have to go on a crazy run through the compound at the crack of dawn.

Kindra, Bear, and Blaze join us a few minutes later. Then Eli strides in, listening intently to something another lieutenant is saying.

When he sees us all waiting on the line, he claps his hands together. "All right! Good morning. I hope you're all limbered up after our run."

Silence.

A few of the other lieutenants still haven't arrived. Most of their cadets are talking and laughing, but a few are watching Eli with apprehension from the other side of the room.

"Why didn't they have to run this morning?" Lenny asks, a serious edge to her voice.

"You're out of line, Horwitz," Eli warns.

Her scowl deepens.

"You shouldn't worry about what the other cadets are doing. Maybe they're in better shape than you . . . maybe their direct commands are nicer than me . . . or maybe their direct commands just don't care if they survive."

Irritation flickers in the pit of my stomach. This "you're all going to die" routine is getting old — especially now that I know that I probably *am* going to die before I hit thirty.

"Can we get on with it, then?" I snap before I can stop myself.

Eli rounds on me. "You got something to say, Harvard?"

"Just getting a little sick of this life-and-death crap."

I know mouthing off is a bad move, and when Eli's eyes darken, I know I've pushed my luck too far. "Congratulations, Harvard. You just earned everyone two laps around the track."

Bear and Lenny groan, and I mentally slap myself for opening my mouth.

"Go! Last one back does twice as many push-ups."

Before I can think — before I give in to the urge to put my fist through Eli's face — I sprint toward the metal stairs in the corner.

The "track" is actually a grated metal gangway suspended ten feet in the air along the edge of the training center.

Blaze is already two paces ahead, springing along like an insect, and Lenny is right on my heels. I can hear her huffing by the time we clear the top of the stairs, but my legs are thrumming with nervous energy.

The whole track shakes as we run, and I worry it won't support all our weight. All I can hear is the bang of my feet on metal, and all I can think is *don't be last.* I will not give Eli the satisfaction.

After one lap, my lungs are burning, and there's a knife lodged in the side of my abdomen. I ignore it. My legs don't need to consult my lungs or my brain. They move on their own.

Lenny has disappeared. She's twenty yards behind me clinging to the railing, but Blaze is still hotfooting it a few paces ahead. He's so tall and skinny; I'm not even sure how he stands upright.

Halfway into the second lap, I start wishing I'd visited the rec center more often. My chest is on fire, and my legs are jelly.

Blaze is already taking the stairs two at a time, as though he has rubber bands where his joints should be.

"Let's go, Harvard!" Eli belts from the ground. "Get your ass down here!"

I nearly trip over my own feet careening down the shaky stairs and fly over to where Blaze is standing on the tape line.

"Give me twenty."

Hating Eli, I drop down to the filthy mat and will my toddler-sized biceps to hold me off the ground.

"Jesus Christ, Harvard. Stop. Just stop. That's pathetic."

I don't stop. I let myself drop back down until my chin touches the mat and push myself back up.

Lenny and Kindra arrive panting, and Bear is still nowhere in sight.

"You two!" Eli snaps. "Over there."

My arms are shaking — refusing to hold my weight — but I don't stop. I can't even breathe, but I realize I don't need to. My body keeps moving.

Blaze is already finished, that son of a bitch.

There's a small earthquake as Bear shuffles over, heaving as though he's going to die. I finish my push-ups and stagger to my feet, sweating and panting but feeling gratified. I'm not the weakest one here.

Eli lets out a sigh, and I try not to roll my eyes. He's such an asshole he's become ridiculous to me.

"Congratulations, Adams. You get to live." He rounds on me. "Harvard. Those push-ups were so weak I'm not really sure how you pull yourself out of bed in the morning. The rest of you . . . give me forty."

Nobody grumbles. No one argues. Their willpower is already so shot that all three of them drop down to attempt forty push-ups when I know they can't be capable of more than ten.

Kindra looks as though she still has no idea how she got here. Bear looks embarrassed, defeated, and hopelessly sad. Lenny, on the other hand, is a flaming ball of red-hot fury.

After the push-ups, there's more running. After the running, we do sit-ups, planks, and up-downs. My body is a tight cord of pain.

On the second set of planks, I feel a boot on the small of my back. Eli pushes down, and my whole body shakes.

I refuse to look up. I will not give him the satisfaction.

I bite down, gritting my teeth so the poisonous words I long to hurl at him won't escape. The boot lifts.

"Two more laps!" he yells. "Then you can go to lunch."

I nearly fall over when I try to stand. My legs are jelly. My arms are hanging limp and useless at my sides. My back feels as though Eli took a sledgehammer to it.

As I pull myself up the rickety metal stairs to the track, I realize Lenny, Kindra, and Bear are still on the mat. Bear's shoulders are quaking in his plank, and Kindra has collapsed in on herself. Lenny is retching in the corner of the gym.

Blaze appears at my elbow, drenched in sweat. "Come on," he says in his slow voice. "If he sees us looking, he won't let us leave."

He slips ahead of me, and I follow him at a jog. I don't even feel my lungs or the stitch in my side anymore. I'm entirely numb — my body is destroyed.

By the time we finish our lap, we've already wasted ten precious minutes of our lunch hour. I shuffle over cautiously to Lenny, who's still propped against the cinderblock wall, trying not to vomit.

"Leave her, Harvard!" barks Eli. "We don't waste food on quitters."

"She needs to eat," I say, fighting to keep my voice even.

"She'll learn. If she wants to eat, she has to earn it."

He's standing right in front of me now, those dark blue eyes boring into mine. I feel the rage humming in my chest — the cumulative effect of learning how I ended up in Recon, being short on sleep, and annoyance at Eli's sadistic training methods.

"Get the hell out of here before I revoke your canteen privileges, too."

I walk away — mostly because I don't think I can do another push-up — and hear him yelling at Bear.

I don't turn around. I know it's cowardly, but in that moment, I just want to get away from him.

I barely notice my feet carrying me up the stairs. I'm so lost in the anger consuming my every thought.

When I get to the canteen, a group of Systems recruits are standing in the entryway, waiting for their friends. They're laughing and joking, looking as cool and pristine as models in their crisp white blazers. The girls are shiny and clean, their makeup impeccable, not a hair out of place.

As I approach, their voices falter. Their eyes follow me across the foyer, identical looks of disgust written all over their pretty faces.

I know I must look like hell. My hair is falling out of its ponytail and sticking to my sweaty neck. My black tank top is completely soaked. I ditched my gray overshirt hours ago.

One of the guys is standing right in the middle of the entryway, blocking it with his tall frame. He has a mess of chocolate curls obscuring half his face and a handsome smirk. I elbow past him, not bothering to be polite, and catch the name on his ID badge: Jacob Morsey.

That's unfortunate.

I suddenly have the strange impulse to turn and apologize — even though he has no idea what Celdon and I did. But then I hear him mutter something nasty under his breath about Recon girls and laugh. I'm genuinely shocked by his creative innuendo, which is rare.

Then the others burst into snickers — a terrible, grating sound that wears on my composure and drowns out the gentle din of chatter from the canteen.

I stop and turn to see Jacob Morsey standing there in his stupid white blazer: shiny teeth, pretty face, perfect genetics. He's an entitled asshole, and yet he just spent his morning behind the computer that should have been mine. He thinks it's pure skills and smarts that landed him there, when it's really just an accident of birth.

The hatred is building inside me at an uncontrollable rate. I try to push it down, but I've already reached my breaking point.

I'm run down and defeated from Eli's demands.

Before I know what I'm doing, I'm striding toward Jacob Morsey. He takes a step back, but not fast enough. When I get within two feet of him, my fist swings out of its own accord and crashes into his face. He staggers back, knocking into his friends. I hit him harder than I meant to, and his eyes are tearing up.

A few EnComm people standing in the mess line look around in interest, and pretty soon, everyone is staring.

Jacob is groaning and holding his nose. I see a trickle of blood escape between his fingers and dribble all over the front of his blazer. The girl nearest him is looking at me with pure horror. Jacob's male friends are jabbering angrily, their voices rising in disbelief.

I see them closing in, their bodies slow to react to the fury I've been suppressing for the last twenty-four hours.

I need to get out of here.

I stagger backward, nearly tripping over my own feet, horrified at my loss of self-control. I turn to leave but catch a sharp pair of blue eyes watching me from the to-go line.

Eli is leaning against the wall, looking annoyingly amused.

eleven

Harper

I don't even realize my knuckles are scraped up until I'm standing back on the tape line in the training center. I must have grazed the asshole's teeth.

My blood is still boiling, though I have no idea why. I've heard the things people say about Recon before, of course. Even I looked down on them, but I'd never anticipated open contempt.

More than anything, I'm confused by my own outburst. Since when did I go around punching people in the canteen? I've hit people before, sure, but only when I had no other choice.

I was out of control this time — a threat to public safety. Control should lock me up and throw away the key.

Lenny, Kindra, and Bear are the last to arrive. They look okay, which makes me think Eli let them go eat after all.

Finally Eli walks in, looking smug as can be.

"Well, look who it is," he says, a dangerous smirk playing on his lips. "How you feeling, slugger?"

I realize he's staring at me, and so is everyone else. I don't say anything, though I can feel Eli's eyes burning a hole through me. He looks happier than I've ever seen him, as though my display in the canteen was just the reaction he'd been probing for.

"Everybody grab a bag!" he yells.

The others scramble over to a line of punching bags against one wall. I take my place between Blaze and Lenny, watching Eli weave between the bags.

"Since Riley is so eager to start beating the shit out of people, I think it's time you cadets learned how to fight."

His use of my real name is enough to shake me out of my numb rage. I chance a look at him. He's standing with his arms folded across his chest, that smirk directed right at me.

"What?"

"I can't have you picking fights all over the compound if you don't know how to win, Riley. You've got one hell of an arm, but you won't always be beating up idiots like Jacob Morsey."

I stare at him. Eli laughs, and it's a real laugh. His eyes crinkle in amusement, but he closes his mouth quickly, as if he knows he *shouldn't* laugh.

Suddenly he's all business again — Eli the asshole. He shows us the right way to throw a straight punch — leading with our shoulder — and how to get a full extension.

Then we're at the bags, and I'm beating my hands sore through my gloves. It feels good until Eli appears over my shoulder to remind me how weak I am — how I'm not throwing my full strength behind each blow.

He watches me carefully and mutters instructions under his breath. "Tuck your chin. Roll your shoulders. Keep your hands up at all times."

His snapping commands are surprisingly effective. After a few minutes, I feel like a real fighter. He nods once and moves on to Bear.

That's when the yelling starts. It seems as though he's targeting Bear now — seeing how far he can push him before he breaks.

But Bear is a brick wall of muscle and determination. I know Eli's words bother him, but rather than shutting him down, they're beginning to stir something inside him — ferocity I haven't seen before.

Eli sees this too and doesn't let up. He keeps yelling at Bear until he grows bored of watching us. He shows us two defense maneuvers to block punches and pairs us up to practice.

I work with Kindra and Lenny in a group of three, and we take turns blocking. I've been dodging punches my whole life, so being instructed on the best way to fight back feels natural. I get my rhythm down almost immediately.

But watching Lenny and Kindra go through the motions is painful. I can tell they're tired — that they don't want to be here.

None of us is here by choice, but I can tell it wears on the others more. Maybe I never really expected to escape the fights and the ugliness. And truthfully, spending my day hitting things seems about right.

Eli hovers nearby, watching us spar and making adjustments. When he passes our group a third time, he sighs aloud and tells us we can stop.

For a second, I think he might let us out of training early, but he strides into the center of the room and calls Bear into the tape outline of a ring.

Bear lets out a loud groan that makes my heart ache. This isn't going to be good. His shirt is completely soaked with sweat, his face is pale from exhaustion, and he's eyeing Eli as though he's facing down his executioner.

Eli mutters something to Bear, and the two square off in the ring. Bear throws a halfhearted punch, but Eli dodges it easily.

He tries again. His second punch is even slower than the first, and Eli slips a few inches to the side and plants his fist in Bear's well-padded belly.

It didn't hurt much — it couldn't have — but Bear seems to fold in on himself more. He whimpers, clutching his side, and I know he's trying not to cry.

"Come on, Kelso!" Eli yells, smacking his gloves together. He circles around Bear, egging him on in a way that's almost encouraging, but Bear's shoulders just sag lower.

Eli's fist flies out again, slowly enough to give him time to react, but Bear just takes the hit. His baby face crinkles in a grimace, and something snaps inside me.

I realize I'm angry, but not at Eli. Mostly, I'm furious and disgusted with Bear. He's completely given up.

As Eli wears out the mat circling him, the larger boy just shuffles around like a blob on his heels.

Several tense seconds pass as we wait for Eli to hit him again, but he just stops and shakes his head until Bear staggers away.

Eli works through each of us one by one, trying to provoke aggression and speed.

Blaze is quick and sharp-eyed, but he's so hyper and nervous he practically punches himself out trying to get past Eli's defenses. Lenny is angry and uncontrolled, and Eli lays her out with one good bop to the nose.

Kindra might as well have lain down on the mat for how well she defends herself. Despite her obvious determination, every trip around the ring looks as though it pains her, and she seems to grow paler by the second.

When Eli calls me to the ring and slaps a mouth guard into my hand, I know I'm about to get my ass handed to me. But there's another part of me, a louder, defiant part, that wants to knock Eli off his high horse.

The other cadets were pathetic. One of us should be able to get a good hit in.

I square off against him and take a split second to gauge his mood. He's irritable and drained but seems to perk up when I raise my fists and get in my fighting stance. He's barely breaking a sweat, but his sharp eyes are bright with adrenalin.

Eli tucks his chin and rolls his shoulders, and I can tell it's a natural posture for him. I expect him to circle me slowly and wait for me to make the first move, but he doesn't give me a chance to throw a punch.

His fist flies out first, and I barely slip the brunt of his hit and feel his knuckles glance off the side of my face.

I recover quickly and go straight for his nose — anxious to wipe that smug look off his face — but he swats my glove away forcefully with the blade of his forearm. The bone-on-bone contact sends a deep, throbbing pain down my arm, but I grit my teeth and ignore it.

His second punch is too fast and hits me right in the nose. Eli knocks his gloves together in frustration.

"Come on, Riley! Focus!"

I clamp down on my mouth guard. The slow burn of hatred is spreading up my chest, and I swallow down my urge to yell. My eyes are watering from his hit, but it could be a lot worse.

Miraculously, I block Eli's third punch, but he gets me in the abdomen with a left hook. I try to suck in my shudder of pain, but it escapes as a whimper.

He thinks I'm down for the count. He looks . . . concerned? He's distracted enough that his glove has slipped down ever so slightly. What an idiot.

I don't hesitate. I throw my arm forward with all the strength I have left. My glove connects with the side of his face, but he throws another reflexive punch.

Now I know he was holding back on his other hits. Those were the training wheels of punches. This was just a reflex. I surprised him, and he probably ruptured my kidney.

My knees hit the mat before I even realize I've fallen, and a second later, I'm curled up on the sweaty, discolored foam that smells like feet.

I'm going to throw up, I think. *I'm going to throw up and die of internal bleeding.*

"Dismissed!" Eli barks.

I stare at him in confusion, but then I realize he was talking to the others. I'd forgotten all about them, but they're staring at me with a mixture of shock and admiration.

I squeeze my eyes shut and will myself not to cry or throw up.

"Do you need to go to the medical ward?" Eli asks in an anxious voice.

I shake my head. My throat is too tight to speak.

"Are you all right?"

I nod, hating him.

"Sorry," he mutters. "You just surprised me."

He bends down and takes my gloved hands, and for a second, I think he's going to help me up. But he just yanks off my gloves and walks away.

He knocks me to the ground and then *leaves*? He thinks this is what will prepare us for the Fringe? Getting beaten up and berated?

No. He just enjoys being cruel. I think back to the way he came at me yesterday.

You're First Gen, Harvard. I'm surprised you haven't asked before.

That's when it occurs to me: Eli *knows* something.

I can't catch my breath. I can barely stand. I feel shaky and reckless from the surge of adrenalin. I know I shouldn't give in to my impulse to follow him, but I spit out my mouth guard and stagger out of the gym.

Storming down the tunnel toward the officers' compartments, I don't stop to form a plan or decide how I will confront him.

All I know is that my legs are propelling me down the tunnel, and I'm gaining on him. I can see the confident arch of his back. He thinks I'm not a threat. He expects me to cower and take orders and say thank you when he punches me. He expects —

All pretense vanishes when he whips around to face me. His brows knit together in confusion. He really didn't expect me to follow him. He doesn't expect me to still be standing.

But all traces of shock disappear in an instant, and suddenly he's moving toward me with purpose, controlling my footwork, until he's backed me up against the wall.

I wonder if he can hear my loud, angry thoughts.

"What is it, Cadet?" he hisses.

"You know," I snarl, shoving him in the chest and surprising myself.

"What? Why are you following me, Riley?"

"I want answers. Why did Recon bid so high on me? Why did you pick me?"

Eli's mouth is a hard, angry line. His eyes dart down the tunnel. "*I* don't have a say in who receives bids."

"I know. But you read my file. You know why they did it."

He sighs, and I know he's going to feed me a line of crap before he even opens his mouth. "No, Riley. I do not know why Jayden would pick *you* to go out and defend this compound on the Fringe. Clearly she had no idea what a disaster you'd be when she bid on you."

I glare at him. His words sound canned and rehearsed. "You can't bullshit a bullshitter, Eli."

He laughs a cold, empty laugh. "Watch it, Cadet. That's Lieutenant Parker to you."

"You *know*," I snarl. "Otherwise you wouldn't be so afraid to tell me."

"Keep your voice down."

"What?" I snap, my voice rising a decibel. "Why should I keep quiet? What are you hiding?"

Before I can draw a breath, I'm off my feet. Eli has grabbed me around the waist, his arm like a steel vice around my body. I kick and flail, but he holds me easily with one hand as he punches in a door code. The door flies open, and he yanks me into the dark compartment and slams the door closed.

Wild fear flashes through me. We're completely alone in here. He's crazy. But suddenly I'm awake — alive — too curious to be truly afraid.

Eli slams me bodily against the closed door, his forearm pressed against my windpipe. My feet are barely touching the ground, and I'm gasping for air. His face is so close that I can feel his breath stirring my hair.

An automatic light flickers on. Eli is in my face, his eyebrows drawn together so tightly that his brow has creased to form three deep divots. His blue eyes are alight in full threat mode.

But then he hears my ragged breath, and the pressure of his arm on my throat eases up.

When he speaks, his voice is a low growl. But it isn't the aggressive voice he uses during training. It's low and panicked.

"Riley, if you value your life at all, you need to cool it."

I struggle to get the words out of my scratchy windpipe. "Why did Recon bid so high on a forty-six?"

"I — don't — know."

His eyes are so wide that I know he doesn't know about the thirty-three. He's breathing hard, barely containing his fear and frustration. Eli Parker is *afraid*, though I'm not sure why.

"Do you think I failed my VocAps?" I ask. "Do you think I failed all the Systems tests?"

He shrugs, but his shoulders are still stiff. "I don't care. All I do is train what they give me. What you learned about Systems is of little to no use to me."

"Well, I didn't. Did you know that eighty percent of the VocAps score is based on how soon they think you're going to die? Your genetics and your health history. It doesn't matter how high you score on the aptitude test. If they think you might get sick, you can't score high enough for tier one."

His face pales, and his grip on me loosens.

"I'm — a ticking — time bomb," I say, punctuating each word as if I'm throwing a punch. "I have a thirty-three percent chance of living past the age of thirty. So *why* did Recon bid sixty thousand on me?"

Eli's eyes are flitting quickly across my face, as though he's trying to discern if I'm telling the truth.

Then his expression turns stormy and urgent. He believes me. His hands grip my arms, and he pushes me harder into the door.

"Listen. I don't know why Jayden bid on you, and I don't want to know. But if what you're saying is true, then just the fact that you know means you're already in too deep."

He pushes against me and leans down. "Riley, you need to *stop looking*. Now. Don't tell anyone what you found out. You shouldn't even have told me. If this gets out —"

"Don't you think people deserve to know how they're being ranked? This goes against everything we've been told. They're determining people's worth based on their genes — it's completely beyond their control."

But Eli is still shaking his head.

For the first time, I glance over his shoulder at the room he's dragged me into. This must be his compartment. It's larger and nicer than mine. The bed is bigger, and the furniture looks newer and industrial.

"Riley," he says, trying to regain my attention. "Promise me you'll drop this. Promise me you'll stop looking and stop asking around."

I stare up at him, frustrated by his cowardice. If the board can inflict this much fear in Eli Parker . . .

"Don't you care that you probably ended up here because of a genetic accident?" I blurt, my mouth completely hijacking my brain. "You could have done something else, but you ended up here."

Eli's mouth tightens, and I know I've gone too far. He's shutting down.

"You don't know anything about me. And whatever you *think* you know . . . about all this . . . it's making you reckless. Your stupidity is going to get you killed."

Before I can open my mouth to retort, the door flies open behind me, and Eli shoves me out into the tunnel. Steadying myself against the opposite wall, I try to catch my breath. I try to think of something to say to make him listen to me, but his closed door is as good an answer as any.

As I walk back to my own tunnel, two facts solidify in my mind: One, that Eli is terrified of the board, which means I should be, too. And two, that Eli knows a lot more than he's telling me.

twelve

Eli

As soon as I toss her out of my room, I know I should go after her.

She's a loose cannon, and she knows too much. She's going to get herself killed.

But going after her is basically an open invitation for her to drag me down with her. I have no idea how she found out that the scores were weighted — or even if she's right. But it makes sense. That's what scares me the most.

I studied day and night for the Control test. I knew the laws of the compound backward and forward. I was in peak physical condition, but I couldn't hide my genetic deficiencies — the result of Fringe breeding. And since I spent fourteen years soaking up the radiation, I'm probably a fucking mosaic of mutated cells.

And then there's the other thing she said. It makes no sense that Jayden would bid sixty thousand on a scrawny Systems-track girl with a forty-six — even with her good marks and record. The girl's tougher than any meathead recruit I've ever trained and too smart for her own good, but Jayden didn't see what I see.

Unless Jayden was in on the whole thing. She had to be. I've never trusted Jayden as far as I could throw her, but if she's deep enough to know how things really work, she's more dangerous than I thought.

There's only one person I trust to find out, and luckily, he's sleeping with someone who might be able to follow the money.

Before stopping to consider that getting involved in Harper's Bid Day drama means almost certain death, I'm banging on Miles's door.

He doesn't answer, but I can hear his stupid video game playing behind the thin walls.

The door's unlocked, so I walk right in. Miles is the biggest guy in our year. He's not worried about burnouts breaking into his place. He's sprawled out on his couch wearing nothing but a pair of athletic shorts. His shiner from our fight has faded slightly from the last time I saw him, but he still looks pretty intimidating.

"Hey, shut the door!" he yells over the sound of gunfire blaring from his speakers. "Rumor has it Jayden's shopping for a new crew to deploy early."

"So you're hiding?"

"Call it what you want, man, but I'll take being a pussy any day over going out for the second time this month. Fuck that shit."

"You are being a pussy," I say, vaulting the couch and settling down next to him.

He shakes his head, but I can see how worried he is. It doesn't matter how badass you are; no Recon operative *wants* to be deployed. Even on normal rotation, that week leading up to a mission feels like being on death row.

"Hey. I need a favor," I say.

"You need me to go all 'scared straight' on your new recruits?"

I try not to laugh. "No."

"Man, I will never know how you got stuck babysitting cadets all day. You should sleep with Jayden so she'll give you a better assignment."

I shrug. "At least I get three months without deployment."

"But then you have to make it up when your cadets are trained. You couldn't get me to do two-a-months. No way."

I sit back on the couch so he can't see my face. Any time deployment comes up, every muscle in my body tightens until I can hardly breathe.

"So what is it?" he presses.

"I need you to ask Brooke to do something for me."

Miles snickers. "I know it must get lonely being Lieutenant Asshole, but I am *not* sharing."

I kick him in the leg. "No, I just need her to check on a transaction for me."

Brooke is an Operations worker in the financial department. If anyone can access Recon's financial statements, it's her.

Miles raises an eyebrow. "A transaction?"

"From the board."

For a second, I can tell I've shocked Miles, but he recovers his sarcasm almost immediately. "Oh, you want my girlfriend to break the law for you and risk cage time? No problem." His voice is light, but it has deadly "don't fuck with me" undertones.

I roll my eyes. "It's important."

"No. No way. I'm already on thin ice with her. I can't ask her to do this!"

I swallow. I know Miles and Brooke have been fighting lately. They were sweethearts before our Bid Day, and getting placed in different tiers almost broke them up.

Brooke wants to get married, but she doesn't understand the rules. Tier-three guys don't marry tier-two girls. Tier-three guys don't marry anyone.

Miles would be shunned down here if he was lucky — sent out on a suicide mission if he wasn't. If they had a kid, it would end up in the Institute and would never know them — same as any Fringe baby, same as Miles.

"Please. Just ask her. I want to find out how we got sixty thousand credits to bid on a recruit and where the money went."

"Are you serious? You want my girlfriend to risk everything to satisfy your curiosity?"

"She got a forty-six, Miles. It doesn't make sense."

"Is this about that hot little Systems dropout? Shit, I'd pay sixty thousand for her."

I wince, fighting the image of Miles going to town on Harper. "You know what I mean. It's weird that Jayden bid so much."

"I'm going to need more than 'it's weird' to get me to ask Brooke to do this. What's really going on with this girl?"

I take a deep breath, wondering how much I dare tell Miles. "She says she found out that eighty percent of your VocAps score is based on your genes. All the people they think aren't going to live long are scored low so they end up in tier three."

"Shit. How does she know?"

"I didn't ask."

Miles shakes his head. I can tell he's just as shocked as I am, probably wondering where he could have ended up if it weren't for his genes.

Miles is smart — smart enough to have ended up in Health and Rehab, probably. But he wanted to become a merchant so he could run his own business. Instead, he got stuck taking orders and trying to be okay with the three weeks between hell every month.

We're silent for several minutes, and then he lets out a low stream of profanity. I know he's connecting the dots. He's wondering what he's going to die from. Miles is Second Gen, and Second Gen is a crapshoot.

Finally he sighs. "All right. I'll see what Brooke can find out about your girl."

I slap him on the shoulder, not bothering to correct him.

Harper's not *my* anything, and I'm not even sure why I'm so wrapped up in her problems. I barely know her, but I know enough to know she's trouble.

thirteen

Eli

It's surprisingly easy to train this recruit class, even knowing what I know.

They're weak, but they aren't lazy. I can beat weakness out of them, but I can't cure lazy or stupid.

I'm secretly grateful for Lenny's limp and Bear's fat ass because it gives them just enough self-loathing to berate themselves until they can throw a perfect round kick. It's a shame it isn't going to help them much.

Bear could be incredibly strong and deadly, but there isn't time to turn him into the machine he needs to be to survive. Lenny is the angriest, meanest cadet I've ever trained, but she's a painfully slow runner.

Still, their physical deficiencies give them the edge of mental toughness. On the Fringe, that can go a long way.

Kindra tries harder than anyone, but she's so breakable and weak that sending her out to the Fringe will feel almost like a mercy killing. Her white-blond hair and porcelain skin make me feel as though I'm looking right through her. I don't even yell at her, because she doesn't stand much of a chance.

Blaze always looks stoned, but he's fast on his feet with reflexes to match. He'll probably live if he doesn't zone out in the middle of a raid.

And then there's Harper. She's still just as reckless and abrasive as the day I met her, but now instead of letting me get under her skin, she acts as though I'm not even there.

If I tell her to run laps, she runs. If I say do ten extra push-ups, she does. But she's determined to ignore me after our confrontation in my compartment.

She's getting good. *Fast.* In fact, she's getting too good, too fast.

I want to yell at her and tell her to try less and fuck up more, because if Jayden gets wind of just how quickly Harper is progressing, there's a good chance she'll be sent out early. The year for training isn't guaranteed — not if we need people on the ground. A year to train has always been a luxury we could afford, until recently.

I only got three months with Juan and Kara before they were sent out. We lost so many of that class that we doubled down after six months, "promoting" a handful of the ExCon recruits to Recon and giving them only the minimum amount of training.

It was the first double recruitment in nearly a decade, and it was a disaster. The ExCon kids were cocksure and aggressive, convinced they'd been promoted because they were somehow *special,* when in reality, the compound just needed more moving targets. That was the class I needed Miles to scare shitless to get them ready for the Fringe in three months.

Ten months into my first year as lieutenant, I'd lost twelve of the fourteen recruits I'd been given.

Jayden told me this class wouldn't be like that, but I don't believe her. I'm pushing them harder than my previous two classes, hoping it won't mean they're sent out early.

Three weeks in, they're ready to spar with each other. Jayden likes them fighting from week one, but I haven't done anything except static drills since the day I roughed them up a little. Seeing Harper hit the mat like that was awful.

When I tell them to pair up, Kindra latches on to Lenny, and Blaze faces off against Bear.

Harper's eyes drift over to me, and I realize I'm going to have to spar with her. I'm nervous and excited. I've been laying off her since that first week to avoid any more confrontations, but I know she isn't going to hold back all her pent-up anger.

I consider going without the pads, but she's wearing an expression that tells me she wants me dead, so I grab a pair of shin guards, a mouth guard, and a padded vest just in case.

I join her in the ring and square off against her.

"Clean fighting," I remind her, shoving in the mouth guard.

She cocks an eyebrow, and that little gesture makes my stomach do a weird flip. I'm both annoyed and a little turned on.

She swings at me, and I block her easily. She tries a nice little combo that I taught them last week — jab, cross, uppercut, hook — and her hips move at just the right angles. Textbook. Her punches have power, and I'm surprised how fast I need to move to get out of the way.

She smiles around the bulky piece of plastic between her teeth, so I come at her next. She blocks and even throws in her counterstrikes.

I'm actually impressed. Most cadets freeze up in their first real sparring session, but not Harper. Her body knows what to do.

After getting a feel for my rhythm, she becomes more confident. She's soaking in my every movement, watching for a weakness, waiting for me to drop my glove.

I shouldn't be surprised. In the Institute, she broke several kids' noses and a few ribs with no training whatsoever.

Suddenly I hear a thud, and I turn my head just as Harper's fist flies out. She's got a longer reach than I realize, and her fist collides with my jaw — hard.

I swear and step out of the way, still trying to figure out what happened in the next ring over. Bear is sprawled on his back, and my jaw is on fire. Harper doesn't hit like a girl, that's for sure.

She goes red in the face and spits out her mouth guard. "Sorry! I'm sorry. I wasn't going for a cheap shot."

"I know," I mutter, grinning despite the fact that Bear is lying on the ground, possibly unconscious. There's a strange, glowing feeling in my chest, and I'm trying really hard not to smile. I realize I'm *proud* of her. Harper kicks serious ass.

Slightly dazed, I run over to see what happened to Bear. He has a beefy arm draped over his puffy red face, and I know he's trying to hide the tears.

Blaze is muttering a stream of apologies and practically bouncing off the walls, all arms and legs. With his copper and green-tinged hair sticking up all over the place, he looks like a mad scientist.

There's blood trickling out from under Bear's head, and I realize in a panic that Blaze backed him right off the mat. When he went down, Bear must have cracked his head open on the concrete.

I drag in a deep breath, trying to stay calm. "Guys, stay on the mats. *Please.*" I hunker down and shovel Bear's arm onto my shoulder. "Get his other side, will you?"

Blaze looks as though he wants to run away and throw himself onto a sharp spike somewhere, but he does what I tell him, and we pull Bear to his feet.

"What the hell is this?" cracks an angry voice from the door.

I glance over, feeling annoyed.

Jayden is standing in the entrance to the training center, drawn up to her full puny height and still managing to look terrifying. She *would* show up at the worst possible time.

"Had a bit of an accident," I say, struggling under Bear's mass. "It's under control."

"I'm talking about Cadet Crybaby, Lieutenant." She crosses the mats and comes right up to Bear, who looks as though he would rather be anywhere else but here. "What the hell is the matter with you?" she snaps.

"He split his head open," I say, not bothering to keep the contempt out of my voice. Jayden can be such a bitch sometimes.

"I don't care," she scoffs. She looks at Bear, her eyes narrowing into slits. "You're a disgrace, you know that?" Jayden pokes her finger into his broad chest, and he's unable to meet her cold gaze.

"Commander, unless you want another dead cadet on your hands, you're going to have to let me take him to the medical ward."

"Let him bleed to death. Better here than out on the Fringe." She offers an icy smile. "Less paperwork that way."

I try to hold in the angry growl that's burning in my throat. Jayden is the only woman alive who gives me homicidal thoughts.

"Commander —"

"What kind of training program are you running here, Lieutenant? I didn't realize this was fat camp. He's a useless waste of space."

"He's doing fine," I growl, completely aware that all five cadets are watching this exchange and wondering who's going to win.

What they don't know is that this is a lose-lose situation for everyone involved. If Jayden thinks they're actually making progress, she'll send them out early to look good to the board. If Jayden thinks they're worthless, she'll send them all out to die in a single month just so she can get a replacement class.

But in that moment, I realize that what they really need is someone to stand up for them.

"They're all making progress — faster than the other squads," I say, staring her down.

"Don't kid yourself, Lieutenant." She throws a withering glance at Bear. "Cut his rations down to fifteen hundred calories. Hopefully that will make him less of a fatass."

"He's doing six hours of physical a day."

"Then the fat should come right off, won't it?"

I sigh. "Can I take him to the medical ward before he passes out?"

"Yes. I suppose." She's looking at Bear again with the most intense loathing I've ever seen. "If I see you blubbering like a baby in my training center again, you're done here."

Bear sniffles and bobs his head. He looks pitiful. His face is burning and covered in snot, but the public humiliation isn't the worst of it. No one can make you feel like shit quite like Jayden.

Then she whips her head around again, drinking in the look of the sweaty, exhausted cadets. "The rest of you . . . completely useless."

Her eyes land on Harper, and I feel my insides tense automatically. "I should have let *you* go to ExCon, Riley. Sixty thousand for a forty-six?" Jayden tsks. "I was told you might actually be useful out there. Too bad."

Harper's face scrunches in confusion, and I'm torn between apprehension and relief. I can see Harper's mind working, but her curiosity is the only thing preventing her from lashing out at Jayden.

As Jayden turns to leave, I have the overwhelming urge to dropkick her out the door. This is what she does: storm into the training center, make my cadets feel like garbage, and undo all the work I've done.

Blaze and I drag Bear out of the room, but my mind is back with Harper. I didn't like that suspicious look on her face. It lit a fire in her eyes that reminded me of me. It's the look I get right before I do something incredibly stupid.

* * *

The rest of the cadets are subdued when Blaze and I return to the training center. Harper's running Lenny around the ring, and Kindra is determinedly jogging slow laps around the track.

They all stop what they're doing when I come into the room, and for a moment, I see that look in their eyes — the look that tells me they *know* I'm on their side.

I can't afford that.

It's fine if they think Jayden is a complete bitch, but I can't have them looking at me as though I've earned their loyalty by standing up to her. If they respect me — if they like me — it will be that much harder to break them, and it will break me when I have to watch them die one by one.

I made the mistake of liking Juan and Kara. I even volunteered to take them out on their first deployment. I won't make that mistake again.

"Sparring is over," I say. "Hit the showers and report to the shooting range after lunch."

Harper holds out a hand to pull Lenny to her feet, and they shuffle toward the door.

On her way out, Harper stops. She's searching my face with those big stormy eyes, as though she can see everything I'm hiding.

"How is he?" she asks.

"He'll live."

"What's with Jayden?"

I swallow. "She doesn't tolerate weakness."

Harper frowns. "Bear isn't weak anymore."

"He can't afford to be if he wants to live."

She narrows her gaze. I realize we're completely alone in the training center, which doesn't help me keep my thoughts in check.

Her face is flushed from fighting, and her collarbone is glistening with sweat. I can see a few strands of damp hair that have twisted around her neck and stuck to the skin.

"Would she get rid of him?" she asks quietly.

"You mean send him out to die so she can get a replacement?" I meet her gaze. "Yeah. She would."

Harper looks taken aback. "What did Jayden mean when she said 'I was told you might be useful'?"

My stomach drops, but I shrug. "You know . . . the list. Every senior leader receives a list of cadets who fit —"

She shakes her head impatiently, her dark ponytail whipping around. "I mean, useful for what?"

"You know what's out there, Riley."

"No," she says in a firm voice. "It's the way she said it. She got this look on her face . . . almost like she was scared. What's really going on out on the Fringe?"

Harper's words send a jolt of apprehension down my spine. I noticed Jayden's expression, too, but I can't think about what she's hiding now. Harper shouldn't either.

"You're being paranoid."

"No, I'm not." Those gray eyes are blazing, and I know there's nothing I can say to extinguish her curiosity now that she's caught the scent. "You saw it, but you don't know what's got Jayden worried."

I raise my eyebrows, glancing back at the doors to make sure we're alone. "You need to drop it, Riley. I mean it. The only way you're going to survive here is by keeping your head down."

"Is that what you do?" she snaps. "Eli Parker, legendary fighter. Eli Parker, Recon's youngest lieutenant. Is that what you call keeping your head down?"

I glare at her, and for a moment, she looks intimidated. "I give them what they want," I say. "And you should, too. They're gonna take it from you anyway."

A strange expression flickers across Harper's face. It isn't anger or fear, so I almost don't recognize it.

Her eyes soften, but before she can speak, I straighten up and pull myself together.

"Beat it, Riley. I expect you back here at thirteen hundred hours. Don't be late."

And just like that, the warmth is gone from her eyes. Harper is cold and cocky again. She shoves past me, practically bodychecking me as she leaves.

She's not like the rest of them, I realize. She isn't lost. She hasn't resigned herself to the Fringe. If anything, training has awakened something inside her. She's fighting back.

That sobers me and fills me with a strength I can't explain. It spreads from my chest all the way to my limbs.

Harper gives me hope, and that scares the shit out of me.

fourteen

Harper

Up until Jayden's visit, I was coping all right in Recon. I was learning, making friends, and trying hard to forget about the factors that landed me here.

But after my conversation with Eli, that gnawing feeling is back in the pit of my stomach. There's something Jayden isn't saying — something about Bid Day that even Eli doesn't know.

He won't help me figure it out, though. That's the most disappointing part. Even if he resents Jayden, Eli won't work against Recon.

I need to know more, and something tells me that Sullivan Taylor, Undersecretary of Vocational Placement, holds all the answers. I can't exactly ask Taylor, but getting on his computer is the next best thing, and there's only one person who can help me with that.

I knock on Celdon's door after dinner and feel a little hurt when Sawyer answers. She and Celdon barely get along half the time, and yet she decided to visit him instead of me.

But when the door swings open, she grins broadly and throws an arm around me. As she pulls away, her expression turns serious. She glances at Celdon, and I realize why she's there.

He's completely passed out on the sleek white couch, with an untouched water bottle and a reheated to-go box in front of him — Sawyer's handiwork, no doubt. He's got more dirty laundry draped over the furniture than usual, empty food containers piled everywhere, and a pill bottle stuffed between the couch cushions.

Judging by his wrinkled clothing and mussed hair, he hit Neverland earlier — probably when he was supposed to be in Systems — and he's coming down from his high.

Sawyer and I talk in hushed voices for more than an hour. Her hair looks as though it hasn't been washed in a few days, and she has bags under her eyes from pulling back-to-back shifts in the medical ward, but I can see she loves Health and Rehab.

She tells me about the different doctors she gets to work with — how brilliant they are, how they let her assist with patients. She says she doesn't mind the long hours because it never feels as though she's been there that long. When she talks, she has the tired, satisfied smile of someone who's worked a long day at a job she finds important.

My heart aches for more nights like this — just the two of us talking about our lives. I try to keep the conversation on her because I can't talk about my life. I can't tell her the truth about VocAps, and I don't want to talk about Recon. My life is nothing like the life I had planned.

After a while, Sawyer yawns and leaves to get some sleep, and I take over babysitting Celdon. He doesn't stir once, and I figure he won't be up for several hours.

I wait until twenty-three hundred to swipe his key card from the ceramic turtle on the coffee table and let myself out. It's easy — almost too easy — but I feel pretty shitty about it.

Heart thundering in my chest, I shove down my guilt and slip through the residential tunnel. I take the stairs up one level and head for Systems headquarters. Nobody's around this time of night, and the lights tick on automatically as I walk.

I feel jumpy and exposed in the bright white tunnel. Celdon

in his white Systems clothes would blend in, but I stick out like a speck of dirt in my gray uniform.

Glancing behind me to make sure I wasn't followed, I pull on a pair of gloves I swiped from the Operations cart and let myself into the room.

Once inside, I make a beeline for Jacob Morsey's computer. I may have felt guilty about using his login before, but after seeing his smug face in person, it doesn't bother me as much as it should.

I know Celdon always uses the same dummy password to set up new accounts for people, and I know Jacob is probably too stupid to change his.

Logging on to his computer is easy; remotely overriding Taylor's office access protocol isn't. Any Systems operative can do it to access the room for routine malware updates, but it takes me a while to figure out how to make the room accessible by key code alone. Most high-level security rooms require a code and an all-access card.

While I'm pretty sure Celdon's security clearance is high enough to get me in, it's too risky. Plus, I need it to automatically reset to its default code as soon as I'm finished.

I start to sweat in Jacob Morsey's stupid ergonomic chair, and tiny fans mounted on the half-moon partition kick on automatically.

I groan. Systems' relentless pursuit of comfort and productivity is sickening.

Finally, I remotely override the lock on Taylor's door. I don't hang around any longer than I have to. Something about being inside Systems among hundreds of sleeping monitors and the barely audible *tick* of blinking server lights gives me the creepy feeling I'm being watched.

I head out into the tunnel and hurry toward the board members' offices. They're situated directly above their swanky compartments so the leaders can access their offices without mingling in the tunnels with everyone else.

I don't encounter a single living soul in the tunnel, which unnerves me. My luck is *never* this good when I'm attempting something illegal. I definitely should have screwed up by now.

Struggling to get a grip on my fried nerves, I tap my interface twice so I can read the silvery plaques on the doors. A little chill rolls down my spine when I reach Sullivan Taylor's door. I can't believe I'm doing this.

My code works, and I let myself in. The smell of new chipboard and fake mahogany finish hits my nostrils, and I go straight for his computer. It's the same model Systems uses, and I get another kick of envy. I'm sure Taylor only ever uses it for messaging.

I turn on the computer, and my heart sinks a little when I realize it's password protected. I'm not as good at hacking into people's accounts as Celdon is, but I've been around him long enough to pick up some of his tricks.

Plenty of people use their birthday. I flip on my interface and perform a quick search through compound records. I try Taylor's, but the little password field just shudders, telling me I got it wrong.

I type in "thisismypassword," but apparently even Taylor isn't that stupid.

I have one more shot at this before the system locks me out. Taylor is the only one who uses this computer. It's in his locked private office, meaning he probably thinks it's safe.

I hold my breath and hit enter, leaving the field completely blank.

I hear the friendly login note and collapse back into his chair in relief.

His application icons pop up on the desktop, and I click on his messaging app. There are thousands of messages clogging up his inbox, but I do a quick search for "bid day."

Scanning the messages, I see they're mainly correspondence about the bidding ceremony itself: a draft of his speech, the schedule, and the new recruits' VocAps scores.

Nothing.

I search for messages containing "Harper Riley," but nothing turns up except for the information about my education and my score.

I sigh in frustration. After all this, Sullivan Taylor might be a dead end after all.

Just as I'm about to leave, I type "Recon" into the search bar. There's one message that sticks out from his trash bin, and I open it first.

It's a message to the rest of the board about the number of recruits for Recon this year. One part catches my eye:

I think it may be wise to reevaluate the number of recruits for Recon. The rapid death of so many cadets last year has created strong animosity for compound leadership, which could spread to the rest of the sections if this continues.

Despite recent threats on the Fringe, internal discord may be a bigger concern at the present time.

I scroll down to President Ferguson's reply, and my blood goes cold.

Your concerns are understandable, but we believe the recent surge in Fringe violence calls for more Recon operatives in the field. I stand by my recommendation to increase recruitment by twenty-five percent.

Somewhere out in the tunnel, a door slams shut. My heart

stutters in my chest, but my head is clear.

I close out of Taylor's messages and hastily shut off the computer. Careful not to make a sound, I creep to the door and put my ear against the cold metal, listening for footsteps outside the office. Nothing.

I open the door a crack and peer out into the tunnel. The lights are on, which means someone must have walked through here recently.

Seeing no one, I slip out of Taylor's office and close the door behind me. I walk as fast as I can without making too much noise, yanking off the gloves and tossing them into the first wastebin I see.

I'm halfway down the tunnel when I hear it: the soft scuffle of controller boots coming from the adjacent tunnel.

The air goes frigid in my lungs, and I stop, listening to hear which direction the steps are coming from.

"Hey!" he yells. "Who's there?"

I know that voice.

My heart flies into my throat. I'm not alone up here after all. The controller on duty heard me shut the office door, and he's close enough to find me up here breaking into a board member's office.

Without pausing to think, I sprint toward the megalift.

The footsteps quicken, drawing closer. There's a chance he'll see me, but the only way out of this tunnel is to run *toward* the controller.

The door to the emergency stairwell is situated out of his line of sight, so I throw myself into it and take the stairs two at a time. It's too dark to see where I'm going, but I can't turn on my interface.

Suddenly I remember Celdon's key card. If I'm caught, I can't let him find it on me. Celdon will probably have his clearance revoked, and I'll be prosecuted for identity theft. I shove it into my bra and hope to god Control doesn't perform strip searches.

I can hear the controller behind me, and I see the blue light of his interface bouncing off the walls. He's only a flight behind me, and he's catching up fast.

The stitch in my side is stabbing me like a knife, but the controller isn't even breathing hard. He's enjoying this. This is what they train for, yet they so seldom get to chase down criminals in the compound.

And then, I don't have time to think about anything else. Someone tackles me from behind, and my feet fly out from under me.

I'm airborne for a second, and then I hit the landing with enough force to shatter every bone in my body.

I feel the oppressive weight of a fully grown man pinning me down and smell something familiar. My face scrapes against the filthy concrete, and the man yanks my arm behind my back.

Panicked, I throw my elbow back just as Eli taught us, and the controller's groan tells me I hit him hard.

"Well, well. Hey there, Riley." The familiar voice is so full of cold delight that it freezes me in place.

I turn away from the blinding blue interface light, but the man seizes me roughly by the hair and yanks my head sideways to get a good look at me. The white-blond waves come into focus around his pointed, weasel-y face.

I almost throw up.

Of all the controllers to be sitting on top of me in a deserted stairwell, Paxton Dellwood is the one who makes my blood curdle in fear.

I feel something hard poking me in the side — his electric

nightstick — and suddenly every part of my body is convulsing against the concrete.

I cry out a little but instantly clamp my mouth shut. I won't give him the satisfaction.

"I've wanted to do that for a while," he says, brushing my hair back with a creepy-soft, clammy hand. He cuffs me tightly and yanks me to my feet. But before I can regain my balance, he throws out his forearm and slams me bodily against the handrail, pinning my back against the wall.

"What were you doing in the upper tunnels?" he growls.

"I don't know what you're talking about," I say automatically.

He lets out a frustrated little laugh of air through his nose. "Of course. Because the Recon recruit with the biggest bone to pick with the board just happens to take her midnight walks past Sullivan Taylor's office."

"I sleepwalk," I say, not even bothering to come up with a convincing lie.

I know I should really be worried about ending up in the cages — about the fact that I actually *did* break the law. But with the biggest slimeball in our year pressing every part of himself against me in the dark, I just want to show him he doesn't have the power to scare me. So I lie shamelessly.

Paxton rearranges himself so his hips are grinding against me even harder, and I feel his holster digging into my abdomen. His hands trail up my thighs, and I swallow down the bile in my throat. His spidery fingers brush the inside of my legs longer than they need to, searching for weapons, and he takes his time rubbing his way up my waist and chest.

I think of the key card shoved in my bra and hope he's too preoccupied with what's going on in his pants to notice the rectangular piece of plastic stuck to my side.

"Hmm. Not going to shank me? That's nice of you."

His breath is laced with so much coffee and spearmint that it makes my eyes water a little.

"Why were you up there, then? Trying to sleep your way into Systems?"

I swallow. Maybe I should tell him that's what I was doing. He might actually believe it, but I can't bring myself to tell such a humiliating lie to Paxton Dellwood.

"No."

"Were you trying to tamper with your test results?"

"No."

"Just tell the truth," he says, trying a seductive tone that just comes out like a snarl.

Now that the adrenalin has worn off, I'm starting to feel genuinely afraid. My hands are cuffed together, and though Paxton is about my height, he's built like a bull. I'm completely powerless against him.

"You have no proof I did anything," I snarl. "I didn't break into any of those offices."

He shoves me harder against the wall. My eyes water as our combined weight slams against my cuffed hands, but I set my jaw and refuse to show weakness.

"Someone did. We got a tipoff that someone from Recon was lurking around the restricted access rooms. And do you really think Control doesn't get an alert every time a high-level security protocol is overridden?"

My chest constricts in horror. I had no idea.

"Well, it wasn't me," I say, trying to sound offhand. Part of me thinks I should confess, in case Paxton is smart enough to link Jacob Morsey's code back to Celdon. I'll take the fall before I let Celdon get dragged into this.

Paxton is leaning against the wall looking smug — as though he can't believe his luck that I'm his first arrest.

"What I can't figure out," he says, unable to hide his smirk, "is *why* you broke in."

"You can't tie me to his office. I wasn't there. I have no way to override the security protocol or whatever."

I know my bluff isn't very convincing, but at this point, I'm just lying my ass off, hoping something sticks.

But Paxton's got the bit between his teeth.

"You know, if I wanted to tie you to Taylor's office, I'd call the best hacker in this place to figure out how you overrode security." He lets out a derisive laugh. "But the best hacker in the compound happens to be your best friend. Now, I'm no hearing board, but I like my chances of —"

I never hear what Paxton says next.

A deafening rumble shakes the level above us. The tremor throws us against the wall, causing Paxton to nearly dislocate my wrist as we're jolted sideways.

He looks up in alarm, clearly thrown off by the unexpected turn of events, but he doesn't let go of me. For a moment, we both just stare at the walls and ceiling, waiting for another tremor.

Then I hear a faint garble coming from his interface, which seems to shake him out of his stupor.

"Copy that," says Paxton, speaking to the controller on the other end. "No. But —"

The speaker seems to cut him off, because Paxton drags in an annoyed breath.

"Captain, I've apprehended a suspect."

"What?" I yell, twisting to glare at him. I have no idea what just happened, but he isn't going to pin it on me.

"Yes. Caught her breaking into one of the board members'

offices just a few minutes ago. Right. Yes, sir . . . yes, sir. I'm on it. Over."

Paxton ends the conversation, glancing at the concrete steps above us apprehensively. But then his expression flips into a smirk, and he tightens his grip on my wrist.

"Well, it looks like my lucky day."

"What are you talking about?" I growl.

"I've gotta say, Riley. I never thought you had it in you to *bomb* a board member's compartment."

"*What?*"

"Oh, yeah." He yanks my handcuffed arms backward, dragging me up half a flight of stairs toward the level just below Systems. "Let's go have a look at your handiwork, shall we? I'm curious."

There's a morbid edge to his voice, and the panic starts spilling into my gut like acid. If there really was an explosion, I'm going to be a suspect. Talk about shitty timing.

Paxton flings the emergency door open, and my stomach falls to my knees.

The destruction is unimaginable. I've never seen anything like it. One tunnel is completely caved in, the ceiling and walls crumpled like a box of broken chalk. I hear yelling and moaning coming from every direction, but I can't see any people among the destroyed compartments.

There's a thick cloud of plaster dust in the air, and as it clears, the realization sinks in.

This is the tunnel I was in less than an hour ago. This is Celdon's tunnel, where I left him passed out on his couch.

Celdon.

"No!" I scream, lunging toward the ruins. I feel the handcuffs dig into my flesh, and Paxton yanks me back roughly.

He's staring at the rubble — utterly transfixed — but his face isn't twisted in shock and horror. He's barely containing his glee.

"I can't believe —"

"Let me go!" I yell, nearly ripping my vocal cords in my anguish. I yank forward hard enough to cause him to stumble, but he rights himself and tugs me backward. The handcuffs dig into my wrists, but I don't care.

"That's Celdon's compartment!" I yell. "Right — there! I have to see —"

"That's cold, Riley. Even for you."

He tsks loudly, and I twist around to face him, wanting nothing more in that moment than to kill him.

More cries and yells drift from the wreckage. A few people are stumbling from the mounds of twisted steel and broken walls, bleeding and covered in dust.

My eyes search desperately for a familiar blond head in the rubble, but Paxton pulls me backward.

"Where are you taking me?" I scream. "We have to help them! I have to see if Celdon's all right."

Paxton ignores me and stabs the button for the megalift, utterly oblivious to the helpless, injured people crying for their loved ones. Nothing happens.

"Damn!" he mutters. "The lift's out."

He tugs me back toward the stairwell, and I feel the tears spilling down my cheeks. I don't even care that Paxton can see. Celdon can't be dead. My brain won't accept it.

I'm sure I'm going to have permanent scars on my wrists from fighting against the handcuffs to return to Celdon's tunnel, but it's completely useless. Paxton wants to be praised for bringing me in; he doesn't care what really happened or who was killed in the explosion.

I kick and scream and drag my feet all the way down the emergency stairwell, but Paxton manages to yank me down to the Control station.

Though Control is a tier-two section, it's almost as crummy as Recon. The walls are a dull yellow color, and all the plaques along the tunnel are coated in a thick blanket of dust.

Controllers are running everywhere, speaking into their interfaces and putting on helmets to venture into the wreckage.

As soon as we turn down the east tunnel, I can smell the sweat, urine, and unwashed bodies crammed together in the cages. My stomach clenches automatically as Paxton drags me toward the ungodly stench.

I try not to look at the vacant faces of the burnouts from Neverland, but their haunting eyes follow me down the tunnel as Paxton frog-marches me to the cage at the end.

He swipes his access card, and the door opens with a clang. Paxton shoves me roughly inside, and I barely have time to duck to avoid cracking my head on the low ceiling. With my hands cuffed behind me, I hit the filthy concrete shoulder-first, and a wave of pain shoots up my right side.

"Enjoy it here while you can," says Paxton. "From what I hear, they've got much worse in mind for you."

The look in his cold eyes is enough to send a jolt of fear through me. Then he slams the door shut with a bang, leaving me all alone.

fifteen

Harper

I don't know how long I've been lying on the filthy concrete in my cage. There's a heavy knot of dread coiled deep down in the pit of my stomach. Part of it has to do with imagining what Control does to suspected terrorists, and part of it is the terrible, sinking feeling that Celdon is dead.

I don't know if they've had me here for minutes or hours. The cage lights don't change the way they do in the rest of the compound, so I can't judge the time. I can't even think.

Moans and whispers drift down the tunnel from the other prisoners, and I crush my hands against my ears to block out the sounds of suffering. They don't know what happened in the upper tunnels. They're trapped here in their own personal hell.

Eventually, Paxton reappears from the shadows and yanks me out of the cage. At first I think he might release me, but instead of heading back out into the foyer, he leads me down a dim, dirty tunnel.

There are a few offices, an evidence locker, and several unmarked steel doors with tiny safety-glass windows.

Before I can process what's about to happen, he shoves me headfirst into a small, windowless room and slams the door.

There are two controllers standing in the corner. One is the portly captain with a heavy scowl and a uniform that strains across his generous midsection. The other man is tall, muscular, and completely silent.

All the walls are bare, apart from a dirty, distorted mirror. I know it's one-way glass. I can feel the prickle of eyes watching me from the other side.

"Cadet Riley," says the captain. "Please have a seat."

There's a single metal chair in the middle of the room under a bare strip of florescent lighting. I shiver.

Before I have a chance to cross the room, the burlier controller grabs my arms and pulls me toward it. He shoves me down into the chair and jerks my arms roughly over the back. Panic grips me as he pulls plastic cords from his belt and straps them over my upper arms.

"I'm sure you know why you're here," says the captain once I'm bound motionless in the chair.

"You think I was involved in the bombing."

"Smart girl."

My eyes dart from the captain to the glass partition separating me from the watchers. It suddenly occurs to me that I'm being interrogated for a crime I didn't commit — a crime they think I'm responsible for.

That's when the terror sinks in.

I'm no longer watching as a detached observer. My body has betrayed me — heart pounding, throat dry, hands shaking uncontrollably.

I'm locked in the dark corners of the compound with two corrupt men who think I'm guilty. Paxton Dellwood is plotting my death just down the tunnel. I'm in a heap of trouble, and I have no one here to vouch for me.

What can I possibly say to clear my name? I had no reason to be in the upper tunnels after breaking into Taylor's office — other than the fact that I'd just been *breaking into Taylor's office* — and I have no alibi to explain where I was just before the explosion.

"Cadet Riley," says the captain. "Where were you this evening?"

"What time?" I croak.

"Say . . . twenty-three hundred."

"I was with my friend Celdon."

That's true. He can confirm my story — if he's alive.

"And then where did you go?"

"I headed back to my compartment," I lie automatically.

"What time?"

My mouth is impossibly dry. "I don't know . . . I-I lost track."

"But you didn't go straight back to your compartment, did you?"

My heart rate speeds up. I am in such deep shit. "What are you saying?" I ask sharply.

"I'm asking if you broke into Systems so you could remotely override Sullivan Taylor's security settings."

My mind is racing. Every instinct is telling me to lie — lie convincingly. "No. I was going straight home."

"We know you broke into Sullivan Taylor's office, Riley. Now did you also plant the bomb in his compartment?"

"No!" I shout.

This is horrible. It won't be a difficult leap to link me to the office break-in, and then they'll use that to tie me to the bombing.

The captain sighs. "Cadet, this can be easy, or this can be difficult."

I don't say anything.

"Irving!" He snaps his fingers, and the other controller slaps something into his hand.

"Do you know what this is, Riley?" he asks.

I squint at the skinny, flexible object in his hand. A cold smirk ghosts across his face.

He takes a step toward me, and I recoil automatically. He pulls my hair roughly out of the way and clips it around my neck.

It's too tight and pulls at my skin. It's made of rubber, but on the inside, two silver probes dig into my flesh. It's a shock collar.

I don't realize I'm hyperventilating until the collar starts to choke me. I clench and unclench my fists, trying to stifle the raw panic that's making my body go haywire. I can't afford to lose my shit — not now.

In that moment, I have the most bizarre flashback: Eli choking me on my first day in Recon, yelling at me to fight back.

The captain regards me with amusement and pulls a tiny fob out of his pocket. Every muscle in my body clenches, bracing for the shock.

He steps in front of me and lifts the corners of his mouth into a grimace I'm sure is supposed to be a smile. "Would you like to tell the truth now?"

"I told you," I gasp. "I was headed straight back to Recon. I didn't have anything to do with the bombing."

If I tell them I did break into Taylor's office and why, whatever they choose to do with me will be much worse than the pain the captain is about to inflict.

He sighs and clicks the fob once.

Even though I watch him press the button, I'm unprepared for the jolt of electricity that shoots into my neck. My muscles seize, and I'm throttled back against the chair.

It's over quickly, but the pain feels permanent. Every muscle in my body is screaming.

"Let's try this again," drawls the captain. "Where did you go after you left Celdon's compartment?"

"I — told — you," I gasp, my fear turning to hatred. There's a funny metallic taste on my tongue. "I went home."

I'm prepared for another jolt of electricity. I'm not prepared for the back of the captain's hand when it snakes back and slaps the side of my face. "Stop — lying! We know you were in the upper tunnels at the time of the explosion! What were you doing in Sullivan Taylor's office?"

For a second, I'm completely frozen in shock. My face burns where he struck me. I can practically feel the red outline of his hand.

"I'm not . . . lying," I say through gritted teeth.

He hits the fob again, and this time, all I feel is raw pain from the convulsions — as though someone is pounding my already-sore muscles. It's worse than being beaten into the scratchy concrete. It's worse than the scorching Fringe from my nightmares.

My vision goes blurry, and I envision smoke emanating from my skin. The taste in my mouth is getting worse, and my skin feels funny.

I think of Eli, talking in his low, urgent voice. He's giving me directions, just as in practice. He's telling me to be stronger, tougher.

Don't show weakness. Don't drop your hands. Don't back down.

I hear the fob click again.

The shock is different this time. I'm no longer sitting there absorbing the pain. I've gone outside myself as I've only done a few times in my life when a fistfight took a particularly nasty turn.

The pain feels very far away now. The less I feel, the more dangerous it becomes. I'm on the brink of passing out. The shadows are pressing in on the edges of my vision like dark thumbprints.

When the pain slips over me again like heavy armor and the full force of it hits me, my feeble brain decides it's had enough.

My last thought is of Celdon and if he's still alive. I see him in his stupid mesh shirt, smiling at me with that hazy expression.

I only have a few more seconds to take in the grimy walls around me — and the captain's face, now purple with rage — before my mind abandons my body and slips away.

sixteen

Eli

It's the middle of the night when I get the call. I've been having nightmares again, and the buzzing of my interface yanks me back to reality, making me feel unsettled and disoriented. It's flashing from my nightstand, so I yank it onto my ear and hit the talk button, still in the fog of sleep.

"Hello?"

"Lieutenant Parker?"

"Yes."

"This is Captain Hutch of Control. We have one of your new recruits . . . Cadet Harper Riley? You might want to come up."

"What?" I splutter. His mention of Harper makes me wonder if I'm still dreaming.

But he's already disconnected. I swear and fling the interface across the room, jumping out of bed to pull on my fatigues.

How the hell did Harper get herself arrested? I wonder as I fumble with my belt.

My brain is working in fits and starts. I'm sure it has to do with her mysterious bid, though I can't think what she could have done. Before I met Harper Riley, I would never have believed that one cadet could cause so much trouble.

I barely have my boots laced when someone bangs on my door, rattling the walls.

I stiffen automatically. Nothing good ever happens after midnight this close to Neverland, but I'm not worried about some burnout. My thoughts go to what I know about the VocAps scores and how dangerous that knowledge is.

Heart pounding, I grab my gun from under the bed and fling the door open.

It's Miles.

He raises his arms at the sight of the gun pointed at his chest and stumbles back. "Whoa. Whoa! Jesus Christ."

"Sorry," I breathe, lowering the gun. "I'm sorry."

"Were you planning to shoot me?"

I wipe my hand down the side of my face, trying to get a grip. "No. I don't know. It's just been a weird night."

"Weird, like, shooting people weird?"

"She's been arrested, Miles."

"*What?*" Miles shoves past me and slams the door shut. When he turns around, his face is contorted in fear and rage. "Shit! Then you need to forget what I'm about to tell you. This never happened. Do you understand me?"

I nod, wondering how his news could possibly top Harper being arrested.

He points his interface toward my computer, and the monitor flickers on. I punch in my password to give him permission to access the device, and he beams a file to my desktop.

I'm staring at a screenshot of an account statement.

"You were right about the shady accounting. Look at this." Miles reaches out to point at a line item, his voice rising with excitement. "Somebody transferred sixty grand to the Recon budget the day before Bid Day."

"You're kidding." But it's right there in front of me. I can see it. "Who made the transaction?"

"This is where it gets really creepy. The transaction didn't go through the proper channels. Sometimes, the board will transfer funds to a section's account if they need to bring on an unusual amount of new recruits, but Recon never sees a piece of that action. This transfer wasn't from the board. It happened way under the radar."

A choking cold dread grips me, and suddenly it feels as though all my extremities are made of lead. Now that I know the facts, the danger is confirmed. I shouldn't have dragged Miles and Brooke into this. This kind of information gets you killed.

I trash the file quickly and delete all traces of it from my hard drive.

"Thanks for finding that," I say. "You should wipe your interface. This is dangerous."

"You think I don't know that?" Miles retorts, an edge of hostility in his voice. "Christ, I thought you were smarter than this. Why did you go get yourself wrapped up in this girl's problems?"

I shrug. "I had to know, Miles. The stuff she's found out . . ."

Miles raises an eyebrow. He's curious, but I can tell he doesn't want to know. "Whatever, Eli. Just please don't ask me for any more illegal favors. And Brooke stays out of this. You don't know her. Got it?"

I nod, still too numb to think straight. Miles leaves, and I remember Harper's been arrested.

A horrible thought occurs to me: What if Brooke attracted attention digging into the transaction and they blamed Harper? What if she'd been caught trying to find that information herself?

Harper's a top-notch developer, and she's friends with the best hacker in the compound. It's possible she tried to hack into the financials, but she of all people must know the encryption would make the file impossible for any outsider to access.

I shake away all thoughts of Harper digging into illegal files and take the stairs up to the Control station. By the time I reach the right level, I'm out of breath and completely panicked.

The stench of piss and vomit hits my nostrils, and I know something isn't right. Dozens of controllers are running in and out of the station, talking in urgent voices. Red lights are flashing on all the screens behind the dispatch desk, signaling an emergency.

"Well, well. Look who it is."

I turn to see a stocky blond guy in a crisp navy uniform coming down the adjacent tunnel, a disgusting grin plastered all over his smug face.

I see "Dellwood" stitched on his uniform, and the pieces start to come together. He's the new Control recruit who taunted Harper and Lenny in the canteen that first day.

"I'm Lieutenant Parker," I say, not bothering to extend my hand. "What's going on?"

"I'm surprised you don't know," he replies in a sharp voice, not offering his hand or saluting. Though rank isn't recognized outside your section, it's considered a sign of respect in Control and Recon to salute when you're outranked. Dellwood doesn't bother. "There's been a bombing in the upper tunnels."

"*What?*"

"The target was a board member's compartment, but an entire Systems tunnel was destroyed."

"Who was the target?"

"Sullivan Taylor. The undersecretary is dead."

I drag a hand down my face, a thousand thoughts firing at once. If Sullivan Taylor has been killed, this thing goes a lot deeper than some Recon bid money.

He was in charge of deciding how many recruits went to each section. He handled the VocAps results, the recruit lists, and allocated each section's recruitment budget. It's possible that he stumbled into something he shouldn't have — like sixty thousand credits mysteriously appearing in Recon's account.

I take a deep breath. "I got a call that you picked up one of my cadets."

"Ah. You're Riley's commanding officer." He breaks into a satisfied sneer. "Captain Hutch called you up here, hoping you could persuade her to confess."

"*What?*"

"She's being held as a suspect."

Suddenly everything clicks, and the panic rips through my veins. "Wait. You think *Harper* was involved in the bombing?"

"We have it on record that Taylor's office code was overridden remotely, and I caught Riley fleeing the upper tunnels."

My heart feels as though it's going to beat its way out of my rib cage. I know why Harper was in Taylor's office, but if he's been killed, it doesn't look good. I swallow several times before I can form a coherent response. "How did she manage to break into his office?"

"I'm still working on that."

"Does Riley have any special security clearance I don't know about? They typically don't hand those out to Recon cadets."

"She had to be using someone else's," he says defensively. "Probably her friend Celdon's. His card was the last one used to access Systems this evening."

Right now, my concern for Harper is the only thing keeping me from putting my fist through Dellwood's teeth.

"So what I'm getting from this is that you have no actual proof that Riley was even involved in the break-in," I say. "And if you don't have any evidence, you have to release her."

Dellwood smirks. "Actually, we don't. Now that Constance is

involved, we can hold her indefinitely."

My blood goes cold. Dellwood sees the change in my expression and knows he's said the magic words.

Constance is the compound espionage unit, comprised of unknown individuals from every section. It was founded at the very beginning to work independently of the board to preserve human life at all costs.

The board likes to assure everyone that Constance exists to maintain checks and balances, but those who serve Constance play by their own set of rules. They have absolute power to terminate any individual they perceive as a threat to compound life.

If Constance has taken an interest in Harper's case, she's as good as dead. Nobody ever gets this close to a Constance investigation and lives to tell about it.

"Where is she?" I growl.

"She's still being questioned. She won't admit to any of it." Dellwood leans over the desk, and I catch a whiff of coffee breath. "Tell her to confess, Lieutenant. Otherwise, this is going to get a lot worse for her and anyone she's involved with."

"She didn't do anything."

"How do *you* know?"

"I just know," I say between gritted teeth. "Either release her, or go get your captain."

"Can't," he says, reclining in his chair and putting his hands behind his head. "He's busy."

I see why Harper hates this kid. I've only spent five minutes with him, and I already want to kill him.

"Get — off — your fucking ass — and get me the captain."

"Watch it, Lieutenant," he says lazily. "Don't make me call *your* commanding officer."

The thought of Jayden schlepping up here to spring me from

the cages is laughable, but I've about reached my breaking point. This kid doesn't know when to shut up.

"You know, I hope Riley can stay conscious for a little longer," he jeers. "I'm kind of enjoying this."

He arches an eyebrow, and before I have time to consider what I'm doing, I've vaulted the desk and grabbed the little prick by the collar.

He makes a pathetic gurgling sound in his throat, and I yank him closer. "Get your captain now, or I swear I will put your head through this wall."

Dellwood's lower lip twitches, but I can't tell if he's trying to smirk or if he's going to cry like a little bitch.

Disgusted, I shove him away from me into the rolling chair behind the desk. He crashes against the wall on four wheels and sits there, red-faced and dumbfounded.

When he recovers, he throws me a terrified look, staggers to his feet, and walks clumsily down the tunnel.

I wait for a few minutes, mentally preparing for a day in the cages for assaulting a controller. But when the captain appears alone, I know Dellwood's too much of a coward to arrest me.

The captain looks pissed. His face is a splotchy reddish-purple color, and he's wheezing as though he tried to run a mile. He's not a handsome man on his best day, but today he looks like shit.

"What is it, Parker?" he growls.

"You need to release Harper Riley," I say in a rush. "She wasn't involved in the bombing."

He fixes me with a glare. "I don't *need* to do a goddamn thing, Lieutenant. I don't care if you're some big deal in Recon. You're in my house now, boy."

I blow out an angry stream of air through my nose. "You have no proof she had anything to do with the bombing. She wasn't even *there.*"

"Even if she wasn't physically present — which I have every reason to believe she was — she could've easily triggered the explosion from anywhere in the compound."

"But she didn't."

Suddenly the pig man looks suspicious. "How do you know?"

"I just know."

What am I doing? I can't tell them that Harper probably *was* breaking into Sullivan Taylor's office, and I can't tell them what she was looking for.

"Parker, I've been a controller for a long time. I know when something ain't right."

I swallow. What I'm about to do isn't smart. It could get Harper dishonorably discharged before she ever sees the Fringe. I'll probably be court-martialed, but I don't have a choice. The words are spilling out before I can stop them.

"I know because . . . Harper was with me all night."

The captain's face goes slack with shock. I see his shifty brain working to connect the dots. Then his jowls lift into a sneer. "What do you mean *with you?*"

I fix him with a look that makes him actually take a step back from the desk. "What do you think I mean?"

His sneer broadens. "I'm going to need you to be more specific . . . for the official report."

What a creep.

"I mean, we were sleeping together. Up on the observation deck."

Sell it, Parker.

"She's a hot recruit." I force myself to shrug. "What would you have done?"

Bingo.

The captain guffaws — actually guffaws — and starts moving his fat, greasy fingers over the keyboard on the desk.

"I'll have to put your name in the report," he says, in the tone of a man who's looking out for another man. "You'll see disciplinary action for this. You sure she's worth it?"

I try to find an expression of cool indifference. "No. But once you realize she doesn't fit as a suspect, every Recon operative's ass is going to be on the line. I figured I should come clean now so I don't accidentally get pinned for this."

The captain starts clacking away at the keyboard with his sausage-y fingers, nodding a little as though my explanation makes sense.

I feel a little sick when his upper lip twitches at the good parts of the report. I hope he isn't embellishing my testimony.

Harper is going to hate me for this, and I'll never hear the end of it from Jayden.

"Hey!" shouts a frantic voice from down the tunnel.

I turn automatically.

"Hey! Harper Riley is innocent!"

I squint through the dim lighting and see a tall, skinny guy with messy blond hair sprinting from the emergency stairwell. He's wearing a rumpled white blazer and pants that have some suspicious purple liquid spilled on them.

The captain and I both stare at him as he careens into the desk, breathing hard.

This kid is a total mess. There's plaster dust in his pale hair, and his eyes are red and bloodshot. By the looks of it, he hasn't shaved in days, and his hands are a little shaky.

"Harper Riley — didn't steal my key card," he pants.

"Who are you?" asks the captain, who looks just as shocked as I feel.

"Celdon Reynolds. I got a call saying my identity had been stolen, but Harper never stole anything."

That name rings a bell, and I realize this is the gifted hacker who'd made several guest appearances in Harper's disciplinary file from the Institute.

The captain huffs loudly, plainly annoyed that I've given Harper an alibi and he now has to pay attention to the testimony of a tier-one worker.

"Mr. Reynolds, we have record of someone entering Systems and remotely overriding Sullivan Taylor's security code. Somebody was in his office tonight."

"Yeah," says Celdon in a shaky voice. I can tell he's making this up as he goes along. "That was me."

He winces, as if to say it's regrettable that he was at the scene of the crime mere minutes before Sullivan Taylor was blown sky-high. He's a terrible liar, but I appreciate the effort. Between the two of us, we might get Harper's name cleared after all.

The captain arches an eyebrow. "*You* were in Systems at twenty-three hundred this evening?"

Celdon looks up, as though trying to recall the details of his made-up jaunt to Systems. "Uh, yeah . . . I was. And I was in Undersecretary Taylor's office this evening."

The captain's face blanches. "Why?"

"I . . . I realized I forgot to update his malware, so I figured I should take care of that."

"And you decided to do this in the middle of the night?"

Celdon shrugs and flashes a disarming smile, as though he's quite used to pulling it out to get people to do what he wants. "I'm kind of an insomniac."

"Hmm. So you understand why we thought someone was acting as you. Not many Systems workers are so . . . dedicated."

The captain is still suspicious. "How did you know we suspected Cadet Riley of stealing your identity?"

My heart sinks. I'd noticed Celdon's slip at once, but I'd hoped the captain wouldn't.

Celdon's eyes widen in an "oh shit" expression, but he recovers quickly. "He called me," he says, jerking a thumb in my direction and glancing at the name on my uniform. "Parker said Harper had been arrested. I put two and two together."

The captain stares between us. I give a quick nod, and he starts typing again. "Are you *both* fucking her?"

"What?" Celdon's jaw drops, and I silently beg him not to say anything stupid. He gives me a strange look bordering on delight but drops it. I know he's probably going to tease Harper about this later.

Once the captain's finished with his data entry, he drags his fat ass down the tunnel toward the room where they're keeping Harper. I swear he's moving extra slow on purpose.

"Well," says Celdon, leaning against the desk and shooting me a sidelong glance. "That was . . . unexpected."

I don't say anything. I'm too wound up. I can't believe what I just did.

After several minutes of strained silence, the captain waddles back down the tunnel toward me. "Parker," he barks, beckoning me to follow him.

I practically bowl him over on my way into the interrogation room. There's another controller guarding her in the corner, and I stifle the urge to hit him when I see her.

Harper is passed out, bound to a chair. Her dark hair is falling around her like a curtain, and she has a fine sheen of sweat glistening on her brow. Even unconscious, I can read the agony in her expression.

She's got a horrible skid mark running down her right cheek, and there's a bruise forming along her hairline as though she hit a brick wall. She looks so much worse than she ever has after sparring.

"What did you *do?*" I snarl.

"Routine interview," the captain says defensively. But he looks vaguely alarmed himself.

He leaves us alone with the brawny controller and slams the door behind him. Harper jerks her head up in alarm, her eyes opening just enough to assess the threat.

Her eyes land first on the controller and then slide over to me.

"Hey," I whisper. *Since when do I whisper?* "Everything's okay."

"What are you doing here?" she groans. But I swear she looks relieved. She's not worried about being in trouble — Harper never is — but she also doesn't have that familiar animosity in her eyes anymore. She knows who the real threat is now.

"I'm getting you out of here," I say.

I can't even manage an expression that's appropriate for a lieutenant. I can't feign irritation or indifference when she looks as though she's been through hell.

I guess that's okay. If Constance is watching us right now, they might actually believe my testimony.

I bend down and touch her arm, and she recoils slightly when I move up to unfasten the plastic restraints that are making deep divots in her biceps.

She shudders, and I throw a poisonous glance over my shoulder at the beefy controller who's standing there like a moron. He makes a strange mumbling noise in the back of his throat and shuffles out of the room.

"Can you stand?" I ask.

She drags in a breath that looks as though it takes an extraordinary amount of effort and moves a little. She doesn't make it all the way into an upright position, but her hair falls back enough for me to see two bright red dots on the side of her neck. Probe marks.

I swear loudly and scoop her into my arms, too angry to wait around here until she regains her strength. If I stay here a minute longer, I'm going to lose it and kill every controller in this place.

Harper lets out a little noise of protest, which floods me with relief. I grip her tighter under the shoulders and knees and kick the door shut behind me.

seventeen

Harper

The pain in my limbs subsides to a dull ache as Eli carries me down the tunnel and away from that horrible room. I can feel the fury pouring off him in waves. He's holding me tightly to his strong chest, and his arms are surprisingly soothing.

As we walk, I chance a look over his shoulder and see the captain jogging down the tunnel to keep up with us.

"I'll need her to fill out some release forms," he says.

I shudder involuntarily at the captain's cold eyes, and Eli's grip tightens.

"That sounds like your job," he growls.

Go Eli.

"This is an official investigation, Parker," says the captain.

I can tell Eli is gearing up for one of his shitstorms of rage, but then a flash of messy blond hair catches my eye.

I gasp and practically roll out of Eli's arms to get a better look, and for a moment, I'm certain I'm seeing things.

Celdon is standing outside the station by the megalift. I'd recognize that wrinkled blazer anywhere. His hair is carelessly tussled as always, but there's a tightness to his eyes that I'm not used to.

Relief like nothing I've ever known floods through me.

"Oh my god," I yelp, thrashing toward Celdon until Eli places me on the ground.

I'm more unsteady than I realize and wobble a little as I half run, half limp toward Celdon. He catches me, and I fall into his arms. I'm not much of a hugger, but today I squeeze him as though my life depends on it.

"Hey, Riles!"

"Celdon! Oh my god," I murmur into his shoulder. "I thought you were dead. I saw your compartment, and I —"

"Hey, hey," he says in an uncharacteristically gentle voice. "Everything's okay . . . I'm okay."

"But your compartment —"

I pull away slightly, and he shakes his head. "I wasn't in there."

Behind me, someone clears his throat. I turn to see Eli at my elbow, and I suddenly remember where we are.

"I talked to them, and it looks like you're free to go," says Eli, raking a nervous hand through his hair.

Celdon smirks and slinks away with a new spring in his step. I move toward the megalift, forgetting it's out of order, and suddenly feel a little dizzy. Eli must have been watching me, because his arm flies out just as I pitch forward.

"Okay, we're taking you to the medical ward," he says, lifting me back into his arms and carrying me toward the emergency stairs.

As his warm arms tighten around my back and legs, I feel off-balance for reasons that have nothing to do with my dizziness. Eli came to bail me out of Control, and here he is. He's not wearing his trademark look of superiority. He actually looks . . . concerned.

Celdon waggles a knowing eyebrow at me, and he doesn't bother to hide his enthusiasm as he drinks in all six-plus feet of Eli.

"Care to introduce us, Riles?"

"This is Eli, my commanding officer."

"Whoa. Going straight for the top, are we? Nice."

I have no idea what he's talking about, but I want to punch him in the face. Celdon has that effect on me. One minute I want to hug him, and the next I want to kill him.

Eli clears his throat uncomfortably.

"You really don't have to carry me," I say, my face burning.

"You were electrocuted and god knows what else," he says in that commanding voice of his, not even panting as he lugs me up the stairs. "Don't fight it."

I roll my eyes, trying to process everything that's happened tonight. "Hang on. How are you okay right now?" I ask Celdon. "I saw your tunnel. It was completely demolished. And when I left —"

"I told you. I wasn't there." He looks over the railing to make sure there's no one below us who could overhear. "I was thinking about what you said and decided to look into your bid some more. I was on my way up to Systems when the explosion hit. Good thing, too, since Taylor was blown to smithereens."

"Oh, shit."

"Yeah. So thanks for saving my life, I guess."

"How did you know I was here?"

He grins. "I knew you'd taken my card. It was gone when I woke up. Then your buddy Paxton pinged me to say my identity had been stolen."

I sigh, feeling a stab of guilt. "I'm sorry. I just had to get into Taylor's office and find out what he knew."

Celdon chuckles. "I know. It's okay. I do need that card back, though."

"Oh, right." Feeling awkward, I reach under my shirt to fish the card out of my sports bra.

Eli averts his gaze and clears his throat uncomfortably, which is almost as amusing as it is embarrassing.

Celdon takes the card and wrinkles his nose. "Gross. It's all sweaty."

I want to smack him, but my curiosity gets the better of me. "Wait. How did you get back into Systems?"

"My illegal backup key," he says, as though this is obvious.

I feel the tears burning in the back of my throat, making my eyes itch, but I swallow them down and take a second just to relish the fact that Celdon is alive. "I'm so glad you're okay. I was so worried."

He grins. "It takes a helluva lot more than an exploding board member to get rid of me. Anyway, I knew they must have arrested you, so I hightailed it down to Control to clear your good name. It looks like somebody beat me to the punch, though." He shoots an amused look in Eli's direction.

"You did?" I ask, twisting in his arms. I instantly wish I hadn't, though, because now our faces are only inches apart.

He shrugs as if this is no big deal, and I get an odd fluttery feeling in my stomach.

Celdon is watching the two of us as though we all share a private joke, and I'm relieved when we reach the medical ward.

The lobby is a swarm of chaos. Systems people are everywhere — moaning, crying, and bleeding all over the place as nurses flit between them. I realize these must be all of the people who were caught in the explosion. The screens along the walls are filled with talking heads from Information giving a play-by-play of the explosion and speculating about what happened.

"Harper!" calls a familiar voice.

I turn in Eli's arms and see Sawyer rushing toward me. Warm relief spills into my chest at the sight of her.

It doesn't look as though she got to sleep after all; they must have called her in after the explosion hit. She's wearing a fresh set of blood-red scrubs, and she's got a stethoscope draped around her neck. Even with all the nurses running around, the incessant beeping of machines, and having to fight off a few injured people tugging at her sleeve as she passes, I can tell she's completely in her element.

"What happened?" she asks, throwing a sharp look at Celdon, as though it's his fault I'm hurt.

When she meets his gaze, it seems to take her a minute to realize he's standing before her — and that he shouldn't be. She lets out a strange little noise like a sob and throws an arm around his neck — a difficult feat given their height difference. She yanks him down until his back bows, and Celdon throws me a puzzled look over her shoulder.

When she pulls away, Sawyer's wearing her trademark irritated scowl. "How are you here?" she asks, punching Celdon in the ribs. "I thought your compartment had been hit in the explosion. I was worried!"

"It's a long story."

She glances from me to Celdon to Eli, utterly bewildered, and summons an electric wheelchair from against the wall. Eli sits me on the edge, and I crumple in on myself, exhausted by all the attention.

Sawyer is suddenly businesslike again. "As you can see, we're completely swamped. It's going to take a while for the doctor to see you, but I can get you a room, at least."

I glance over at the long, crooked line of bedraggled Systems people slumped around the lobby. "Can you *do* that?"

"There aren't many perks to being an intern, but controlling the admissions charts is one of them," she says proudly, flipping on her interface and making a few deft swipes in no-nonsense

Sawyer fashion. "Let's go."

She wheels me down a tunnel crowded with injured people on gurneys into a tiny private room. I feel a little bad for jumping the line when these people are clearly in worse shape, but I'm too exhausted to protest.

Once he sees that I'm in good hands, Celdon pats my head and leaves to go reboot Systems' security. Sawyer takes my vital signs like a pro and then dashes off to help triage the remaining bombing victims.

I'm left alone with Eli, and the weight of everything hits me at once. I drag in a deep breath. I can't even absorb it all: what I learned in Sullivan Taylor's office, the bombing, thinking Celdon was dead, finding him alive, Eli coming to my rescue. It's all so strange, and I suddenly feel very exposed with him hovering over me like a sentry.

Summoning the shredded remains of my courage, I look up into his intense blue eyes. "I never had a chance to say thank you. I don't know what you told them, but —"

I expect Eli to shrug it off or just say "you're welcome," but a wary expression clouds his face. He swallows once and glances at the closed door. Maybe I'm imagining it, but he looks worried.

"Don't thank me yet," he says in a rough voice. "There's something you need to know."

eighteen

Eli

The room suddenly feels much too small. Harper's sitting there in the hospital bed, looking like hell — probably hours away from being dishonorably discharged — and she's *thanking* me.

I don't know what to say. I don't know what drove me to lie for her — to risk my rank to save her from Constance — and I certainly don't know how to explain it. So I deflect.

"What was that all about?" I ask, though I already know.

"What do you mean?"

I raise an eyebrow. "The arrest. You broke into Sullivan Taylor's office."

"They can't prove that."

I throw her a look that says "drop the bullshit," and I see a flicker of fear behind those startling eyes.

She sighs heavily. "Okay. I did. But you can't tell anyone!"

"Why would I tell anyone?"

She looks a little lost for words. I'm sure being detained, tortured, and thinking her best friend was dead has made whatever she was searching for seem very insignificant. "I wanted to get a look at his computer to see if there was anything about the bid money."

Glancing at the door and back at Harper, I know it's time to come clean. "I might know something about that, actually."

Her eyes grow wide. "What? How? You told me —"

"I know what I said. But I did some investigating."

Now I've got her attention.

"You were right," I say. "Something was fixed. Somebody transferred sixty thousand credits to Recon the day before the bidding, but they didn't go through the proper channels. You were at the top of Jayden's recruit list. Whoever it was always intended for Jayden to bid high on you, but I don't know why."

"How did you find this out?"

"Does it matter?" I throw a glance over my shoulder. I have this weird feeling that we're being watched. "The point is . . . this goes up to the top. You need to stop digging before you get yourself killed."

She looks shocked, even a little scared. "Do you think whoever planted the bomb knew about the bid?"

"I think it's a safe assumption. We don't even know if yours was the only one that was fixed."

"Who would know that, though?"

I shake my head. I don't have time to worry about who might be trying to take out board members, but it's terrifying nonetheless. You'd have to be a maniac to plant a bomb in the compound.

"How did you get me out of Control?" Harper asks suddenly. "They think I had something to do with the bombing. They wouldn't just let me go unless there was a good reason."

I clench my jaw, contemplating lying my ass off. But I know Celdon will tell her what happened. He seems like the overly chatty type. "I . . . gave you an alibi."

She looks confused again and then suspicious. "What did you tell them?"

I swallow, fighting the words that are about to come out of my mouth. "I told them we were together."

"Oh." She studies me for a moment, and then her face goes

red as she catches my meaning. "Wait. *What?* What do you mean 'together'?"

I clear my throat, trying to look anywhere but at her. "Uh . . . sleeping together."

She sinks back into the pillows, looking horrified. "You didn't."

"I *had* to. It was either that or let them think you could be the bomber. They need someone to blame, and they'd sure like for it to be someone in Recon."

"Why couldn't you say something else?" she cries. "*Anything* else?"

For a moment, I almost feel insulted. "They wouldn't have believed me. There's no reason for me to be with a new recruit in the middle of the night. But incriminating us both by saying we were fraternizing throws suspicion off you."

"You had no right," she snaps, eyes sparkling with anger.

"They were *torturing* you. What was I supposed to do?"

She looks flustered. Her face is still all pink, which is doing something weird to my stomach. "They're going to discharge me. They'll put me in ExCon."

"Better ExCon than dead."

"That's a lie, and you know it." She levels me with a furious glare.

"Relax," I say, even though I'm a tangle of nerves. "Jayden isn't going to discharge you."

"Why wouldn't she? I would discharge me. And what about you?"

I smirk, which just seems to make her angrier. "Trust me, Jayden will just give me a slap on the wrist."

"How do you know? Have you done this before? I mean, actually slept with one of your cadets?"

"No!"

I can't believe she'd even think that. I just risked everything to save her, and she's being a brat. This girl is a land mine of trouble, and it's as if I'm skipping through the Fringe with my head up my ass, about to get my legs blown off.

I take a deep breath, letting out all my pent-up frustration. "Trust me, whatever Jayden does to you is going to be inconsequential compared to what would have happened to you if you were the best suspect they had," I snarl.

"What do you mean?"

I lean in and lower my voice. "It wasn't just Control investigating. Constance is involved now."

That does it. Everything seems to hit her at once, and her expression melts from fury to pure terror. I instantly feel guilty for yelling at her, though I don't know why. I have absolutely no problem yelling at her in training.

She meets my gaze with a look of terrified acceptance. "Celdon," she says. "What if they suspect him? He was up in Systems right before it happened."

"Celdon's not really my problem," I say as nicely as I can. "You are."

That was the wrong thing to say. She's staring at me with a look of disbelief. I try not to care.

She's naïve if she thinks anyone in the compound can afford to care about people who aren't their own. I can tell they're close, but he's not her problem anymore. It's Systems' job to break him out of Control if they haul him in for questioning.

But her anger melts almost instantly. She buries her red face in her hands, and for once, Harper isn't acting tough. "Oh my god," she groans in a muffled voice. "Paxton Dellwood is going to give me so much shit for this."

I'm shocked by the rage that flashes through me when I think of him saying *anything* to her.

"Did he hurt you?" I ask before I can stop myself. I shouldn't be this furious — this protective — but I can't help it.

Harper shrugs. "He tried. He's a piece of shit."

"Come on. You look like hell."

"Why are you suddenly so concerned?" she snaps.

I don't have an answer for that — at least not one that will make any sense to her. But Harper's waiting for an answer, so I shrug. "You're still my cadet."

"So?"

"So I'm not heartless," I say, feeling a little defensive.

She cocks an eyebrow.

"Look, Jayden makes us single out a cadet to scare half to death. If it wasn't me, it would have been someone else. Trust me, you should be glad it was me."

She seems to consider this for a moment. "And all the 'Harvard' stuff?"

I laugh before I can stop myself. "That was pretty much just to get under your skin so you'd fight better. Encouragement works for some people, but anger is usually the best motivator."

"Sounds like you make a lot of people angry on purpose."

"You're the third recruit class I've trained."

"Your third?" Her eyebrows scrunch together, and my stomach sinks. I shouldn't have told her that. Now she's doing the math. "But you're only . . . wait, you had two recruit classes last year?"

I nod reluctantly.

"But how?"

"Jayden drafted up from ExCon midyear."

"Why?"

I fix her with a look, but she doesn't want to make the leap — doesn't want to consider the possibility. "The first class was sent out early, and most of them didn't make it."

She sinks back onto the bed, looking shocked and terrified.

"I have to be hard on cadets," I say slowly. "I don't have very much time to train you guys, and you don't understand the danger. I have to break you down and build you back up *fast*. The easiest way to do that is —"

"Intimidation," she finishes, raising an eyebrow. "Being a bully."

"Is that what you think? I'm trying to keep you all *alive*." I take a deep breath. "A bunch of you are going to die. I've seen it. I meant it when I said at least three of you would be dead after your first year of active duty. Numbers don't lie."

Harper's gray eyes are fixed on me, and I cringe at the pity in her gaze.

"You detach yourself," she whispers. "I get it now."

"No, you don't," I snap, more harshly than I mean to. I hate that she's analyzing me — feeling sorry for me. I'd rather she hate me.

"Yes, I do," she says, her eyes turning to steel. "You think it will hurt less if you act like you don't give a shit about us. You push people away because the people around you die, and there's nothing you can do about it."

Unnerved by her forceful tone — her understanding — I feel myself withdrawing. Lieutenant Parker is back. "Well, I'm more worried about you dying *inside* this compound than outside, to be honest. You have no idea what you've stepped in."

I expect her to look panicked, but her clear indifference makes me want to throw something. "They have no proof I broke into Taylor's office, and I didn't have anything to do with the explosion."

"*Proof?* You think proof matters to them? You're in danger as long as they think you're hiding something. If they knew what you know, they wouldn't bother building a criminal case against you."

"What would they do to me, Eli? Seriously. Send me out to the Fringe? They might be rid of me soon whether they want to be or not."

"Don't say that," I say in a low warning voice.

"Why not? What are they going to do to me, Eli?" She shakes her long dark hair. Between the skid mark slashed down her cheek, the bruises, and the exhaustion taking hold, she looks a little crazy. "If I'm going to die anyway, I might as well take Constance down with me."

And that does it for me. I knew I'd push Harper too far. She's too much like me.

In a few weeks, she's gone from being a survivor who didn't take shit from anyone to someone who's accepted death as an inevitability.

I can't be around her anymore. I had hope for her — probably too much. I thought she might live, but Harper Riley is just like the others.

In a year, she'll be dead, and everything will be the way it was before.

nineteen

Harper

Eli leaves abruptly after my little declaration. I really only said what I said to be dramatic, but the way he looked at me, you'd have thought I said I was going to jump off the observation deck.

I'm a little put out when he leaves. I still haven't figured Eli out, and even though he can be an asshole, I liked talking to him.

Sawyer reappears to tell me I've got a few bruised ribs but no permanent damage. She thinks I was caught in the explosion and doesn't ask too many questions.

When the attending physician finally makes his rounds, he orders a week out of training and discharges me without a second glance. Part of me wishes I could stay longer to spend some more time with Sawyer, but she's busy taking care of the people who were wounded in the upper tunnels.

I go back to Recon and spend most of my time watching the newscast on my interface. According to the report, Control is still investigating the bombing. Other than Sullivan Taylor, there were only two other casualties — both high-level Systems workers I've never met.

Now that I'm no longer the primary suspect, I can't help but feel unnerved by the bombing. As the days drag on, the reports speculate about who might have had motive to target Sullivan Taylor, but they never say if Control has brought in any suspects. I can't understand who would want Taylor gone badly enough to risk bringing down the entire compound.

Sawyer, Celdon, Lenny, and Kindra all visit me during my recovery. I don't talk about the arrest. Instead, I elaborate on Sawyer's assumption that I was in the upper tunnels visiting Celdon during the explosion. Nobody questions how I was injured when Celdon walked away unscathed. In fact, they absorb my story all too eagerly.

Everyone was shaken by the explosion. There hasn't been an act of terrorism within the compound for more than a decade. In fact, I haven't heard of a bombing within any compound in years.

I'm dreading returning to the real world. I know Eli wouldn't tell a soul about my fake alibi, but I have no doubt that Paxton Dellwood has already spread it around that I'm sleeping with my commanding officer.

As soon as I emerge from my bunker, I'll be assaulted by the rumors and mocking looks. All the other cadets will probably hate me.

I avoid the canteen on my first day back for that very reason. But when I pull myself out of bed and shuffle into the training center breakfast-less, I'm met by a tide of relief.

Lenny rushes over to me with a huge smile plastered all over her face.

"You're back!" says Bear brightly. I haven't been gone that long, but he already looks a little stronger and slimmer since I last saw him.

I roll my eyes and grin. "With bells on."

"I'm glad," says Lenny. "Eli's been extra moody with you gone."

I stifle a laugh.

Luckily, Lenny told the boys the details of my absence, so I don't have to recount the lie I told her and Kindra. Seeing them all together in the training center makes me happy, and I realize I've actually missed them.

"Well, well. Look who it is," says a sharp, familiar voice from the doorway.

I turn quickly to see Eli staring me down with his arms crossed over his chest. He's wearing a strange expression: half amusement, half wariness.

"Done playing hooky?" he asks.

"I wasn't —"

"On the line," snaps Eli. "Now."

The others skitter over to the line on the mat. I follow them but keep my eyes trained on Eli.

Whatever concern I saw in his eyes after he bailed me out of Control is gone. Now he's back in pissed-off drill sergeant mode, walking toward us with long, purposeful strides.

As he passes me, I whisper, "You should really take something for these mood swings of yours."

"What did you say, Riley?"

My stomach drops. I hadn't expected him to comment on my remark.

Eli's standing in front of me now, glowering down with those unforgiving blue eyes. His jaw is stiff, his dark eyebrows pulled down in fury. Even though I've seen the human side of Eli, a tremor of fear shoots down my spine.

My face flushes automatically as the other cadets' eyes swivel toward me. "Nothing . . . sir."

"No, no. Please, Riley. If you've got something to say, you should share it with the class."

I stare straight ahead, and out of the corner of my eye, I watch his expression harden.

"Two laps," he growls. "And everyone else will do push-ups

until you return. Go."

Lenny shoots me a look that's a perplexing mix of annoyance and pity, and I take off for the rickety metal stairs. I'm hyper-aware of Eli's eyes following me around the room, burning a hole in my back.

As I run, I feel the instant stab of the stitch in my side. My legs are weak from days of inactivity, and my ribs and back are still tender.

By the time I return, I'm gasping for air, and the others are sweating and shaking through their push-ups. Eli still looks pissed.

"The rest of you, up!" he yells. "Give me two miles. Riley, push-ups."

I drop onto the filthy mat, anger coursing through me. He's isolating me from the others, pitting me against them to make me miserable.

I start doing push-ups, counting each one even though he hasn't given me a specific number. I know he'll make me keep going until I collapse.

As soon as the others are out of earshot, Eli hunkers down in front of me. "If you value your life, you need to keep your mouth shut."

"Afraid — I'm going — to tell the others what you said to Control?" I pant.

His jaw tightens, and he looks away. Under his infuriated ex-pression, I can tell he's nervous. "Like you would tell any of them what I said."

"I wouldn't," I pant. "But you don't have to be an asshole."

"I'm your commanding officer, Riley. Don't forget it."

Now I'm pissed. It's not the push-ups-as-punishment that bothers me; it's his attitude. He acts as though he cares — finds me in Control and lies to protect me — and then has a complete personality change the next time I see him.

It must be written all over my face, because it gets a reaction from Eli. "What's the matter with you?" he asks in an angry whisper. "Do you want to live?"

I glare at him out of the corner of my eye before dipping down and touching my chin to the mat.

"I'm asking because I'm curious. You keep doing stupid things. You start poking around to find out about your VocAps score. You break into a board member's office. You get yourself arrested by Paxton Dellwood, of all people —"

"Yes, I want to live," I snap back at him. I don't like being on the ground with him hovering above me like this. With Eli, I have a strange instinct to be on my feet and moving at all times.

"You can't afford these angry little outbursts, Riley. You keep this up, and you're going to say something that throws suspicion back on both of us."

"Oh . . . I see," I pant, sweat rolling off my forehead. I can't pretend it doesn't sting a little, him being nice to me and then turning on me again.

Eli is staring at my face, trying to work out what I'm thinking. I purposely look over at the others running laps instead of at him. I don't need Eli in my head.

I stop the push-ups and rest on my stomach for a moment. I expect Eli to yell at me, but his eyes widen, and a look of clarity spreads across his face. "What? You think that because I saved you, we're supposed to be best friends now?"

I roll my eyes to tell him he's way off the mark. I can't have him thinking he's hurt my feelings or anything.

"Riley, you don't want people thinking I did you any favors. If anyone suspects I was lying to cover up what you did, Jayden will have no choice but to discharge you."

I swallow down my resentment and try to keep my tone neutral. It doesn't work. "What did *she* say?"

"Nothing yet. She's been out on assignment."

It seems strange to me that the commander would be out on the Fringe doing grunt work, but I don't say anything.

"Go," he says quietly. But the edge in his voice is softer now. "Two miles, just like everybody else."

And that's the end of it. Eli switches gears again, and as far as everyone else is concerned, I'm back to being the cadet he hates. I know better, but it still grates on my nerves that it's so easy for him to flip his switch and be an ass after everything he did for me.

I take the stairs at a sprint to catch up with the others, but I'm behind on their workout for the rest of the morning, thanks to Eli's one-on-one attention. The others don't suspect a thing; they think he singled me out just because of my snide remark.

Eli barks orders at us until we're all bone-sore and soaked with sweat. My body feels as though it's been through a meat grinder, and I'm slightly dizzy.

Eli doesn't take it easy on me just because I was injured. This is Recon. Even after deadly radiation exposure, one week of rehab is all you get before you're expected to be training and fighting again.

But when we break for lunch, I catch Eli staring at me from across the room. He looks almost . . . protective. I haven't figured him out yet, but I can tell that something has definitely changed for Lieutenant Parker.

twenty

Eli

The rest of the day's training is awful. Harper takes everything I dish out, glaring at me with those accusing gray eyes the entire time.

She must think I'm such an asshole, but that's the safest way for both of us. The board doesn't care about tier-three workers sleeping together — not really. Not enough to make us disappear, at least. They don't want us making babies or getting married, but casual sex is something they expect.

It's camaraderie they can't see. Protection. Friendship. Lust. All of those things would throw suspicion on me and Harper.

People who lust after each other are unpredictable — uncontrollable. It's why Neverland exists. When tier-three workers can get what they need from strangers in the dark, they don't think about falling in love. They don't take stupid risks.

The rules within Recon are a different story. Sleeping with a fellow operative — especially someone below your rank — is serious shit.

That's why I have to treat her as though she's just another cadet. If Recon buys my testimony, me freezing out Harper will seem normal. Her capture forced me to expose myself, risking discharge or getting my ranks stripped. If they don't believe it, all they'll see is a lieutenant being rough on his cadet.

By the time training is over, I'm completely drained. All the cadets listen to me now, which should make me happy. But all I feel is the irritation coming off Harper in waves.

I send them all to dinner an hour early, before I completely lose my grip on the asshole persona that has taken over my life.

I shut myself in my compartment and run the wash cycle on my shower four times at piping hot, trying to forget the deep hole I've dug for myself.

Miles was right when he said it gets lonely. Not many lower-ranked Recon want anything to do with me, and the other lieutenants think I take training too seriously. They don't care if their recruits get blown up or shot their first time out. They know it's inevitable, so they don't feel responsible.

I'd be lying if I said it didn't suck sometimes. Miles was my only friend in the Institute, so he's the only person who really knew me before I became Lieutenant Parker.

I had some friends in higher ed and my recruit class, but most of them are dead now.

The way I see it, it's just extra motivation. I'm only good at fighting. It's all I've ever been good at. If I can use that to make sure fewer cadets die out there, then I don't mind being the asshole that everybody hates.

Yeah, right.

I climb out of the shower and dry off, trying to shake the weirdness that has come over me since seeing Harper in Control. Someone clears her throat nearby, and I nearly have a heart attack.

"Holy shit!"

There's someone sitting on my bed, facing the opposite wall. I tighten the towel around my waist automatically, but my alarm is downgraded to wary curiosity when I see a dark head of hair around the corner.

Then the woman turns, and my stomach clenches with dread and disgust.

It's Jayden. She's wearing her hair in a tight bun as always, which wouldn't look good on a normal woman. But Jayden isn't normal. She's scary hot.

"All the cold showers in the world can't wash off the stupidity, Parker," she croons, swinging her legs around and springing up to her full height of five foot four.

I frown. "Commander."

Jayden scowls. She hates when I call her "Commander." She'd like us to be on first-name terms, but I'm not stupid enough to give her what she wants.

Jayden doesn't think the rules apply to her. She didn't achieve her rank by keeping her head down and working hard in Recon. She became commander by kissing the board's ass — and by being the last bitch standing.

"What do you want?" I ask.

"I want to know why there's a report on my interface about my best lieutenant fraternizing with a cadet."

I shrug and pretend to clear the water from my ears. "What can I say? It was a mistake. Do whatever you have to do."

Jayden raises a triumphant eyebrow, her mouth curling into a smirk. "*Really?* You're not even going to deny the allegations?"

"Why would I?" I say, trying to keep my expression completely neutral. We both know she isn't going to discharge me. I'm her favorite. "I confessed. There's no getting out of this."

"And why would you confess?" she asks. "The rest of the file is sealed, and I have no idea what circumstances would get Constance involved in an open-and-shut case like this. Control wouldn't even bring you in for fraternizing with Cadet Riley."

My blood goes cold. Jayden's too smart for her own good.

"So enlighten me, Parker. What happened?"

I take a deep breath, praying I can get to Harper before Jayden does so we can get our stories straight.

I clear my throat. "Uh, we were doing it in the upper tunnels when the explosion happened. They brought us in, thinking we might have seen something. When we told them we hadn't, they got angry and decided to pin us with the only charge they could."

Jayden stares at me for a long time, and I can practically see her mind working. She's turning my story over in her head, searching for holes. She's deciding if she believes me.

"Where were you doing it?" she asks finally.

"The observation deck," I lie automatically.

She lets out a little huff of laughter. "That's ballsy of you. Why up there? There are closets and empty compartments all over this compound."

Because it's a public place. You can't prove I wasn't there.

"We knew we wouldn't get caught," I say. "Recon officers never go up there."

"You're lying," she whispers, so quietly I'm sure I've misunderstood.

"What?"

"I said you're *lying*, Parker. You've never been one for details. When you found that cell of terrorists on the Fringe, I had to practically drag the information out of you."

I stare at her, trying to gauge if she really knows I'm bluffing. Jayden is a master manipulator.

"What can I say? This was slightly more memorable than Fringe terrain."

I grin like a dog to hide my worry, but I know my face is beet red. Before I can get a good read on her, Jayden's in my face, stretched up to her full height so she can jab me in the chest.

"You're full of shit, Parker. I don't know why you're lying, but it makes me think you're using this to cover up something worse."

"You think I need a deeper motive to sleep with Riley?" I snap. "Have you seen her?"

This rankles her more than anything. She doesn't like the insinuation that there's anyone hotter than her. "Like I said —"

"What? You think I was involved in the bombing? You can ask Riley —"

"That's all right," she sighs. Her voice is deadly calm. "I don't want to draw any more attention to this than I have to."

Of course. Jayden is all about looking good to the board. She'd never discharge Harper, because it would mean making this public.

She takes a step back, and suddenly, all signs of superiority are gone. She looks serious. "Parker, whatever it is that you're involved with, you need to stop."

"What makes you think I'm involved in anything?"

"Because I know you better than you know yourself. You're not stupid, and you're too moral to sleep with one of your cadets. You're already racked with guilt that you're training them up for their death march. You wouldn't add to that guilt."

I don't say a word. Jayden's right. She does know me well. Too well.

It was Jayden who recruited me when I was eighteen and she had my job. I told her I wanted to test for Control, but she never cared. She knew I'd end up in Recon.

When I don't respond, she seems satisfied with whatever twisted conclusion she's drawn and breezes out of my compartment as though she owns the place.

I don't like to think about the fact that she has universal clearance in Recon and can just magically appear in here whenever she wants.

I slide the defunct chain lock into place and put on my clothes. I know it's risky to go see Harper, but Jayden has an annoying habit of doing the exact opposite of what she says she's going to do.

Now may be my only chance to get to Harper before Jayden does. She has her mission debriefing, which should keep her busy for a few hours.

Before I have time to think about how stupid I'm being, I'm banging on Harper's door. She doesn't answer right away, which makes me cagey. I don't like being out here in the cadet wing, knocking on a female subordinate's door. It looks bad — though not as bad as what I willingly told Control.

Harper takes her time coming to the door — either that or she saw me through the peep hole and is thinking about not answering.

Finally, she cracks the door open.

"I need to come in," I say in a low voice.

In her eyes, I can see the storm rolling in. She wants to slam the door in my face just to demonstrate that I can't tell her what to do outside of training.

"Please," I say, hoping my voice conveys my regret. "It's important."

Finally she steps aside, and I push my way into her compartment. It's even more of a shithole than I remember my cadet living quarters being.

"What do you want, Lieutenant?"

"Really?"

She folds her arms across her chest and cocks an eyebrow at me. For some reason, that little eyebrow thing she does nearly unravels me. I shove down the heat rising in the pit of my stomach and clench my hands to try to regain some control.

"Listen. Jayden's back from her mission, and she might be questioning you soon. We need to have our story straight."

Harper rolls her eyes. "Sure, Eli. We slept together. I've got it."

"No, you don't. Jayden's not an idiot. We need our facts to match up."

"Those are the facts," she says lazily, gesturing around her as though she's laying it all out for me.

"*Do you think this is a game?*" I yell.

"No, I don't, Eli. Not since everyone in the compound is saying I slept with my commanding officer! Do you know how *humiliating* that is? I'm already a failure as far as they're concerned, and now I throw myself at a Recon officer?"

I feel a slight pang of guilt when I realize my lie has made her life harder, but I push it down.

"Harper, I'm sorry. But you'd have a lot worse than the rumor mill to deal with if I hadn't lied."

"I know that," she snaps. "And I can handle myself. I don't need you bursting in here —"

"Hey!" I yell, sounding more like an angry lieutenant than ever. "This is serious shit, and now my ass is on the line, too. You need to fucking *listen* so we don't both get pulled into the bombing just because you botched a routine B&E."

I realize too late that I sound like a lunatic and that I've come way too close to her.

She's got her back against the wall, but she isn't scared of me. She's jutting out her chin and glaring up at me with those big beautiful eyes. She's pissed, and she's playing me like a cheap piano — getting me worked up on purpose.

Suddenly, I realize what a dick I've been to her. She was tortured by Constance just last week, and I gave her a rough time in training.

I treated her like shit just so no one would be suspicious. I have to apologize — even if it means undoing everything I've done to push her over the edge in training.

Taking a deep breath, I force my shoulders to relax and take a step back from her.

"I'm sorry about today," I say. "I was trying to keep things normal in training, but I might have overcorrected."

"You think?" she mutters. She's still huffy, but she's calming down.

I grin because my instincts were right, and that seems to piss her off more.

"What are you smiling about?"

"Nothing." I sigh. "You just . . . *challenge* me as a leader."

A crack appears in her rough demeanor, and a slight smile starts to play on her lips.

"I was universally feared before you came around. Now I'm not sure I have any authority whatsoever," I say quietly, my eyes still focused on those lips.

Her smile fades a little. She looks as though she wants to say something but then stops herself.

"I guess I should really thank you," she says finally. "You put your own job at risk to protect me, so . . . thanks."

I nod, feeling as though I've crossed some line that I shouldn't have. "Look, you have to convince Jayden. It's not enough to make up an alibi for Constance. You have to sell it now.

"If she thinks you made it up, you can't trust her to lie for you. She's senior leadership, which means if she thinks you were actually involved in the bombing, she's going to turn you in." I glance down at her face quickly. "She'd throw you under the bus in a second."

Harper swallows as the realization dawns on her. For the first time since I've known her, she looks genuinely worried. She nods quickly and becomes very serious. "Okay. What do I tell her?"

I run through the story I told Jayden, recounting the details as if I'm giving an official report. My face is burning hot. Harper listens with rapt attention, nodding as she files away the information to use later.

When I finish, she looks at the ground, turning the story over in her mind the same way Jayden had. She may be a pain in the ass, but if she doesn't get herself killed in the next year, Harper's going to be a killer Recon operative.

"How was it?" she asks finally.

"What?"

"How — was — it?" she repeats slowly.

I just stare at her. I have no clue what she's talking about.

Harper rolls her eyes. "The sex, Eli. If she asks about it, what should I say?"

"Oh." I shift my weight from one foot to the other, wishing I could extricate myself from this conversation. "Uh . . . tell her it was great, but you won't be doing it again."

For some reason, she grins at this, and my ears suddenly feel as though they're on fire.

"Why wouldn't I want to do it again if it was great?"

Now it's my turn to smirk. "Because I'm your commanding officer, and it was a stupid thing to do."

She nods, but that look she's giving me is making me nervous.

"Jayden won't ask," I say quickly. "And you shouldn't give her any more details than you have to. She's a trained interrogator. She'll do anything she can to trip you up."

"Did she trip you up?"

"She didn't have to. She knows me too well."

"What do you mean?"

I sigh. I don't want to tell her the truth, but I know I don't have a choice. "She thought I was lying."

The color drains from Harper's face, but she just nods. "Well, I guess I'll just have to sell it better, won't I?"

twenty-one

Eli

After my conversation with Harper, I'm way too wound up to go back to my compartment.

I head to Miles's instead, and we go up to the canteen to grab an early dinner. He stares at me the entire time, and I know he's waiting for me to tell him about everything that's happened.

Harper was right: Everyone is talking about her sleeping with one of her commanding officers. Constance may have sealed a portion of the report, but that hasn't stopped rumor of her arrest from leaking out of Control. I'm sure Paxton Dellwood is to blame, but he's too much of a coward to rub it in my face directly.

So far, my own name hasn't been tied to the story at all. I suppose I'm not interesting enough.

Harper, the smart Systems-track girl who was knocked down a few pegs by scoring a forty-six on her VocAps, makes for a much more entertaining rumor.

People are speculating about who it could be, and hearing the names of random Recon men whispered across the canteen, along with all the dirty things they think Harper might have done, makes me clench my fists on the table until my knuckles whiten.

I'm irrationally defensive about her, and even though I know it's more than normal protectiveness, I tell myself I'm just looking out for my cadet. I can't consider any other possibility.

I don't say anything to Miles the whole way back down to the lower tunnels. I know I'm being paranoid, but I have this weird feeling that I'm being watched — if not by Constance, then by Jayden. She didn't buy the alibi I created for Harper, and Jayden knows enough about counterintelligence to know that some times you just have to wait for your target to screw up.

But instead of going back to one of our compartments, I head for the training center. Miles is still too messed up to spar, but at least I can work off some steam.

It's after hours, so Miles slams the heavy doors shut and wheels around, his eyes bugging out at me in a "spill your guts" kind of way.

"What is going on? Please tell me you are not the officer who was stupid enough to get caught sleeping with that pretty little stick of dynamite?"

I groan and toss Miles a pair of punching mitts. "I didn't sleep with her."

Miles misses one of the mitts, and his jaw drops to the floor. "So you *are* the guy? Man, that girl is *trouble*. What were you thinking? I mean, I know she's hot, but —"

"I told you. I didn't sleep with her. I didn't do anything with her. I just . . . gave her an alibi."

He picks up the mitt and puts his hand in. "Yeah. I give Brooke 'an alibi' all the time."

I raise an eyebrow and shove my hands into a pair of gloves.

Miles stares at me for a long second and then lets out an in-credulous laugh. "Oh. Oh my god. You're serious. You're sayin' you got yourself written up for sleeping with her without actu-ally getting to do anything?" He doubles over and slaps his knee. "You're even dumber than I thought!"

I've had enough. I jab, and the mitt appears not a second too soon to keep my glove from colliding with Miles's broken nose.

"Easy," he snaps, looking around the gym as though he's suddenly worried about being overheard. "Why did you do that?"

I do a jab-cross-uppercut combo and work Miles in a circle. "They thought she was involved in the bombing."

"Why would they think she was involved?"

"Sullivan Taylor was the target of the explosion, and Harper was arrested for breaking into his office."

Miles's eyes grow wide, and he's too slow with the mitt to block my left hook. It sinks into his side, and he makes a pained gurgling noise in his throat.

"Shit!" But I know he isn't talking about my kidney strike. He's thinking about Brooke digging up the Bid Day money. "Why would she do that?"

"To find out what he knew about her placement in Recon. She was targeted specifically. It doesn't make sense."

Miles lets out a low whistle. "Talk about bad timing. And they think the bombing was an inside job?"

"It has to be. It's not as if we wouldn't have seen a bunch of drifters scaling the outer wall."

"You don't think . . . you don't think someone let one in, do you?"

"No, I don't."

The idea that anyone in the compound would willingly let a drifter in gives me a chill. Fringe babies are one thing, but blood-thirsty people who want us all dead? That would be the height of stupidity and nearly impossible to do.

"But if it was someone in the compound, who do you think it is?"

"I have no idea."

"You know they're going to try to pin it on Recon . . . or Ex-Con."

"Probably."

"What if it was the board?" Miles asks suddenly. "What if they want everyone to think it was Recon so they'll have the compound on their side when they decide to send more of us out there?"

I snort, shaking my head in disbelief. "The board took out one of their own?"

"I don't know! Maybe."

I throw another jab-cross combo. "Why would they do that?"

"Maybe they thought Taylor was getting cold feet about something. Maybe he was about to get really chatty."

I force a grin. "You're getting more paranoid than I am."

But I don't think he is. I've already entertained this possibility, but bombing a tunnel within the compound is extreme, even for the board.

I can tell Miles is worried. He's worried about Brooke, and he knows something bigger is coming. Recon can always sense looming disasters because preventing them is a matter of life and death.

When I'm tired enough to sleep, Miles and I walk back to our tunnel in silence. Even though I said he was paranoid, we both know it's best to tread with a little healthy fear.

When I get back to my compartment, I shower again and climb into bed. My muscles are sore, but my brain is still wired from our conversation.

I know I'm going crazy, but the fact that the board hasn't come out with a suspect for the bombing is unnerving. Either they have no idea what's going on, or they were behind it in the first place.

There's also a gnawing unrest in my gut that's completely separate from the quiet panic rumbling just beneath the surface.

I realize I'm worried about Harper, which isn't good. The last time I felt personally invested in another cadet, I let my guard down. I lost my edge. I can't let that happen again. I can't let it change the way I train them.

I turn over onto my side to go to sleep, but a tiny pulse of light from across the room catches my eye.

Everything is pitch black for a moment, and I'm almost sure I imagined it. But then it pulsates again — a tiny red light coming from my computer.

That's weird. I never leave my computer on sleep mode.

I hop out of bed and tread over to the desk, hitting the power button. Instead of flashing to life immediately, I see the welcome screen.

My computer is booting up. It was off, yet the idle light was still blinking.

I turn it off again and back up to the edge of my bed to wait.

Sure enough, that little red light illuminates again, throwing a soft red glow over the monitor. It's not the light that goes on when the computer is on; it's the light that flashes whenever you video chat with someone.

My heart starts pounding in my chest, and I lunge for my interface resting on the nightstand. I clip it over my ear and turn it on. The device floods my bedroom with its unearthly blue light, and my dashboard flickers in front of my eyes. Up in the right-hand corner of the display, next to the battery icon, is a tiny red light.

I desperately double-click the home button to pull up my open apps, but the chat app isn't even running in the background. I click off the device and throw it onto the bed, breathing hard.

They're watching me.

I want to run. I want to throw my computer against the wall and watch it shatter into a million pieces. But then my instincts kick in — basic, mechanical good sense hardwired by years of stress drills and field training.

I need to act normal.

Heart still pounding, I force myself to lie down and slow my breathing. If I'm being recorded, any freak-out will look suspicious. As long as they don't know I know I'm being watched, I still have an advantage.

I clench and unclench my fists under the covers. When did I make the leap from slightly paranoid to crazy town?

I don't actually have any way of knowing if that's what the red light means. I don't know anything about computers.

But Harper does. And if they're watching me, there's a good chance they're watching her, too.

I should stay away from her. That would be the safest option. But the moment Constance suspected enough to put me under surveillance, any hope of keeping myself or Harper out of danger disappeared. They know I've done something I shouldn't have. They know I've learned too much.

I thought giving Harper a harmless alibi would take suspicion off her, but it just aroused Constance's suspicion of me. And since my involvement all circles back to digging into Harper's bid, it's still going to come back to hurt her.

Instead of protecting Harper as I'd intended, I just gave Constance two messes to clean up instead of one.

twenty-two

Harper

On Saturday morning, I'm still half-asleep when I hear the knock on my door. Oh-seven hundred seems a little early for Jayden to come interrogate me about Eli's half-baked sex story, so I roll out of bed to answer.

I throw open the door and let out an involuntary sigh of relief when I see it's him. I'm not sure when I became *glad* to see Eli — probably around the same time I was tortured by Constance.

Eli doesn't wait for me to invite him in. He doesn't even say hi. He just pushes past me to get out of the tunnel and heads straight for my computer — but not before I've gotten a look at his face.

He isn't wearing the hard, smug look he always has in training. His expression is strained, almost panicked. He has dark shadows under his eyes and looks as though he hasn't slept.

"What are you —"

"You missed a full week of training," he says. "You need to catch up."

"Now?"

This is getting weird. He's standing in front of my computer, staring at it as though he's never seen one before. I suppose I should be glad he's preoccupied with my computer, since I'm only wearing a tank top and a pair of tight black Spandex shorts that go under my fatigues.

"Were you thinking you'd just get to skate by in training for the next few weeks without doing some extra work to catch up?" he asks loudly.

I stare at him in disbelief. "I was tackled down a flight of stairs and electrocuted repeatedly. I think that's a good excuse for taking a few sick days."

He's silent for a moment, grabbing my interface off the desk and examining it. For a second, I think he's trying to read my messages, but he sets it back down quickly.

He turns to look at me, and his eyes jerk involuntarily to my tight shorts and wander up my tank top before snapping back to my face. "You think drifters aren't going to blow you up because you had fewer days to prepare than everyone else?"

His voice isn't harsh. It's low, quiet, and matter-of-fact.

"No," I say sheepishly, crossing my arms over my chest. I know I'm blushing, which only makes me angrier and redder.

Eli doesn't say anything, but there's a satisfied glimmer dancing in his piercing blue eyes. He just nods and crosses to the door. "Put some pants on and meet me in the training center."

He leaves as abruptly as he came, and I stand there for nearly a full minute, trying to get a read on this weird situation.

Eli's been douchey to say the least, yet he risked his own career to investigate my bid and covered for me when I should have been in deep shit. Then he shows up in my room at the crack of dawn to give me private one-on-one training sessions?

If he hates me, he sure has a weird way of showing it. Part of me thinks I'm winning him over, and my ultra-cocky alter ego roars in approval.

Feeling a little giddy, I pull on my fatigues and boots. By the time I join Eli in the training center, he's practically climbing the walls.

"How long does it take to get dressed?" he snaps, prowling

over to me like a panther.

I take an automatic step back, wondering if I was way off-base thinking he might actually be growing fond of me.

"Sorry. I move a little slow in the morning," I say, examining his face carefully. He still looks really flustered, which isn't like him.

He slams the door shut, and I'm automatically suspicious. "What's this really about?"

Eli looks taken aback, and then I swear he goes a little red. He lowers his voice and glances around the training center. "I have to tell you something."

I stare at him, utterly bewildered.

He sighs and meets my gaze dead-on. "I think I'm being watched."

That's the last thing I expected him to say.

"What?"

He drags in a deep breath, eyes flitting from me to the closed door. "I think my computer and interface have been hacked."

Suddenly his weird behavior in my room makes sense. "That's why . . . hang on, have mine been hacked, too?"

"It doesn't look like it. But I'm not sure if that's what they're doing. I don't know enough about computers. The red light — the one that comes on when you video chat — that's on all the time. Even when the computer is turned off."

I let out a long sigh, still trying to process the creepy fact that someone might be watching Eli's every move. "You think it's Constance?"

"It has to be."

I shake my head. "They have to have somebody from Systems working for them. Hacking a device with the antivirus and anti-malware software we install isn't kid stuff."

I sink down onto the mat and rest my elbows on my knees. I feel a little dizzy. "Why, though? Is it because of what you told them about me?"

Eli shakes his head. "No way. They must not have bought my story. Now they think I know something I shouldn't."

I think I'm going to be sick. "But if they're spying on you, that's a *huge* breach of personal liberty. It's against the law. Systems would never —"

"Not if Constance has cause to believe I could be endangering the compound."

He's right. Hell, I'd probably learn to do something similar if I were in Systems — just in case Constance ever called on my services. "This is wrong."

Eli laughs — really laughs. "You're concerned with the ethics of Systems all of the sudden?"

"Well, *yeah*. I never wanted to do stuff like this. I'm a developer, not a spy."

Eli breaks into a grin, which is startling. He's actually incredibly good-looking when he isn't yelling at me. "Good to know."

"I'm serious. This is crazy. They can't just spy on you."

"I wish this was the worst thing Constance has ever done." He levels me with a serious gaze, and I can't look away. "I need to know, Harper. If they're watching me, I have an advantage. But only as long as they don't know I know."

I nod, a little startled. He's never called me Harper before. I almost say something, but I don't want to ruin the moment. I don't want him to pile on all his layers of indifference again.

"You need me to look at your computer," I say, following his train of thought. "Won't that make them suspicious?"

He sighs and drags a hand through his short hair. I can tell he's stressed and that this is the first time that idea has occurred to him. "Yeah. You have no reason to be in my compartment in the first place."

Suddenly an idea pops into my head — a good one.

"Sure I do."

As soon as I open my mouth, I realize I'm going to have to say it aloud, and I'm embarrassed. I feel myself going red, and Eli looks confused. It's bad enough that he made up the lie in the first place.

When I finally open my mouth, my voice sounds strangely small. "You told them we were together."

"Yeah, but . . ."

It takes him about two seconds to get it, and his whole body freezes. The look on his face is priceless — panicked and embarrassed. His ears are burning red.

I want to laugh and run at the same time. Eli Parker is afraid of bringing a girl back to his compartment.

"No. No way. It's too dangerous."

"Why?"

"Because if they're recording, they'll have proof."

"They already have proof. You confessed. Plus, if they see us . . . you know, making out or whatever . . . they'll have every reason to think you were telling the truth. It'll throw suspicion off you for whatever they think you did."

Eli's still staring at me, but by the calculating look on his face, I can tell he's giving it some thought. Finally, he takes a deep breath and swallows. He knows I'm right. It will work.

"Harper, you don't have to do this," he says in a low voice. "We can find some other reason for you to come to my room to use my computer."

"But confirming that they're spying on you isn't going to stop them from investigating. Even if they never find any dirt on you, do you really think they're going to just give up? They're not going to let you live if they still suspect you."

Judging by his expression, he's already made it through this thought process. He knows he's screwed if he can't throw suspicion off himself.

He's pacing back and forth in front of the doors, and I can tell he's considering my proposition. Then he stops and stares at me, and I feel the flush spreading up my neck. "Harper, you don't *owe* me anything for bailing you out of Control."

I nod, even though I owe him big.

But that isn't why I feel compelled to help him. Somehow, being co-conspirators in uncovering the truth about Bid Day has made me feel connected to him.

"I'm not helping you because I feel guilty," I say finally.

Eli sighs and runs a hand through his hair. I know he's giving in. "We can't do it right now. It will look suspicious since we just left. Come by later tonight."

"What's your password?"

"What?"

"Your system password. It would be great if I could root around to find the source of whatever they put on your computer."

He buys this explanation, but really, the developer in me is just curious about how Constance could have corrupted the device.

"Oh. It's fifty-eight, O, O, lowercase m, two, Q, S, forty-seven."

I grin. He's got a good password, which kind of turns me on in a bizarre way. "You should wear your interface today."

His eyebrows knit together. "Why?"

"Most people wear theirs everywhere, but you barely ever wear yours. It makes you seem weird."

He cocks an eyebrow. "How do you know I never wear it?"

I shrug. "I've just seen you around. But if you wear it as if nothing's wrong, they'll think you don't know."

For a second, Eli looks irritated at the prospect of wearing his interface, but then he rolls his eyes and gives me a sideways look. "For not being a spy, you sure think like one."

twenty-three

Harper

After our fake training session, I'm too wound up to go back to my compartment. I can't stop thinking about the fact that Eli's being watched or that I volunteered to fake a romantic relationship with him tonight to find out if his devices have actually been tampered with.

I'm dying to tell Celdon what I've found out and ask him what kind of malware could penetrate Systems' defenses, but I know it's too risky. For all I know, they could be watching him, too, since I used his key code to break into Systems that night.

In any case, he won't be awake this early.

I take the megalift to the upper tunnels and hit the nicer rec center to let off some steam. Even though Eli said what he said to get me into the training center alone, he's right. I've lost time, and I don't want to be behind the other recruits.

By lunchtime, I've pretty much exhausted all my excuses to avoid my compartment, so I go back down to take a shower.

I try to work on one of the side projects I started before Bid Day, but now it seems pretty pointless. What am I refining my skills for? All the awesome programs in the world won't get me into Systems.

The hours crawl by, and I force myself to grab a flavorless to-go box from the canteen. I can't risk hanging around in the dining room and seeing Celdon. He'll know something is up, and I'd never be able to live down what I'm about to do.

Plus, I've been avoiding the canteen at peak times on the off chance I'll run into Paxton. I can't risk getting a citation for assault tonight.

By the time I return to my compartment, I'm in full-on panic mode. What does one wear to a fake rendezvous with her commanding officer? I've only worn my Recon uniform since Bid Day, but all my old clothes are still shoved in the back of my closet.

I have one really slinky dress that Celdon made me buy for his Bid Day Eve party last year, but something about it feels all wrong for meeting Eli. I'm sure under his rough exterior he's just a guy, but something tells me he doesn't go for girls who try too hard.

I collapse onto my bed and smack my hand against my forehead.

I'm going crazy. This isn't even real. It doesn't matter what I wear. Constance isn't going to be dissecting my wardrobe for signs that it's all a ruse. But this feels important for another reason — one that's absolutely ridiculous and even dangerous to admit.

I remember the way Eli's eyes drifted down to my shorts this morning. I shouldn't even be thinking about it, but my hand has a mind of its own when it reaches in the back of my closet for the deadliest pair of shorts I own.

They're made from a silky blue fabric and go perfectly with a strappy black tank top I haven't worn before. I want to wear it tonight because, after all the push-ups and pull-ups Eli's been making us do, my arms look fantastic.

Feeling reckless, I leave my hair down and spritz a little bit of body spray that I haven't bothered with since I joined Recon. The chance to be a girl again is actually making me giddy.

Around nineteen hundred, I hear a lot of noise out in the tunnel as the other cadets head off to Neverland or to watch the early amateur fights. I'm sure there are plenty of parties going on in the upper tunnels, too, but Recon cadets won't be invited to those. Their Saturday night entertainment is pretty much restricted to underground debauchery and bloodshed.

Finally the noise dies down, and I check my reflection one last time before heading out for Eli's compartment.

Last chance, I think to myself. *Last chance to turn around and pretend none of this ever happened.*

But even though I'm having a hard time breathing, I know I couldn't back out now even if I wanted to.

It's my fault that Eli drew attention to himself. I was the one he was protecting when he constructed that ridiculous alibi.

And I have to admit I'm a little curious to see if he's a good kisser. Even though he's moody and standoffish, if I had a type, Eli would be it.

Suddenly I'm right in front of his door, and the most obvious question pops into my head — one that I probably should have gotten an answer to this morning: What are we *doing?*

I have no qualms about making out with Eli a little — even letting him cop a feel for realism — but I have no intention of making an amateur porno for the surveillance guys in Constance.

I think I'm having a heart attack. Every muscle in my body is coiled, prepared to flee.

No. *This is Eli*, I tell myself. He bailed me out of Control. He won't let this go too far. I trust him.

I glance up and down the tunnel. It's totally deserted. Either Recon officers have no life, or they've already left to go see the fights.

I knock.

The door flies open so fast that I'm sure Eli's been waiting — probably as antsy as I am. Somehow, that makes me feel a lot less stupid for picking out an outfit and everything.

His eyes are wide and bright with . . . excitement? Nerves? I'm not really sure. They grow wider when they land on me, and I see them flicker down my body again.

I flush, but I don't feel embarrassed. I'm actually glad. It will make this whole exchange so much easier if —

Holy hell. I've just gotten an eyeful of Eli. He's wearing a snug navy T-shirt that makes his eyes seem even bluer and a pair of light-colored jeans. For some reason, it's this last detail that stumps me. No one wears jeans. They're almost impossible to get since they're made of natural fibers. We don't grow cotton in the ag labs. I have no idea where he got these, but he looks good in them.

"Hey," he says.

I force my eyes to move back up to his face and almost wish I hadn't. He's smiling at me again, and it isn't an act for Constance. He looks a little nervous but genuinely glad to see me. It even makes the corners of his eyes crinkle.

"Hi," I say, feeling really stupid.

He jerks his head nervously, and I suddenly remember I'm not supposed to be in his compartment. I jump inside so he can close the door.

Before I can stop myself, my eyes flit over to his computer. Sure enough, the monitor is dark, but I can see that red light blinking lethargically at the top of the screen. Weird.

I feel his hand on my arm and almost jump out of my skin. I meet his gaze, and he frowns a little. "Are you okay?"

I nod, swallow, and force myself to speak. "Yeah."

His eyes are concerned now. "Did you see anyone on the way here?"

"No."

This is not going to work. Anybody watching this would be able to tell that I am a complete train wreck.

But then Eli smiles, and I sort of forget what we're doing. He has a nice face. He has a nice everything, really.

His hand drifts down my arm, encircles my wrist, and then finds my waist. I draw in a breath, trying to steady myself, and his eyes bore into mine. He's asking me a question, even though he can't verbalize it.

I give him the smallest nod, and he pulls me in for a hug. Even though I hate hugs, I let myself lean in to his chest.

I'm instantly enveloped by a crisp, warm boy smell and feel myself relax as he folds his arms around me.

Then he whispers something in my ear, and I sigh — actually sigh — against him when his breath disturbs my hair.

"You look really beautiful tonight."

My heart is pounding embarrassingly fast against his chest. If he's acting, he's a pro.

His other hand drifts up my arm until he reaches my neck, where I'm sure he can feel my pulse pounding against the flesh. His thumb grazes my jaw, and he pulls away just a little.

This is it.

His eyes meet mine for the briefest second. Then he bends down and touches his lips to mine. They're warm and soft, moving slowly. I fit my lips around his mouth, tasting and exploring. His flutter away, and when he pulls back, he looks *nervous*.

This is shocking. Eli Parker is nervous.

But then his lips find mine again, and they're more sure this time. His fingers thread through my hair and pull me closer.

I love the feel of his strong, calloused hands on the back of my neck. Goosebumps erupt all over my arms as he closes in.

His scent is all around me, and it's like some crazy pheromone that's making me drunk and ridiculous.

My hands are on his chest, and I'm savoring his warm mouth on mine. I push against him, and I hear the softest groan in the back of his throat. A pang of satisfaction rolls through me. I'm not the only one enjoying this.

But then his arm snakes around my waist, pulling me even closer. His tongue works between my lips, and my head starts spinning.

He's better at this than I am, and it irritates me that it's so easy for him to make my brain shut off completely.

We're halfway across the room, pushing and pulling against each other. My hands have completely hijacked my brain and are touching his neck, threading through his hair, and dragging against his scalp.

What am I doing?

His hands are everywhere I want them to be, and suddenly I feel the backs of my legs hit his bed. My brain doesn't even register what that means as we fall backward, still tangled around each other.

I pull him down, and as my head hits his pillow, I remember I didn't come here for this. I'm not supposed to be enjoying this; I'm supposed to be checking out his computer.

I pull my lips away a little and glance at the red light. Eli drags in a ragged breath, which is very distracting.

The light is still blinking. As much as I want whatever is happening to continue, I'm itching to get my hands on his computer.

That's what I should be doing, I think as Eli's lips find my neck.

I groan as a wave of pleasure spreads through me. His warm breath on my skin is making me completely lose my mind.

Before I can give in to the urges rising up inside me, I pull away and slink under his arm.

He looks vaguely surprised that I'm vertical again, and I swear I see his ears go red as he regains his composure. He clears his throat and says for the camera, "What are you doing?"

"Can I borrow your interface? I forgot mine."

He nods, and his eyes go dark.

I grab the device off the nightstand and fit it over my ear so it can project in front of my eye.

Sure enough, there's a blinking red light next to the battery icon, though the chat app isn't open. Now I really want to get into his computer.

"Your battery's about to die," I say. I pull off the device and set it in its charging station. "I'll use your computer instead. I just need to check my messages."

He nods and swallows. What's his deal?

"Don't worry," I say lightly, testing the waters. "I'm not messaging some other guy or anything. Well, I am, but it's just Celdon."

I glance over at him, and his face lights up a little as he catches on. "I didn't say anything. Though I was wondering why you were so desperate to check your interface when we were . . ."

"I'm sorry." I turn his computer on and log in with my username. "I forgot he and I had plans tonight."

My setup appears, but that red light doesn't go away. I quickly pull up my message history and then take the chance of opening up his "applications" menu.

Unsurprisingly, there's nothing unusual in there. I'm positive the malware must have installed itself when he clicked on a link, probably in one of his messages. There are about a million places the malware could be hiding, and it could take hours to find.

I want to get into his message history and find the damn link, but he's right behind me. If they're watching what's going on with his computer, that will look suspicious.

I turn around. He's propped himself on his elbows, watching me with smoky eyes.

"Do you have anything to eat? I'm starving."

He looks perplexed. "Uh, no. Sorry. Do you want something to drink?"

I nod, and he gets up and goes over to the mini fridge. I hope he takes his time. I quickly switch users and pound in his password. His dashboard appears, and I open his message history.

The only recent messages are from someone named Miles, except for one. The sender is labeled as "Office of Walter Cunningham," the Secretary of Security, but I'd bet money it's fake. I click on the message, and it's time-stamped two days ago at eighteen hundred hours. That alone is suspicious. The board's admin people never work overtime.

This has to be it. Eli is observant. He would have noticed the red light if the malware had been installed for longer than a week, and that's as far back as his message history goes.

I scan the email. I can hear Eli messing around across the room, buying me some time. The contents of the message are fairly routine — a blanket PSA sent to officers about reminding their new recruits about the consequences of illegal activities. It also says they're going to have to sign up for a shift to patrol their tunnels for added security.

There's a link to a sign-up form. Bingo.

In a swift stroke of keys, I exit out of his account and pull up mine, just as Eli appears over my shoulder with a bottle of synthetic beer. The cheery "real wheat taste" scrawled across the label isn't fooling anyone. I've never had real beer to compare it to, but synthetic tastes like crap. It was manufactured in a lab.

They can't waste valuable ag space growing wheat and barley for alcohol.

"Did you message Celdon?" he asks, wandering over to the sleek black couch and sitting down. I'm relieved he's off the bed.

"Yeah."

I meet his gaze. Eli's staring at me with a mixture of curiosity and something else I can't quite place. I want to enjoy this time with him, but I know I won't be able to relax knowing we're being watched. It's not as though we can have a real conversation. The only things we've ever talked about have centered around corruption in the compound.

He surprises me by beckoning me over. I turn off his computer and shuffle toward the couch. My heart is pounding against my ribcage.

He holds out an arm, and I turn and lower myself awkwardly into his embrace. I've never been much of a snuggler, and Eli isn't just any guy. He's my commanding officer, and I've never seen him this way.

I try to relax, and as soon as I do, I realize it's nice. The side of his body is hard yet inviting, and his warm breath is soft and gentle against the top of my head. I let myself go limp against him, and his arm tightens around me. I'm feeling pretty relaxed until I see the hawk embroidered on his T-shirt, mocking me in fine blue thread.

"What does it mean?" I blurt out.

He glances down to see what I'm looking at and raises an eyebrow. "Have you heard the story of the hawk and the dove?"

I shake my head.

He grins. "Classic game theory. It's the basis for Recon's philosophy. If there's a hawk and a dove competing for resources — say food — the dove will fight the hawk. But if the fight escalates, the dove will fly away to avoid injury or will try to share the food. The hawk . . . the hawk will fight until he dies or wins."

"And Recon is the hawk."

Eli nods, and an ominous feeling sinks into the pit of my stomach. This is why he is the way he is. Eli is a fighter, through and through.

"What are we fighting over?" I ask absently. "If Recon is the hawk and the drifters are the dove . . . the compound already has everything. The drifters have nothing."

"The board still thinks they pose a threat."

"Not all drifters are terrorists," I murmur, thinking of my parents.

"I know."

I don't have to continue, but I keep talking. "Celdon and I were born on the Fringe. We grew up in the Institute together."

"It was a different place before Death Storm," he murmurs.

I cringe. Even though I'm too young to remember the instability overseas that led to nuclear annihilation, the footage of the attacks they showed us in compound history still gives me nightmares sometimes.

When the compound was founded, the first generation of people to settle here were the smart ones. They took the threats seriously. Once the bombs started dropping in New York, Los Angeles, and Chicago, the ones who could buy their way into the compound were the lucky ones.

The U.S. and its allies struck back, but the attack was too co-ordinated. Eight countries were dropping bombs on the most populated areas in the U.S. and the European Union, driving people out of the cities.

Anyone left after Death Storm . . . well, I hadn't even known there *was* anyone left until recently.

"What happened to your parents?" Eli asks quietly.

"They died a few weeks after entering the compound. They told Celdon his parents were dead, but we think he was abandoned out there." I look over at him quickly. "Don't tell anyone that. He doesn't like people to know."

Eli shakes his head as if to say he would never dream of blabbing Celdon's secret, which I find cute for some inexplicable reason.

"How did he end up in the compound?"

"Some Recon officer heard him crying and brought him in. It was a low birth year."

"It wasn't the last. They brought me in when I was a teenager."

I didn't see *that* coming. I twist around in his arms to look at him. "What?"

"When I was fourteen."

"You were raised on the Fringe until you were *fourteen*?" That never happens.

He nods.

"How are you still *alive*?"

He swallows, and I can tell that Eli, like me, doesn't like to think about where he came from. "There are . . . pockets where the radiation levels are low enough to sustain life. Not that people don't get sick. I just never did."

"Why did they bring you in?"

"The same reason as you. To pad the population . . . to bring in some hearty Fringe survivor genes." He gives me a humorless grin, and I realize he's serious. "They brought me in with a few others. They told everyone we were the only survivors they found after Death Storm, but . . . there were so many people left out there."

My stomach clenches. "So you lived in the Institute?"

"Until I was eighteen. That's where I met Miles."

"That big black guy I always see you with?"

He grins. "Yeah, that's him."

"I heard he made a cadet pee his pants last year in training."

Eli laughs, and I find I'm annoyed.

"I'm so glad it amuses you to scare the shit out of cadets."

His face goes dark, and for a minute, I wonder if I've stepped over the line.

"I don't enjoy it," he says defensively. "I *have* to scare you guys. You all come in completely clueless. You need to be motivated to train hard and prepare yourselves."

"You don't have to be such an asshole all the time."

He pulls his arm off me and inches away, which is difficult on the narrow couch. "Yeah, I do. It's my job to make sure you guys survive." He sighs, running a hand through his short hair. "You don't get it. You've never been out there."

I know he's frustrated and upset, but his tone is pissing me off. I'm not some kid he can talk down to.

"Got it," I say suddenly, jumping to my feet and setting the beer on the side table.

He looks a little surprised, and then his expression clouds over. "What?"

"I'm leaving," I say. "It's obvious you don't need to be with someone who's never been 'out there.' Maybe you should hop in bed with Jayden or something. She's certainly *mature.*" I say the last word with more spite than I mean to, but I don't care. "Find someone else who understands, because I'm done."

Eli looks genuinely shocked.

"I'll see you in training," I snap. Then I stride out of his compartment and slam the door.

Once I'm out of Eli's sexiness splash zone, I can actually think straight again.

I have no idea why I just staged some dramatic exit — if that's what I was doing — or why my blood is pounding in my ears.

I realize I never had a chance to tell Eli what I discovered on his computer. Whatever. If he really wants to know, he can come find me.

As I walk back to my compartment, I realize I'm not prepared to handle stealth spy missions like that. I'm way too emotional. I can't let Eli know, though. It would be embarrassing if he thought that rage fit was real — or anything that came before.

The next time I see him, I have to be cool and collected. I'll act impervious to his good looks and superhuman make-out skills. I have to, because that can never happen again. I won't be the girl who sleeps her way to the top.

In the short time I've been in Recon, competitive, cocky Harper has been running in the background. I've been so busy poking into my bid and resenting Recon for robbing me of my future in Systems that I never noticed that part of me actually wanted to become a kick-ass cadet.

I've been training hard, and I'm getting *good*. Killing drifters isn't what I signed up for, but it's not as though I have a choice. If I'm stuck here, I'm going to be the best cadet they've ever had.

twenty-four

Eli

I have no idea what to expect when I see Harper on Monday. I know I pissed her off Saturday, and I'm furious at myself for turning into Lieutenant Parker.

Even though Harper was only in my room to get on my computer, our conversation felt real. It felt good — until I fucked it all up.

I'm angry at myself for pissing her off, but I'm even angrier about how much I enjoyed kissing her.

I shouldn't be surprised. Harper is hot — beautiful, even — but that's not the only reason I liked it. I like *Harper*, and that's a huge problem.

I don't want to like any of my cadets, not even platonically. Those kinds of feelings cause you to make stupid decisions as a leader. They get you killed on the Fringe.

Besides, I'm positive Harper doesn't share my feelings. I turned her on, but that's it. She's made it perfectly clear that she hates my guts. Part of me wants to see her, but the other part is dreading training.

I delay getting out of bed so long that I have to rush to get breakfast. I scarf down my bowl of bananas and power greens so fast I nearly hurl, and then I end up getting back down to the training center a good twenty minutes early.

I'm too wired to stand around and wait for the cadets to arrive, so I go over to the weights to let off some steam.

I load the bar with about as much weight as I can handle, but I still can't get the image of Harper in shorts out of my head. I'm not picturing her all dolled up, though. I keep envisioning her just after waking up, with her hair all messy and that unsuspecting softness from sleep. She looked so different than she does in training, with that dark hair falling all over her shoulders and back.

God, I love her hair. I love running my fingers through it — the way it smells.

The doors to the training center slam, and I almost drop the bar when I catch a glimpse of a dark, silky ponytail in my peripheral vision.

I act as though I don't see Harper striding toward me in her gray fatigues. They aren't loose enough to make me forget those shorts, but luckily her hair is mostly contained, and the top half of her is swimming in the gray overshirt.

"Hey," she says, a little louder than she needs to. We're the only ones here, but you'd think we had an audience.

She's only a few feet away now, looking slightly rattled.

"Hey," I say, focusing on getting a full extension on my press.

She takes a deep breath, and I can tell she's been dying to tell someone what she found on my computer. "So I didn't have a lot of time to go rooting around on your hard drive, but I'd bet money that malware was downloaded when you clicked that link in your message from Walter Cunningham's office."

"You think Walter Cunningham is part of Constance?"

"I wouldn't put it past him, but no. I think that email was a fake."

"Okay."

"I *could* get the malware off your computer and your interface, but I think that would look suspicious."

I still don't meet her gaze. I don't want to look into those big gray eyes again. "You're probably right."

"You should just leave it on your computer and try not to let them catch you doing anything illegal."

"Sounds good."

My short responses are bound to piss her off, but I need her to leave me alone so I can banish the thoughts of her soft lips on mine.

"Eli?"

"Yeah."

"Is that it?"

"Yep," I say in a businesslike voice. "I don't plan on doing any more illegal stuff, so they'll probably get bored eventually."

"So you don't even care that they're watching you?"

"Should I?"

"*Yes.*" She lets out an irritated sigh and crosses the small distance between us. Before I can prepare myself for what she's about to do, Harper swings her leg over the bench, knocking her knees into mine. All I see is her torso until I feel her hands on the bar, pushing it toward my face.

The weight seems to double, and I freeze with shock.

This girl is trying to kill me.

"What's your deal?" she snaps.

"Nothing," I groan, pushing against the bar to stop it from crushing my chest.

She throws more of her weight on it, and my arms wobble. Not good.

"Why aren't you going to fight this? It's *wrong*, Eli."

"Harper! Get — off!" I grunt. I'm sweating and panting now. I shouldn't have loaded the bar with so much weight.

"When did you turn into such a coward?"

"What?"

Summoning all the energy I have, I thrust the bar up and re-rack it. Harper was already leaning toward me. When the weight disappears, she flies forward, nearly face-planting onto the floor and stabbing me in the chest with her bony elbow in the process.

"Jesus!" I catch her around the waist and steady her.

She huffs, grabbing the side of the bench. She's full-on strad-dling me right now, and she pulls herself off in a hurry.

"What the hell was that?"

"Why are you acting this way?" she asks. "Everything went down just as we planned."

"I know," I say incredulously, still a little stunned.

"Then why don't you care that they're watching your every move? I thought . . . I thought you'd want to *do* something."

I stare at her. "You said yourself that it would make them sus-picious if you removed the malware. I don't really have another option."

Harper crosses her arms, and I know whatever comes out of her mouth next is going to be trouble. "I didn't say that."

I pull myself into a seated position. "What are you saying?"

She grins briefly, and I want to go bang my head against the wall for all the thoughts that come to mind. I realize I want to make her smile like that again — I want her smiling because of me.

"I'm *saying* you could use the surveillance to mess with them."

I shake my head. "No. No way."

"Why?"

"It's too dangerous."

"No, it's not."

I'm standing up, and when she takes a step backward, I realize I'm doing that towering-over-her thing again. I try to relax my shoulders and get out of her face. "They *tortured* you, remember?"

Her mouth tightens into a thin line, and she gives me a nasty look that says she doesn't need to be reminded. "Of course I remember."

"I'm just saying that after what Constance did to you . . . you're lucky to be alive."

I take a step toward her, holding out my hands and trying to keep my voice low and nonthreatening. "We don't want them as our enemy, Harper."

Her eyes widen a little. She's surprised, probably because I said "we." I know I always find it shocking when I'm a part of anybody's "we."

She looks at me and starts to nod when the double doors burst open. Lenny and Kindra saunter in, and Harper takes an automatic step back. She stares at me for a moment and turns to go join them on the other side of the room.

I take a second to pull myself together and force the memory of Harper's lips out of my mind. I'm not succeeding, but the other girls don't pay any attention to me.

Bear and Blaze shuffle in, and I tell them to pair off to work on the maneuver we practiced last week. It's ground defense — the last one the cadets have to master before moving on to disarming attackers with weapons.

Part of me hopes that Harper will grab Lenny or Kindra so I won't have to partner with her again, but I have a feeling they are too intimidated. Harper's advanced much faster than the rest of them, and she doesn't hold back in practice.

Reluctantly, I join her in the empty ring and pull on my gloves. Out of the corner of my eye, I see the other cadets starting the exercise from the ground, but Harper steps up in front of me.

She knows I'm going to make her begin from a fighting stance. I've tried to tell the others that falling the right way is just as important as what you do on the ground, but they don't listen.

Harper shakes out her arms and tucks her chin, giving me this look that says she did try to get away from me. I grin before I can help myself, and she looks pleasantly surprised.

I circle Harper slowly and throw a few warm-up jabs. She deflects them easily and even returns a few well-aimed counterstrikes.

I'm not going as hard or fast as I can, but she still impresses me. It's actually hard to get in close enough to make contact with her shoulder and pull her leg out from under her, but she hits the mat, and I see irritation etched all over her face.

She knew what I was going to do, but takedowns still suck.

I tower over her, straddling her legs, and a sense of dread washes over me. For this self-defense maneuver, I prefer to have the girls practice with girls, and now I'm really thinking I should have insisted. Even though it's just me, I see panic in Harper's eyes right until she throws her hips and flips me back onto the mat.

Suddenly our roles are reversed, and she's straddling me. Her fist flies out, and I'm barely fast enough to deflect her punch.

With most cadets, I would stop and start the exercise from the beginning to give them a chance to catch their breath. But Harper can handle nonstop, so I flip her over and make her go through it all again. We do this a few more times, and I can tell she's getting winded.

On her last flip, her hips don't come up enough, and she barely has the strength to push me off her. She still does, though, which is amazing.

I check the clock and decide she's had enough. I hold out a

hand to help her up, and she takes it uneasily. She stares at me for a moment, and I give her a nod of approval.

"How did I do?" she prompts.

"Pretty good," I lie.

She did great.

Harper nods slowly and opens and closes her mouth. That isn't like her.

"What is it?" I ask.

"Do I get to advance to the next level?"

"What?" I splutter, not sure I heard right. I never told the cadets which maneuvers were the milestones we used to advance them. "Who told you which self-defenses you had to pass before you moved on?"

She shrugs. "Everybody knows."

Now it makes sense that I haven't heard the other cadets talking and laughing. They're actually taking this one seriously because they know they have to pass it.

Harper should advance to the next level, but that means Jayden will start to oversee some of her training. And once Jayden gets a good look at Harper, she's going to want to send her out early. It's been almost nine weeks. Twelve weeks is the minimum amount of training cadets can receive before they're deployed.

"So? Do I get to advance?"

I sigh. "No, Riley. I'm sorry. It wasn't good enough."

Her excitement fades. She looks so crestfallen I wish I could tell her why I'm holding her back, but we're surrounded by people.

She swallows and musters up a little of that cockiness I love. "Why not?"

"You didn't throw your hips like you were supposed to."

Lies, lies, lies.

"On the last one!" she snaps. "I was *tired.* You made me go nonstop."

"You're going to be tired in the field."

Her face clouds over, and I have the sudden impulse to duck and cover. "This is bullshit," she mutters.

I suck in a deep breath, already hating myself for what I'm about to say. "Riley, the truth is if you were fighting a bigger guy, you wouldn't have been able to flip him the way you flipped me."

"Bring Miles in here!" she yells. Kindra and Lenny look over at us but don't say anything. "If I can flip him, you let me move forward."

Reluctantly, I dig down deep and summon my most menacing, authoritative voice. "You're out of line, Riley. And my decision is final."

For one terrifying moment, I think she's going to cry.

"I'm sorry, Harper," I add quietly. "Maybe next week."

I can tell she's furious, but she doesn't lash out the way old Harper would have. In fact, I'm actually astounded by the amount of self-control she's accumulated in the short time she's been here.

"Fine. Let's go again."

"Not ground defense," I say. "You're going to have bruises all over your back."

She shrugs but grabs some pads from the hooks on the wall. Harper fights hard until lunchtime.

When the bell rings, she sulks off without touching gloves to end the sparring session. She knows it's tradition — good sportsmanship — but she's still too angry.

I can't say I blame her. I'd be mad at me, too.

I'm just about to leave when the doors creak open and I hear a low whistle. Miles is leaning half inside the training center, beckoning me over. Something about the look in his eyes makes me nervous.

"Hey!" I call.

"Hey, yourself! I've been waiting on you. Jayden wants to see us in her office."

"For what?" I toss my gloves on the ground and mop the sweat off my face.

I see one shoulder lift into a shrug. "Hell if I know. But I've never been summoned for any good reason, have you?"

"No."

Walking as slowly as I dare, I follow Miles down the tunnel toward the commander's office. With every step we take, the leaden weight in my stomach grows heavier.

This isn't the first time we've marched into trouble together, but this is a lot more serious than getting issued a citation for illegal fighting or breaking into the canteen to steal rations. There's only a handful of reasons Jayden would call me to her office instead of just showing up in my compartment — and only one that would involve Miles.

We reach the end of the tunnel and exchange a look of dread before pounding on the metal door.

"Come in," Jayden calls. Jesus. Even in two syllables, she still manages to sound condescending.

Miles throws the door open and strides in as though he owns the place, but despite his posturing, I can see that even he's intimidated. Jayden doesn't inflict punishments with her fists; she gets you right where it hurts every time. She's used Brooke against Miles more times than I can count, and now she's got Harper to use against me.

Sitting behind her big-ass metal desk in a chair that's about three times too big for her, Jayden looks incredibly imposing for such a delicate, beautiful woman. "Close the door," she snaps.

Miles kicks it shut.

"How are your whiny cadets holding up, Parker?" she asks breezily.

"Fine, Commander. They won't be so whiny once I'm finished with them."

Her dark eyes narrow into a wolfish stare. "And how long do you think that will take?"

"The same as it's always taken, Commander. About fifty-two weeks or so."

She nods. "That's quite a shame. We don't have time on our side the way we used to."

Miles looks confused, and my stomach clenches with dread.

"Right," says Jayden, suddenly nice and professional once again. "I didn't call you in here for a progress report. You're being deployed — both of you."

Even though I expected this, it's always a bit of a shock. "Both of us?"

"That's right." Her eyes are as cold as stone. "I know you were expecting a few more weeks with your cadets, but I trust that Lieutenant Duffy can pick up where you left off. Unless there's some personal reason you'd rather not leave?"

Her fake innocent tone isn't fooling anyone. Miles is looking from me to Jayden, trying to work out whatever sick game she's playing. She's not really offering me an out, and she never feigns thoughtfulness when assigning a mission.

"No, Commander. I'm just surprised you're sending us both out together."

It's common knowledge that Miles and I are close, so Recon generally avoids partnering us for deployment.

"Considering Private Hackman missed a deployment recuperating from an illegal fight last month, I can't think of a better man for the job."

Miles rolls his eyes. "Right."

"You leave at oh-six hundred hours."

Miles's face clouds over. "*What?*"

"Is there a problem, Hackman?"

"No, but . . . we've always had at least twenty-four hours' notice before."

"The situation has changed. We're fighting a losing battle out there. Timing is everything."

"Parker, Lieutenant Duffy will take over your training sessions effective immediately, and you will report to Remy Chaplin's office for a briefing at seventeen hundred hours. Is that understood?"

"Yes, Commander," we say, because we have no choice. There'd be no point in asking for delayed deployment — no point even asking what they want us to do. You don't question your commanding officer. You don't question anything.

Miles and I leave without another word, but we're barely out of earshot when Miles strings together a creative stream of foul names for Jayden. He hates her even more than I do, which isn't surprising. Whoever doles out deployments is the Recon equivalent of the Grim Reaper.

"Brooke is going to kill me," he says.

"I'm sure she'll understand."

But we both know that isn't true. When you're not in Recon, it's hard to understand how you could drop everything and march out into the Fringe without thinking twice. That's one reason it's practically impossible for a Recon worker to maintain a healthy relationship.

I don't tell him that everything will be fine. I don't tell him it doesn't matter if Brooke is angry, since he'll be back in a week.

Nobody says that in Recon. It's an unspoken superstition.

Never count on coming back. If you always deploy as though you're going to die, it's easier to do whatever you have to do to survive. You shoot faster and fight harder. You forget that you might have to live with yourself later.

I have a fleeting thought that I should tell Harper I'm leaving — say goodbye — but the thought is snuffed out almost instantly.

Telling Harper would be stupid. It would imply that she's something more than my cadet, which she isn't. I have no right to burden her with this.

But truthfully, I'd give anything to have someone to tell — someone who'd care that I was being deployed. The impulse is ridiculous, but I can't deny it's there.

* * *

Everything leading up to deployment feels misleadingly benign. It's just like preparing for a long trip.

After Miles and I are briefed on the mission by Remy Chaplin and I'm cleared by Health and Rehab, I eat a late dinner alone in the canteen. The food is cold and gelatinous from sitting out too long — too terrible to be a last meal.

I don't see Miles for the rest of the night. I'm positive he won't leave Brooke's side until he has to. She'll be crying and clinging to him, and when it comes time to leave, he'll be distracted.

Miles doesn't have a lot of weaknesses; Recon beats them out of you pretty fast. But Brooke is his.

It's not just the fact that their relationship — any relationship — is against the rules. Brooke can be kind of a bitch. She has this way of getting under Miles's skin, making him hate the fighter in him — the thing that keeps him alive. And not a day goes by that Brooke doesn't somehow make him feel inadequate for not being able to marry her and pop out a bunch of babies.

That's why we don't have families. They just drag you down.

I pack my rucksack with one change of clothes and as much water and rations as I can carry. There are checkpoints out on the Fringe where we can restock, but I've learned not to depend on those. Too often they're scheduled to be restocked by cadets who never make it that far.

Sleep comes surprisingly easy and doesn't last long enough. I don't have a window in my compartment, but I know it's dark when I lie down and still dark when I dress and leave.

Miles isn't in the tunnel waiting for me — not that I'd expect him to be. He'll run out the clock with Brooke, whereas I'd just rather get this over with.

The sooner we leave, the sooner it will be over. The anticipation is sometimes worse than the mission itself, though not often.

Jayden and Remy Chaplin are already waiting on the ground level inside the first set of doors. Remy is the Undersecretary of Reconnaissance — charged with overseeing Recon on behalf of the board and ensuring we keep our mouths shut. Jayden has been gunning for his job forever.

On the other side of the frosted glass, I can see the outline of an orange jumpsuit — some poor ExCon guy they got out of bed early to open the airlock doors so that neither Jayden nor Remy would have to expose themselves to the elements.

He doesn't mind. He already wears the Fringe like a second skin.

Miles jogs up to us with two minutes to spare, and Remy begins to read us our deployment disclosure:

I am exiting the compound on my own volition, fully aware of the risks that await me on the Fringe. I understand that although I am acting on behalf of the compound, I am a free agent on the Fringe, and the compound bears no liability for any harm that may come to me.

I understand that I am bound by law to reveal whatever I find outside the compound wholly and truthfully to my commanding officers. I understand it is of equal importance that I never discuss what I find with any compound civilians.

Miles and I answer with a flat "yes, sir" and salute Remy and Jayden.

"Good luck, boys," says Remy. "Strength as one is strength for all."

I nod and wait for Remy to punch in the code to unlock the first set of doors. They swing open with a slight hiss, but they're mainly ornamental.

As soon as we cross the threshold, the doors close automatically, and I see a thin red laser line move down the door to show it's been locked.

We're standing in a small entryway encased in steel. There are decontamination chambers on either side, a first aid kit mounted just inside the door, and a big yellow sign stamped with the radioactive symbol — as if we don't know what we're about to face.

Miles and I pull on our masks to avoid breathing in radioactive particles. It suctions to my face, and I feel the familiar panic settling in the pit of my stomach.

The tired ExCon man barely grunts in acknowledgement as he punches in the second key code. This door is stronger than the six-inch glass that encases the compound. It's made of reinforced steel coated with lead.

I hear the loud hiss as it's released and feel a heavy blast of heat. As the doors open, a flurry of dust blows in, coating our black boots with orange dirt. I take my last breath of cold, recycled compound air and step out into the Fringe.

twenty-five

Harper

It's early morning when I receive the summons to Jayden's office on my interface.

I'm only vaguely surprised. I've been waiting for her to crush me with her demon claws ever since Eli's fake confession.

I know I should be worried, but I'm more curious than anything else. I've seen Jayden yell at Bear, push Eli's buttons, and place inhumanly low bids with the cool efficiency of someone ordering a drink. She terrifies me, but I'd be lying if I said I wasn't fascinated by her.

I dress quickly, grab breakfast to go, and arrive outside her office just in time for our meeting at oh-seven hundred.

When I knock, I hear a sharp command from behind the heavy door and let myself in.

I salute quickly and take the opportunity to scope out her office. It's bigger than my compartment, with a huge silvery desk in the middle and award placards mounted across the back wall. Jayden has an impressive computer setup — one I'm sure she uses to process Fringe intelligence and track deployed operatives.

"At ease, Cadet."

I lower my arm stiffly and make eye contact with the diminutive woman behind the war desk.

She's short, but she has sharp, unsympathetic eyes and sky-high cheekbones accentuated by the tight bun she always wears. When she moves, her uniform clings to her like a second skin.

Her posture is meant to intimidate, but everything else about her screams seduction.

"You wanted to see me, Commander?"

"Yes, Riley. Have a seat."

Sinking down into one of those plush chairs seems like a mistake, but I do it anyway. The chair is super comfortable, and I can't fight the image of a black widow spider luring me into her web.

"I had a chance to review Lieutenant Parker's testimony in your case file."

"Oh." My stomach sinks. I'm here to be punished.

"Parker told Control that you and he had . . . relations."

I cringe at the disgust she places on the last word, and she arches one perfectly groomed eyebrow in disapproval. "Is this true?"

My face is burning up, and Jayden is *loving* every second of my discomfort. "Yes."

The corner of her mouth twitches, and I know she's holding back a smirk. "What was the nature of your relationship with Lieutenant Parker?"

"We had sex."

"Right. I suspected. How many times?"

My face is burning even hotter. I'm shocked she's asking. "Just once."

"And was it consensual?"

"*Yes,*" I say, exasperated. "I pursued *him.*"

Jayden finally cracks a smirk and sits up in her chair, looking as though Christmas has come early. "Really?"

"Yes," I say. "And I know he regrets it."

"I'm sure," she says forcefully. "And where did this happen?"

I stare at her computer, willing myself to disappear. I can't believe I'm having this conversation. "Up on the observation deck. It was deserted."

She nods and rests her chin on her linked fingers. She's taking her time — playing with her food. She gets off on this.

"Riley, I'm not sure what the policy is in Systems, but I run a tight ship down here."

Bitch. She knows what the policy is.

"Relations between two Recon operatives — especially relations with your commanding officer — are strictly prohibited."

"Yes, Commander."

"Were you aware of the policy when you engaged in this . . . behavior?"

"Yes."

"And were you aware that relations between two Recon operatives is grounds for discharge?"

I nod, unable to breathe. She's going to throw me to ExCon. I just know it.

"What happened afterward?"

Now I'm getting pissed. What does she want to know? If we cuddled? I wish she would just discharge me and get on with it.

"I'm not sure I know what you mean, Commander."

"I mean are you still involved with him? Even emotionally?"

"No," I say, more aggressively than I mean to. "Believe me — it was a mistake."

"Really? And you haven't been alone with him?"

I shake my head. The look of smug disbelief on her face is making me panic.

She turns to her computer and makes a few swipes on her touchpad. She turns the screen toward me, and I'm horrified to see the inside view of Eli's compartment.

There's Eli in his sexy jeans. His arm is wrapped around me, and we're tripping backward, kissing and touching. I go down onto the bed, and Jayden hits pause.

"You can see why I don't believe you."

I don't even have to fake shock. "How did you —" I splutter.

"Clearly you haven't ended your relationship with him."

"We had a bit of a relapse," I say dismissively. "But that's as far as it went."

"Oh, I know."

The superior look on her face is compounding the fury that's bubbling just beneath the surface. Suddenly I understand how Jayden rose through the ranks so quickly: She enjoys manipulating people, and she's good at it.

"Where did you get this?" I ask, even though I already know.

"Constance has been watching you, Riley. I usually like to think I have better things to do with my time than spy on my officers, but this . . . this is entertaining."

My stomach churns with disgust, and I have the sudden urge to put my fist through her fancy monitor. But whether I'm out of Recon or not, Jayden can definitely kick my ass.

"Why were *you* watching us?"

"You've been asking too many questions, Riley. You and your little friend Celdon were digging into sealed files containing top-secret VocAps data. And now Lieutenant Parker is involved. It has to be taken care of."

"What?" Suddenly my anger is gone. All I can feel is the mounting panic constricting my chest. "What do you mean 'taken care of'?"

"Never you mind. This deployment should do it, I think. Our satellites show that drifters are congregating near the perimeter, waiting to launch an attack. If he comes back, we'll just send him out again."

"You're deploying him?" I choke. "Sending him into trouble to *get rid* of him?"

I have to get out of here. I have to warn Eli.

"It's already done. I sent him out at oh-six hundred."

So many thoughts are firing in my head at once that I can't do anything more than stare dumbfounded at Jayden. Eli was right when he said she was only looking out for herself. Jayden doesn't give a shit about anyone.

I've melted into my chair, and I feel as though I need to put my head between my knees and breathe into a bag.

"You *recruited* him," I say after a while. "How can you do that to him?"

"It's my job, Riley. I have to think about what's best for this compound."

"So that's it?" I splutter. "He's disposable to you? You were just like him once."

"And I did what was best for the compound then, too. It's why I recruited him. He understands. It's the reason he recruited you."

"*What?*"

A slow smile spreads across Jayden's face. Oddly enough, she doesn't look as pretty when she's smiling. "Not quite as aggressively as I recruited him. But when he got the list of recruits who were recommended for Recon, he had to have you."

I feel as though I've been punched in the stomach. This can't be true. That would mean that everything Eli told me from the beginning was a lie.

Jayden must see the devastation written all over my face, because she adds, "He didn't know about your viability score. Only the board and the bid committee are privy to that information."

I drag in a deep breath. So not *everything* had been a lie.

"But when he saw a Systems-track girl who wasn't recommended for Systems, he became obsessed." She drags out the last word, and I can tell torturing me is giving her intense pleasure.

"He dug up your permanent file. He saw you were a Fringe brat, just as he had been — saw you were suspended again and again for fighting in the Institute. And yet you weren't stupid. You had good marks in all your higher-ed classes. He saw what I saw."

"And you didn't care that I only have a thirty-three percent chance of living to the age of thirty?"

"Oh, I'm counting on the fact that you won't live to be thirty. A thirty-three percent chance is much higher than even a genetically perfect person's odds of surviving ninety-six deployments. With an aptitude score that high, why wouldn't I take you? Plus, when Constance decided to subsidize your recruitment, that was that."

"Did Eli know?" I ask. "About the sixty thousand?"

I don't care that I sound wounded or that Jayden's air of satisfaction is growing stronger by the second. I have to know.

"Would it matter if he did? He's still the reason you're here."

So *that's* why she's telling me all this. She wants to break our bond. But there's more coming. I can see her fighting a smile.

"What's going to happen to me?"

"Well, obviously, the arrest didn't go as planned. Even Constance can't prosecute someone based on circumstantial evidence when she has two witnesses come to her defense."

"As planned?"

Jayden lets out a wistful sigh. "It would have been perfect, you know. You would have taken the fall for Taylor, and our little VocAps hiccup would have been wiped away. An act of terrorism within the compound is grounds for lethal injection. We accounted for everything — except your friends coming to your defense."

"We?"

And then it hits me. Jayden is with Constance. Constance is responsible for the bombing. Constance tried to frame me for it.

"You set me up," I murmur.

"Constance set you up," she corrects. "I knew you'd try to hack into Taylor's computer sooner or later. I just didn't think it would take so long. I had to plant the seed."

"That day in training when Bear . . ."

"You're a smart girl. We tracked your interface going from Systems to Taylor's office. I called in a little tip to your friend, Officer Dellwood . . ."

"You killed Taylor?"

"He had to go, Riley. It was regrettable, but he decided to grow a conscience after all these years. He felt guilty about re-cruiting so many for Recon when our fatality rates were rising. He even tried to fight the money coming in from Constance, since influencing the bidding goes against compound law. He be-came a liability."

"So you just *murdered* him?"

Jayden fixes me with a serious look. "Constance is not Con-trol, Riley. It was created to operate independently of the board . . . to step in if the board's decisions could have dire consequences.

"Our sole purpose is to preserve the human race — not just the compound itself. One individual's life . . . even two or three . . . is not relevant. Keeping this compound and others function-ing requires us to make the tough choices to do what we know is good for them. But we do have to move quietly. If people felt they had no control over their lives . . . society would collapse."

I sit completely frozen with shock as it all sinks in. There's an urgency pounding through my veins, though. Deep down, I know Jayden wouldn't be telling me all of this unless she planned to get rid of me.

"What's going to happen now?"

She smiles. "Your time will come. It's too bad. Things are getting much worse out there. We could have used you on the Fringe permanently."

"That's why Constance paid sixty thousand for me to be in Recon?"

Jayden nods. "The drifters are getting smarter, Riley. We needed someone with your skill set . . . someone who wouldn't live long enough to become a liability the way Taylor did. It's lucky Parker brought you to our attention."

"But why would Constance want all the drifters killed if your *duty* is to preserve the human race?"

She fixes me with a blank stare. "There's nothing left for humanity out there, Riley. Those who are left are dying out, but right now . . . they're impeding progress."

I stand up to leave, simultaneously disgusted and stunned that she's letting me walk out of here alive. "Why are you telling me this?" I ask, dreading the answer.

"To show you what happens to people who don't do what they're told. We still need you, Riley . . . for now. I need to make sure you're . . . motivated to make the right choice."

I glare at her, the hatred humming in every cell. "Motivated?"

"You'll be dead soon anyway, but your friend Celdon . . . he could have a long, happy life ahead of him. That's how I know you'll do what needs to be done and keep our little conversation private."

Nausea builds in my stomach. I take two purposeful strides toward the door but stop with my hand on the knob. I have to know. "What's Eli's viability score?"

She sighs, and for the first time, there's genuine regret in her voice. "Ten."

Before she can pile on to what I've learned, I'm flying out of her office and down the tunnel. It's starting to get crowded. People are going to the canteen, coming back, heading to training, or going to the intel rooms to monitor Fringe activity. Nobody pays me any attention as I fight against the wave of people.

My head is spinning, and the blind panic is making my heart feel as though it might jump out of my chest. I stumble through the crowd, holding down the tears and the bile burning in my throat.

I punch in the code to my room and slam the door, breathing hard. Jayden's words are still ringing in my head, and I have this horrible sinking feeling that wasn't there before.

Jayden is with Constance. Constance wants me dead. Jayden threatened Celdon's life and mine. Eli lied. He's the reason I'm here, and now Jayden wants him dead, too.

I can't hold the tears in anymore. I slide back against the cool metal door and bang my head back hard.

Everything is falling apart. I knew I could get into trouble when I started digging into my bid, but I never expected it would get me and Eli killed.

Once the initial shock wears off, I'm pissed by what is bothering me the most. It isn't the fact that Constance wants me and my friends dead or the fact that Jayden played me to get Taylor out of the way. It's the fact that Eli has been lying to me the entire time.

I thought he cared about me. I thought we were friends, at least.

That night in his room, I got caught up in the heat of the moment. I felt something. I thought he enjoyed it, too. Or maybe he was faking it — just as he played dumb when I cornered him about my bid.

Then again, Eli also protected me when I was arrested. Maybe he felt guilty. Maybe he cared about me. Either way, he was deployed early because of what I did, and that guilt neutralizes some of the anger and panic that's raging inside me.

My tears dry up fast — much faster than they would have three months ago. I realize being in Recon has made me tougher. The need for food is winning out over my impulse to sit on the floor feeling sorry for myself.

I splash some cold water on my face so that no one will see that I've been crying and head out the door.

If Constance wants me dead, they're going to have to get their hands dirty. I refuse to die on the Fringe. They won't be able to write my death off as another statistic. Jayden is going to have to put a bullet through my head herself.

twenty-six

Harper

Even though I'm wildly distracted, I can tell something is off the second I step into the brightly lit canteen.

At first I think I'm imagining the drama because Eli is gone, and for the first time since Bid Day, there's no one in Recon looking out for me.

But then a Waste Management guy turns around in the mess line and sneers at me. He nudges his scruffy friends, and the rest of them shift around in line and mutter under their breath.

I don't hear everything they're saying, but I catch the word "bitch."

Any other day I'd shove past them and ignore it, but there's a strange prickle of alarm on the back of my neck. I glance behind me and quickly realize I'm the only Recon worker in line. I'm surrounded by tier-three men who look as though they're out for blood.

Maybe I'm just being paranoid because I know my number is up.

But then a worker in the mess line who smiled at me just the other day shoots me a deadly glare over the glass partition and slops boiled kale all over the rim of my bowl. I throw her a wary look and take my food before she decides to starve me completely.

Looking around for a place to sit, I immediately notice the tight knots of people bunched together at every table. Normally the canteen is a blur of mismatched colors. Today, nobody is mingling with other sections, and Recon has been sequestered to one corner of the canteen. I see a mop of bright red hair whip around, and Lenny gives a little jerk of her head that's anything but subtle.

Relieved, I squeeze in between her and Bear and catch a whiff of a few dozen Recon bodies all crammed in close together.

"What the hell is going on?" I ask.

"It's bad news," Lenny whispers. "The whole compound has turned on us."

"Why?"

"Someone on the board leaked that a bunch of deployed Recon operatives have gone AWOL in the last few weeks."

"What?" My mind instantly goes to Eli, and I panic. But he was just sent out this morning. He can't be missing yet.

"Yeah." Lenny shifts in her seat and looks around as though she doesn't want to be overheard. "And now they're saying that someone in Recon planted the bomb. They think the AWOL Recon have split off from the compound . . . gone rogue."

"That's ridiculous."

"Of course it's ridiculous!" snaps Lenny. "Who the hell would stay out there voluntarily?"

"They're trying to cover something up," says Bear. "That bomb didn't come from anyone inside the compound. Nobody's that stupid . . . not even the ExCon guys."

I resist the urge to shout "Constance" from the top of my lungs and take a deep breath. "What made them decide to leak this now?" I ask.

"Dunno. I guess they couldn't just keep sending guys out there without any coming back and expect that people wouldn't notice."

Dread spills into my gut, and I drag in a heavy stream of air. "Eli's out there now," I whisper.

Their expressions mirror the sucker punch I felt when Jayden told me.

"*What?*"

"They sent him out this morning."

They're silent for a beat, and then Lenny's expression twists from flabbergasted to curious. "Wait . . . how do *you* know he got sent out?"

There's a wicked grin pulling at the corners of her mouth, and I feel my face go red. None of them ever mentioned the ugly rumor circulating about me, but I know they must have heard it.

"I was summoned," I say, trying to keep my expression neutral. "By Jayden."

"What did she want?" Bear asks, keeping his eyes on his food.

I grin. He's probably the only cadet who hates her more than I do. "She wanted to talk about my attitude in training," I lie. "I guess I've been talking back to Eli too much."

"Oh please," scoffs Lenny. "He shouldn't dish it out if he can't take it. He's relentless with you. I would have punched him in his beautiful mouth our very first day. Oh, wait . . . you *did.*"

Lenny dissolves into laughter for a moment but then seems to remember what we were discussing. "But that's terrible he's been sent out," she says quickly. "He was just starting to grow on me."

I swallow, thinking Eli had done more than grow on me in the last few weeks. Even though I'm furious that he lied, I actually *miss* him.

We finish our breakfast and make the long awkward walk through the canteen. I catch a few hateful remarks as we pass, and I'm amazed at how quickly the hostility has escalated in the compound.

As we descend to the lower tunnels, I switch on my interface to check the stream for the board leak. But just as I open the news app, something catches my eye in the corner of my interface. Right next to my battery icon is a flashing red light.

A chill shoots down my spine. I switch my interface off quickly, though I know it doesn't matter. I glance around, but the others haven't noticed anything strange. I can't say what I've found. I can't tell anyone.

I have no idea how Constance got the malware onto my device. I haven't opened a single message from anyone I don't know.

Before I can digest this alarming new development, Bear pushes the doors to the training center open. The other cadets are milling around across the room, but our corner is empty.

Eli is gone, of course, but then my eyes land on a sturdy-looking man going at a punching bag against the far wall. He moves more than Eli does when he boxes. He's short, energetic, and light on his feet. When he sees us enter, he stops what he's doing and bounds up like a golden retriever, mopping the sweat off his ruddy face.

"Good morning, everybody."

Lenny throws me a sideways look that embodies her trademark "What the fuck?"

He's only a few years older than us — probably a year older than Eli — with closely cropped strawberry-blond hair and a pale, freckly complexion. When he smiles, it stretches so wide it looks as if it hurts.

"I'm Lieutenant Seamus Duffy. I'll be overseeing your training."

I lift an eyebrow at his use of the word "overseeing." Eli didn't oversee; he commanded.

"Just until Eli comes back, right?" blurts Lenny.

Seamus gives a slight nod, and Lenny and I exchange a look. The lieutenant doesn't think Eli will be coming back.

"Lieutenant Parker tells me you've already moved on to sparring?"

I nod, feeling the hurt sting my insides. Eli had time to give Seamus a lesson plan, but he didn't bother to tell me he'd been deployed on a death mission.

"Well, that's fantastic. But I'd like to start today with some work on the pads and ease into sparring to get a feel for your capabilities."

Lenny scoffs audibly, and Bear and Blaze exchange an irritated look. Seamus pretends not to notice. He claps his hands together and grins. "All right! Let's go!"

We each grab a pad from a stack in the corner and pair off. I join Kindra and Lenny because Seamus doesn't strike me as the hands-on type of instructor.

He starts us with an easy warm-up of straight punches and a few kicks, which sucks. Today of all days, I could use the distraction of a tough workout.

Seamus moves around the room, praising us for our good technique. My annoyance with him is mounting by the second. Eli never praised us, which bothered me at first, but Seamus sounds like a doting parent. It's tough to concentrate and even harder to take myself seriously when he's being all sunshine-and-rainbows.

Once we're warmed up, he moves us into a drill that Eli never did, where we go down the line one at a time and throw a different combative at everyone holding a pad. Bear almost sends me flying across the room with his side kick, and Seamus looks impressed. I want to hate him, but he seems like a nice guy.

After an hour, he finally lets us split into groups to spar. Kindra is looking pale and feverish, and Seamus quietly tells her to sit out.

I am stunned. Eli never would have let Kindra sit out — not until she passed out.

I find it's much easier to flip Lenny than Eli — almost too easy. She falls forward every time I buck my hips and hits the mat with a resounding *smack* when I flip her over.

After the fifth time, she swears loudly and rubs her shoulder. Her face is almost the same color as her hair, and I can tell she's getting irritated. She's only managed to flip me twice — probably because she's used to working with Kindra, who's roughly the size of a leprechaun.

Her outburst attracts the attention of Seamus, who wanders over to watch us take it from the top. Lenny hasn't quite mastered the takedown that Eli used on me, and I land awkwardly on my shoulder.

Suddenly she's hovered over me, her fist poised to strike. I throw out my forearm to stop her punch and send her flying forward onto her hands. When her weight shifts, I throw her off-balance, and with one quick blitz, our roles are reversed. I throw a slow strike so she has time to block it, but my fist still glances off her jaw.

Lenny lets out an irritated huff, but Seamus is clapping, a ridiculous grin stretching across his face.

"Wow. I'm very impressed. Cadet Riley, is it?"

"Yeah," I pant, getting to my feet and helping Lenny up.

"That was very good. Has Lieutenant Parker seen you do this?"

"Yeah."

Seamus looks puzzled. "Well, his progress report shows you haven't yet mastered that maneuver, but from what I can see, I have to disagree."

I feel as if I should say something to defend Eli, but then I remember that he's been lying to me from the beginning.

"I'll mark this off for you so you can advance to the next level," he says. "That was very well done."

Lenny and I just stare at him, a little taken aback by his praise.

"Why don't you work with Cadet Horwitz on her technique, and then we can see about you moving up?"

I nod, feeling vindicated. But something doesn't feel right. Why would Eli keep me from advancing on purpose? He may be a liar, but nobody can say he doesn't take his job seriously.

Before I can process this fully, I'm distracted by a rush of noise out in the tunnel. It sounds like the normal commotion before mealtimes, but it's the middle of the morning.

Seamus frowns and crosses to the door. Without thinking, we follow him out into the tunnel, where a crowd has formed near the megalift. It's mostly Recon people, but there's an angry mob of ExCon and Waste Management guys pouring out of the lift.

Their shouts echo off the walls, and it's tough to make out what they're saying. I catch a few words here and there — words like "traitors" and "terrorists" — and the crowds are merging. I see accusatory fingers stabbing chests, and a few men throw out their forearms to hold their violent companions back.

Then a fist shoots out. The crowd roars, and a few more men start throwing punches. They're sloppy, but the men are strong and full of rage.

In a matter of seconds, the angry mob has escalated into a full-out brawl. Guys in orange grab men in gray, and I see a Waste Management guy tackle a Recon officer to the ground.

Seamus's cheery face drains of color. He jumps into the crowd to pull the closest Recon man away from the mob, but he just gets swept along with the crowd. I stare transfixed, unable to believe that the animosity at breakfast has actually led to violence.

I'm shaken out of my trance when an ExCon man barrels into a shrimpy new recruit I've never spoken to. I see a familiar look in the cadet's eyes — that moment of freeze you experience when you're caught in a fight and your body doesn't remember how to respond.

He goes down on the ground as his companions stare in horror. I wait a beat for his training to kick in — for him to do something — but clearly he wasn't subjected to Eli Parker's school of hard knocks.

Bear nudges my arm. "Uh, should we . . ."

I give a shaky nod, but part of me is terrified. These men might not have any combat training, but they're strong.

I grit my teeth. "Let's go."

"Uh-uh," says Lenny. "No freaking way."

But I'm not listening. I can't just stand here and do nothing — even if this kid is a moron. Bear and Blaze and I jump in between the flying elbows and jostling shoulders, and I grab the ExCon man around the neck to yank him off the recruit. I get him in the side of the face with my left hook and hear a satisfying groan as I shove him aside.

The recruit is doubled over in pain, but he rolls to his feet and gets the hell out of the way. At least his direct command taught him that.

Up ahead, Bear and Blaze are mowing down men in orange and green and trying to avoid their clumsy punches. I follow in behind them, delivering quick kicks and elbows to the men they yank off Recon guys.

It's a little easier than I expected. The other tier-three workers are strong, but their hits are slow and uncoordinated.

Then I hear a shrill whistle from the megalift. When I look over, there are a dozen controllers streaming out into the tunnel, shocking whomever they can reach with their nightsticks. They don't care who started the fight or why — they're taking everybody down.

Suddenly, I hear Eli's voice in my head telling me to get the hell out of here, and for once, I listen. I don't need to give Control any reason to arrest me again.

I look around for Bear and Blaze and see Bear on the ground. He's buried under two ExCon guys, and I feel a surge of panic. One man is holding him down while the other punches. Bear's face is screwed up in pain.

Not thinking about the controllers or the fact that I'm in way over my head, I launch myself at the two men. I elbow one in the side of the head as hard as I can and grab the other one around the neck the way Eli taught me: by expanding my lungs to tighten the choke. As I crush his windpipe, he panics and tries to buck me off him.

Then everything becomes a blur. I see Bear on the ground, bloody but conscious, and two controllers elbowing their way through the crowd.

I hit the ground — hard — and my already-sore shoulder throbs in protest. The man rolls over on me, and I let out an involuntary yelp. A fist comes out of nowhere and connects with the side of my body. This is nothing like the hits I took in the Institute. This is a fully grown man delivering a strike to the kidney.

I know I should use the move I just learned to flip the man over, but his forearm is crushing my face, and I can barely tell which way is up. Everything is slow and blurry.

Then, from under the man's armpit, I see a blur of blond hair and pale, milky skin. A tiny, sharp elbow flies out, and the man on top of me lets out a guttural yell.

He kind of goes limp, and I use all my remaining strength to shove him off me.

When his weight lifts, I know I wasn't hallucinating. Kindra is standing over the man, looking pissed. He's got an elbow-shaped bruise already forming on the side of his face, and she throws out her foot to connect with his groin.

I jump to my feet, smiling through the gripping pain. She returns my grin with a satisfied nod, and Bear gets slowly to his feet. He looks terrible. His nose is already swelling and dripping blood all over the place.

With the crowd blocking the megalift and Recon people pouring out of the training center, our escape options are limited. Luckily, the controllers are busy with someone else. When the crowd shifts, my jaw drops. They're struggling to restrain Blaze, who's going ballistic on a huge ExCon guy. His coppery hair is sticking up all over the place, and his lanky arms are windmilling in every direction.

Seamus bumps past me, muttering an angry stream of curses. "Adams!" he yells. "What the hell are you doing?"

Blaze barely registers Seamus's voice. I think he's forgotten that we have a new instructor altogether.

The controllers look irritated and exhausted from holding Blaze back. Finally, one of them draws an electric nightstick and zaps him. He yells, and his long body collapses in a heavy convulsion. I'm pretty sure I see sparks fly from his crazy hair.

Seamus is on a rampage, and I can't tell if he's angry with Blaze or angry with the controllers. Either way, it seems like a good time to escape, so the three of us elbow past the crowd toward the east tunnel, grabbing a shell-shocked Lenny on the way.

My compartment is the closest, so we take cover in there.

When I see Bear's face in the sickly florescent light of my compartment, reality punches me in the gut. His nose looks broken — it's gushing blood all over my carpet — and he's going to have one hell of a black eye.

Now jumping into that crowd seems like a really stupid idea. The ExCon and Waste Management guys may not have been trained, but we aren't full-on Recon yet.

I dig an ice pack out of my mini fridge and apply it to Bear's face. He groans, which only confirms my suspicions that his nose is broken. And judging by the way he's holding his side, I would guess he has a few broken ribs, as well.

He needs to go to the medical ward, but it's too risky. Controllers or no controllers, the compound isn't safe for Recon right now.

"Thanks for jumping in there," he mumbles, wincing when he tries to smile.

I laugh at his strange expression. "I would have been in trouble if Kindra hadn't helped me." I turn to look at her, and she slips us a shy smile. "Thanks for that."

She shrugs as if it's no big deal, but I can tell it's a huge deal to her.

"I can't believe they're trying to pin this all on us," Lenny growls. "People can't actually think we'd bomb the compound."

"Apparently they do," says Bear in a muffled voice.

"ExCon and Waste Management are a bunch of morons," she snaps. "How can they not see that the board is just looking for a scapegoat?"

"They probably just don't want to get lumped in with Recon," I say. "That's why they're doing this. They don't want the blame shifting on them."

We fall silent and spend the next several hours on the floor of my compartment. The noise in the tunnel doesn't die down until after lunch, and Control institutes a curfew until sixteen hundred. Nobody is supposed to be roaming the tunnels, and for the first time since I can remember, I actually feel trapped — trapped in this room, trapped in the compound, and trapped by the malware on my interface. I've shoved it under my pillow, but I know Constance can probably still hear everything we're saying.

When the curfew lifts, we head for the megalift in a tight group, quiet and subdued after the violent attack. Bear's steady enough to make it up to the medical ward on his own, but we'll be safer moving as a pack. Even healthy Bear couldn't hold his own against a couple of decent-sized ExCon guys.

There's a long line in the tunnel to reach reception — mostly Recon people sporting similar injuries. There are a few workers from other sections in the mix, but they know they're too outnumbered to pick a fight up here and live.

It's nearly twenty hundred by the time Bear is ushered into a blindingly bright exam room. Kindra and Lenny leave to grab dinner before the canteen closes, but I stay with Bear.

Part of me is hoping to see Sawyer again, and part of me is just worried about him. I don't know why I feel protective of a guy who's literally twice my size, but Bear has always seemed too gentle for Recon.

Finally, an exhausted-looking doctor shuffles in, wearing a wrinkled lab coat. His mouth is sagging in a permanent scowl, and his hair is sticking up in all directions.

He doesn't say a word. He just glances at the notes on his interface and stabs a finger into Bear's ribs. When Bear winces, the doctor's mouth tightens into a hard line of annoyance. He gives Bear a disapproving look, makes a note in the air for his interface to record, and leaves.

As soon as he disappears, an army of interns in red scrubs descend upon Bear to clean up his bloody face and tape his nose straight. I lean back in the little plastic chair next to the door and watch the other interns jog from room to room pushing carts of supplies. I'm so tired I could almost fall asleep right here.

Just when I'm about to drift off, I hear the frantic scuffle of feet and the rattle of a gurney.

The door is open, and I stick my head out in time to see four nurses flitting around a limp body, rolling down the tunnel at breakneck speed.

It's the gray uniform that catches my eye — and something familiar about the dark head of hair.

I don't even realize I'm standing until Bear asks me a question. I mutter an excuse and tear down the tunnel after the gurney, horror spilling into my chest. Nobody tries to stop me, but it wouldn't matter if they did. I'm not paying attention to anything except that gurney.

One of the nurses moves to the side, and I see a dirty, sunburned face I recognize. It's covered in blood and dust from the Fringe, but there's no mistaking Eli.

twenty-seven

Eli

The second I become conscious, all I feel is the pain.

My left arm is on fire, and no one will help me. My throat is so raw and scratchy that it feels as though it might tear if I try to talk.

I feel horrible, though I can't remember why.

Slowly, I peel my eyes open and squint at the bright florescent light overhead. I can't be dead, because I know hell isn't this well-lit. It isn't this cold, either.

I glance down at my body. It looks too clean — pink and perfect, as though they've forcibly scrubbed away the Fringe.

Someone has draped a thin cotton blanket over me, and I'm pretty sure I'm wearing one of those horrible assless hospital gowns. There are tubes everywhere, and someone has cocooned my throbbing arm in soft white bandages.

I wiggle my toes, and I feel them lift the blanket. Thank god those still work.

I turn my head. A Korean girl with big glasses and red scrubs has noticed I'm awake. She's jogging down the long tunnel toward me, looking anxious. I remember she's Harper's friend — the one I met before.

Harper. I have a vague memory of seeing her recently, but she was upside down, and she looked scared. Harper is never scared.

Suddenly the girl stops, and a man in a crisp beige uniform steps in front of my door. He's speaking in a low voice and keeping his body between me and the girl. She's arguing with him, but her eyes are darting around nervously — as though talking back to her superiors isn't something she does on a regular basis. She's scared, but I can tell she's brave.

The pain in my arm is getting worse, and I try to follow the clear plastic tube in my flesh to its source. They better be giving me the good stuff for the pain. Whatever it is, it's wearing off.

I stare at the deceptively neat bandage and wonder what kind of nasty injury it's hiding.

The explosion.

All at once, it starts coming back to me. Miles and I were ambushed just outside the cleared zone, but the drifters didn't just have guns this time; they had explosives. There were only two of us, and we didn't stand a chance.

How did I make it back to the compound? There's no way I walked back.

Miles. I don't remember what happened after the explosion, so I don't know if he made it out alive.

I fumble around on the bed, looking for the call button. I need a nurse or a med intern or someone to tell me what happened. The girl in the glasses has disappeared.

"Oh, relax," says a voice from the door.

I jerk my head up and see Remy standing just inside the room.

"They can't come back in here until I give the all-clear."

"What?"

He sighs. "I need to be sure you don't pose a threat to internal security, Parker."

"Why would you say that? What happened out there?"

He braids his fingers in front of him and looks down at me with a stern expression. "I was hoping you could tell me."

"Where's Miles?" I ask. "Did he make it back?"

Something skirts across Remy's face, and the corner of his mouth quirks.

Is that how this guy smiles? What a creep.

"Yes. Private Hackman got you both back to the compound safely . . . and six days ahead of schedule, I might add. You did not complete your assignment."

"We were ambushed," I say, feeling the anger bubble up to the surface. "Sorry if that threw things a little off schedule."

"So Hackman says." The inflection he's using is one of interest, not alarm, which makes me think he doesn't believe us.

"Have any drifters broken through the perimeter?" I ask.

"Lieutenant, I'm the one asking questions here. Tell me, did you see anything out of the ordinary before you got past the cleared zone?"

"No."

"So you and Hackman made it past the mines, and then . . ."

I sigh in exasperation. "We were patrolling the perimeter around the cleared zone. It was . . . quiet. I should have known it was too quiet. We didn't find any squatters in the first town we checked.

"There's a few rusted-out old cars about half a mile outside the mines. We took it slow, but when we got close enough, the drifters ambushed us. There was an explosion, and —" I break off because I can't remember what happened next.

"What did they look like?"

I shrug, my breath coming faster with the memory of the attack. "They were all men. Thirties and forties. Dirty. I don't know."

"Did they look healthy?"

I stare at him, confused. "I didn't get a great look."

Remy looks irritated for a moment but then smirks. "Well,

that is a convenient story. Can I trust you won't go spreading it around to your little Recon friends?"

"*What?*" At first, I'm not sure what the point of this inter-rogation is if he's just going to disregard everything I've said, but then I realize Remy wants to make sure I don't tell anyone within the compound that the drifters are mobilizing against us.

"Lieutenant, I don't care if you and Hackman skipped out on your assignment or if you really were ambushed by a gang of drifters," says Remy in his cool, clipped voice. "I'm simply here to ensure you are fit to be integrated back into the compound. I cannot release you until I can be sure you do not pose a threat to internal security."

I let out an angry stream of air from between my teeth and slump back. "No, sir," I mutter. "I am not a threat to internal security."

He doesn't look convinced. "And what will you tell people when they ask why you returned from your mission early?"

"What would you like me to tell them, *sir?*" I ask, fitting as much contempt into the last syllable as I dare. I'm starting to sound like Harper, I realize, and the thought makes me want to smile.

"I'm sure you'll think of something that fits within the publi-cized duties of Recon operatives."

"I could tell them an air quality gauge exploded . . . and burned my arm."

Remy smiles humorlessly. "Do whatever works. Just make it convincing."

He stands to leave but turns back to me before reaching the door. "And, Lieutenant, it's in your best interest to keep whatever you *think* happened under wraps. If anyone should start asking questions, I'll be back to continue this conversation. But it won't be as friendly, and it won't end well for you."

"Understood, sir," I growl.

He leaves, and I can finally breathe again. He's gone for less than five seconds before Sawyer flies in, looking harried.

"I'm sorry," she says quietly. "I couldn't get in here to up your pain meds until he cleared you. They were worried you might regain consciousness and start talking before you were debriefed."

"It's okay."

I watch her fumbling with the plastic box by the bed and notice how stressed out she seems.

"You're Harper's friend . . . Sawyer, right?"

Sawyer bobs her head. "She was here, you know." A small smile works its way across her face. "She saw them bring you in. She tried to come see you, but they weren't letting non-medical personnel in."

Something warm and wonderful spreads through my chest when I hear that Harper wanted to see me. "Where is she now?"

Sawyer grins, and I see a spark of mischief that makes me understand why she and Harper are friends.

"She's hanging out in my compartment. I said I'd message her when you could have visitors. I didn't think she should be walking around the compound alone right now . . . especially in the lower levels."

This remark, combined with Sawyer's jumpiness, strikes me as odd. "Why?"

"There's been a riot. Recon operatives have gone AWOL, and people think they're breaking off from the compound."

I stare at the ceiling, trying to process this information. I leave for one day, and everything goes to hell.

"Are you serious?"

"Yeah. One of your cadets got banged up pretty bad. Harper

was here with him when she saw you."

I let out a frustrated groan and bang the back of my head on my flat, uncomfortable pillow. "If Harper came with him, that means she was probably involved, too."

Sawyer nods, and I can tell that nothing about Harper would surprise her. They must have been good friends before Bid Day.

Sawyer leaves to message her, and I lie back to rest my eyes. I'm surprised how tired I am.

I doze off for a minute, and when I wake up, I can feel someone sitting on the bed by my knees. I almost don't want to open my eyes and have my hopes shattered, but I peel them open anyway.

Harper materializes in front of me like a dream. Her uniform is wrinkled, her knuckles are cracked and bloody, and pieces of hair are falling out of her disheveled ponytail. She looks exhausted.

In my foggy state, I smile before I can stop myself, and her face relaxes in relief. She smiles back, but it's strained.

"What are you doing here?" I ask.

"I saw them bring you in. I had to see if you were all right."

Her voice sounds anxious and oddly distant. Even though she's sitting right beside me, she's almost leaning away. I push that thought aside. "I'm fine. Miles brought me back."

"Is he okay?"

I sigh. "I think so. I haven't seen him, though. They just finished debriefing me."

"Who?" Her sharp, panicked tone surprises me, and I wonder if I dare tell her. It will only throw fuel on the Harper conspiracy fire, but I decide not telling her just means she'll find out herself.

"Remy Chaplin, Undersecretary of Reconnaissance," I say in a low voice.

She nods as if she isn't surprised at all. Then she glances around to make sure we aren't being watched and scoots closer on the bed. I'm distracted by the feeling of her leg pressing against mine through the blanket, but I know she's not even paying attention. "Eli . . . what *happened* out there?"

"We were ambushed," I say. "By about a dozen drifters with explosives. They were waiting for us."

Her eyes widen. She understands the significance of this. If gangs of drifters are mobilizing, it's only a matter of time before they breach the cleared zone.

"How long will you be in here?" she asks. Her voice is hollow again.

I shrug. "Probably a week. It's how long they usually give us to recoup before resuming our normal duties. They have to treat me for possible radiation poisoning, but I wasn't even in an orange zone."

This seems to distress her more than anything, and I can tell that there's something else going on besides the riots.

"Don't worry," I say lightly. "I'll still be able to kick your ass when I get back to training."

"That's not what I was worried about. Anyway, I'm not sure you could. Seamus said my ground defense looks good, so . . ."

"What?" I snap, taken aback.

"He passed me on to the next level. I'll get to spar with some of the privates who are out of training and —"

"Harper, *no*." I pull my hand down over my face and squeeze the bridge of my nose, completely failing to hide how worried I am. She has no clue what this means, and it's my fault that it happened. I knew Seamus, the Recon kiss-ass, was taking over their training. I should have warned her.

"What?" she asks finally. There's anger burning low in her

voice, and I can tell I've unleashed something bigger. "Shouldn't you be happy for me? You're the one who taught me everything."

"No," I growl. "Harper, you should have passed that test last week, and you *would have* with any other instructor. Your ground defense was fine."

"So, what? You didn't pass me even though I was good?"

I glance out into the tunnel to make sure we don't have an audience. "*Yes*, okay."

For a moment, Harper looks furious, then confused. "Why?"

"As soon as you pass that test, you're considered trained in the bare necessities of combat. You've had basic weapons training, instruction on Recon strategy, and hand-to-hand combat. As soon as you pass to the next level, Jayden can legally deploy you."

She looks stunned. "What? I haven't even been here three months. I get a full year before —"

"Not in times of crisis. If the board determines there is a real threat, they can deploy more Recon units. We're stretched thin as it is after the last two recruit classes. They were also sent out ahead of their deploy date. You're going to be next."

Harper's face drains of color. For the first time since I've known her, she's completely speechless.

"I'm sorry," I say. "I should have told you to mess up on purpose until I got back. Why do you think I've been keeping Jayden at arm's length? She's been sniffing around, but she was so preoccupied by how bad everyone else was that she ignored you."

Harper takes a shaky breath. "Jayden hasn't been ignoring me." She glances around quickly. "She called me to her office this morning. Eli . . . she's part of Constance."

"*What?*"

Harper rolls on, not pausing for breath. "She showed me the recording of us . . . in your room." Her voice gets so quiet I have to lean in to hear. "Constance is watching me now, too."

I slam my head back, trying not to think about Jayden watching and re-watching me kissing Harper. That evening fills me with shame. I lost control. I took advantage of Harper's plan and savored every second of it.

But if Jayden is part of Constance, we're in more danger than I thought.

"Why have they been watching?" I ask. "They didn't believe your alibi?"

She shakes her head slowly, and I realize it has to be worse than that. "I started asking too many questions, and they tried to frame me for Taylor's death to get me out of the way. And since you gave me an alibi, they think you know, too. Jayden knew you were walking into an ambush. They're trying to get rid of you . . . and me."

None of what Harper is saying makes sense. My brain is working in fits and starts, trying to comprehend what she's telling me. "Jayden is in Constance?"

"*Yes*," she breathes in exasperation.

"Constance . . . wait, Constance was behind the bombing?"

Harper swallows and nods.

"They killed Taylor just to get rid of you?"

Harper shakes her head. "She said he was feeling guilty about recruiting more Recon when the cadets kept dying. And he was against Constance subsidizing bids. They put the sixty thousand in Recon's account so Jayden could make sure I ended up in Recon. Taylor was going to make a scene. He had to go."

I don't believe it. My brain is running through everything that happened the night of the bombing. There were just too many variables for Harper to have been purposely placed in the line of fire.

"How would Constance know you were going to break into Taylor's office?"

"Jayden said she knew I would eventually. She said something that day in training to provoke me. They were tracking my interface, and she tipped off Paxton Dellwood so I'd be caught.

"But then you gave me an alibi, and Celdon said I didn't do it. Constance can only operate outside the law if no one gets suspicious."

"Why would Jayden tell you all of this?"

"She wanted to scare me . . . show me what happens to people who try to fight Constance." Harper takes a short, distressed little breath. "She threatened to kill Celdon to keep me quiet."

All my muscles tighten under the blankets. I want to throttle Jayden for threatening Harper.

When Harper's eyes widen, I realize I'm wearing the face of a killer.

"Say something," she whispers.

"I can't believe Jayden's been playing me all these years," I say finally.

Then her gray eyes turn stormy — not the reaction I expected. "Yeah, I know the feeling," she says sharply.

After everything she just told me, I can't believe she's angry that I purposely held her back in training.

"Harper —"

"Jayden told me everything, Eli," she snaps. "You *lied* to me."

My stomach clenches, and she scoffs at my expression.

"Don't act like you don't know." Harper looks up at the ceiling. "She told me you were the one who pursued me for Recon."

I close my eyes, and I hear Harper drag in a shaky breath, as though my reaction confirmed everything she hoped wasn't true.

"Harper, I didn't know you," I say slowly. "If I had —"

"What? You wouldn't have recruited me?"

When I open my eyes, I'm startled to see that hers are glistening with tears. I've never seen Harper cry — not even in training. Part of me thought I'd never see it. It's like catching a comet that only comes around once in a lifetime.

I unstick my throat with some effort, wondering how much I dare say to her.

My thoughts are loud. *No, I wouldn't have. I would never choose this life for you, and I hate myself for it.*

But I know telling her those things won't make deployment any easier. And now that Jayden has Harper in her crosshairs, part of me thinks it would be better if she had someone to hate — some angry inertia to keep her going.

But my mouth is moving of its own accord, completely abandoning my brain.

"Harper, if I knew you the way I do now, I would have never pursued you for Recon." I take a deep breath. "Not that it would have done any good."

She nods and tries to pull herself together. "I know. I probably would have ended up here anyway."

By her tone, I can tell that rationalizing it doesn't make what I did any less despicable. I nod slowly, unsure if agreeing with her will make things better or worse. "If Constance wanted you in Recon, there would have been no fighting it. I don't know what they're up to, but clearly you are part of their plan."

She draws in another breath, and I can tell that whatever she's going to say next is costing her everything. "I just wish you wouldn't have lied to me . . . I *trusted* you."

Those last three words are like a knife in my chest.

"I'm sorry," I say. My apology feels so inadequate. She'll probably never trust me again.

But then she surprises me. "I'm sorry, too," she sighs. "It's my fault she deployed you early. She was hoping you'd be killed."

"It's not your fault. Jayden decided to punish me the second I lied to her."

We both fall silent, and I wonder how much damage has been done. She did come to visit me, but that doesn't mean she cares about me. Maybe she just feels guilty. There's a lot of that going around.

"Hey," I whisper. "Whatever happens next, promise me you'll be careful."

She lets out a watery laugh. "You mean don't go snooping around sealed Bid Day records? I think that ship has sailed."

"No. You're smarter than they are. You'll be all right."

She nods, but the distant look in her eyes tells me she doesn't believe it. Hell, I don't even believe it. What a mess we've made.

"I'm sorry," I say. "For everything."

She nods, and I'm actually taken aback by how calm she seems.

"I swear . . . that's the only lie I ever told you. You can trust me."

Harper purses her lips together. "I'm not really sure I trust anyone anymore. But I'm okay." Her eyes focus on mine, and they're dead serious. "They aren't going to get me."

That knocks me on my ass. Suddenly I understand the real reason I was so drawn to Harper before I even knew her: She reminds me of me, but she's all the things I wish I *could* be.

She's brave and honest. She doesn't take any shit from people. She doesn't just accept the system. Hell, Harper thinks she can do anything.

I like her a lot, but I can't think about that right now. There's a gun pointed at both our heads. Constance is going to do everything to make sure we die when we step out into the Fringe.

Once Harper leaves, exhaustion sets in. Whatever pain medication they gave me seems to be doing the trick, and I let myself relax until the burning in my arm ebbs away.

My last thought is part nightmare. I'm standing out on the Fringe. The oppressive heat hangs over me like a wool blanket. The miles of nothing press in from every direction, sucking the energy right out of me.

Then the heat haze clears, and I see a dozen drifters looming in the distance. There's an explosion too close, and the wave of heat knocks me backward.

I wait for the searing pain, but when I open my eyes, I'm all in one piece — conscious, alert, and unharmed.

Where Miles should be lying, I see a fan of dark hair spreading over the cracked earth like spilled oil. Instead of me, Harper has caught the brunt of the explosion. She's lying in the dirt, cradling her arm to her chest. She's crying in agony, her arm and stomach covered in angry red burns.

Then the suffocating wave of panic hits me. Harper is going to die.

twenty-eight

Harper

The next few days of training are a complete blur. I was right in thinking that Seamus would be pissed when we returned. He was mad that we ditched the rest of the day's training, but he was even angrier that we'd all been involved in the riot.

I really don't care. Seamus knew what he was doing when he passed me on to the next level. He could have held out like Eli, but he doesn't care enough to fight the system. It gives me a whole new appreciation for Eli's hardball training tactics.

Seamus's nice-guy persona is permanently tarnished after the riots. The tides shifting against Recon in the compound have made him short-tempered and irritable, and I realize his encouragement and smiles only hold out when everything is fine.

When things go to shit, he gets a temper, whereas Eli seems to thrive on things going to shit. If anything, he was calmer in the medical ward with third-degree burns on his arm and chest, knowing that the drifters were encroaching on the compound and that Constance was trying to have him killed.

To escape Seamus, I ask him if I can spend more time in the shooting range. He doesn't put up a fight.

I don't want to admit it, but I'm counting down the days until Eli returns to normal duty. I'd planned to have it out with him when he woke up, but seeing him in that hospital bed made it impossible to keep my emotions in check. When he returns at full strength, I'm going to confront him about his lie.

Plus, angry or not, I know I would feel more at ease with him around. Ever since my talk with Jayden, I've barely slept. When I do, I have nightmares about Eli being sent out into the Fringe or Constance ambushing me in the lower tunnels. Then they shove me into a cage and let me starve.

After six days, my anxiety has reached its peak. I want to go work off my aggression in the training center, but my shoulder is sore after spending the entire day on the simulation course. I overdid it trying to hit every target, and I know I'll have a rifle-shaped bruise on my shoulder from the kickback.

Around twenty-one hundred, there's an urgent knock at my door. My body tenses automatically.

I jump to my feet, heart pounding. For once, I'm not thinking about Constance. Eli should have been discharged today, and it might be him coming to visit.

I peer through the peephole, and my heart sinks. It's Celdon.

Yanking the door open, my jaw drops as I meet his gaze.

Celdon doesn't look like Celdon.

He's pale and sweaty with a huge purple shiner on his left eye, and his hair is matted on one side. His white jacket is dirty and disheveled, as though it hasn't been cleaned in days. He's hunched to one side, clutching his ribs, but it's his shell-shocked expression that makes my blood run cold.

"What happened to you?" I choke.

"Not here," he says in a hoarse voice. His eyes dart down the tunnel. "We can't talk here."

"Okay. Your place, then."

But he just shakes his head and starts walking down the tunnel. I don't think. I just follow him.

"Do you have your interface on you?" he asks, jerking his head back to look behind us.

"N-no. Why?" That crazy look in his eyes is making me panic.

"They're watching you," he whispers. "They're watching you everywhere."

"Who?" I ask, praying he doesn't say it.

"Constance."

My heart seizes. "I know."

Celdon lurches suddenly, fixing me with a cold look that's so unlike him. "You *know?*"

I give a small nod, and he lengthens his stride so that I practically have to jog to keep up. He doesn't stop until we reach the Underground platform. There are no trains coming or going, but the ground is shaking from the heavy bass of Neverland.

Celdon stops and stares at the tunnel as though he might take off running until he reaches another compound.

But then he deflates — just slumps against the wall and sinks down onto the dirty tile.

"They got me, Harper. There was nothing I could do."

He splays his white fingers out on his filthy knees, and his knuckles lighten as he squeezes.

"They came to Systems and arrested me. It was two controllers, but I knew who was behind it. At first I thought this was because I hacked into your records, but they didn't even ask me about that. They barely asked me anything."

The dread seeps into my stomach. "What did they ask you?"

He looks away and waits a beat before he answers. "They asked me about you."

Suddenly, I feel as though I'm going to be sick. My worst fear has come true.

"They took my interface and used it to message you. I didn't know what they were doing at first, but then I guessed. They knew all this stuff about you . . . creepy stuff. Stuff they would only know if they were watching you."

I put my head in my hands and try to breathe. That was why I couldn't identify the source of the malware. They'd sent it to me from Celdon's interface.

"Harper, they used my message to hack your interface so they could spy on you."

I nod. "How long did they have you there?"

"I don't know," he says quietly. "A week? I lost track of time."

I try to think back to the last time I saw Celdon. It was definitely more than a week ago. I'd been so worried about Eli and my own impending deployment that I hadn't even sought out Celdon at mealtimes.

"I'm sorry," I whisper.

"It's not your fault."

"They took you to get to me. It's completely my fault."

Celdon lets out a cold laugh and then winces. "I thought you would blame *me*."

"No. Of course I don't. I should have known this would happen."

"How could you know?"

"Constance found out I was looking into Bid Day," I say. "I was asking too many questions, and they tried to get rid of me."

"*What?*"

I take a shaky breath. Telling him puts him at risk, but he needs to know what happened. They already captured and tortured him. I can't let him walk around not knowing.

"They orchestrated Sullivan Taylor's murder."

Celdon stares at me dumbfounded, but I continue. I tell him everything Jayden told me about the night of the bombing and how she plans to take me and Eli off the map.

When I finish, his eyes are wide and vacant, but I know he's trying to process everything I just told him.

"You have to get out of here," he says. "Now."

I let out a strangled laugh. "Out? Out where? There's nowhere to go but out on the Fringe."

"No." His voice is low and deadly. "I mean to another compound."

I stare at him. His bloodshot eyes are wide, rimmed in dark circles. With his matted hair and stubble, he looks as though he escaped from the mental ward.

"You know my ticket is expired," I say slowly.

"So get another one."

I push this aside, irritated that he makes it sound so easy. "I wouldn't have enough if I saved for a year."

"I don't care how you get the money," he says in a desperate voice. "It doesn't matter. If you don't get out of here, you'll be dead the day you step out on the Fringe."

His stony expression tells me he's completely serious.

"No," I say. "I'm not going to leave you here. You know too much now. They'll kill you, too."

"I'm not staying here!" he says incredulously. "I'll get the money somehow."

"It's easier for you than for me."

"Are you kidding? Between the premium rations and the compartment, there's barely anything left over. But I'll whore myself out to get it. I don't give a shit. They aren't going to get me."

I drag in a shaky breath, turning the idea over in my mind. The idea of leaving the compound terrifies me, but Celdon is right.

If we leave, I'll probably have a short, hard life in ExCon. A few months ago, that was the worst-case scenario. But now, even living a few more years seems like my best option.

It's his shaking hands that finally do me in. I've never seen him this scared.

"Okay," I say finally. "We'll find a way to transfer. Just . . . please don't leave without me."

Celdon's hard, terrified expression softens slightly, and just then, it's as though we're back in the Institute, talking late into the night about getting bids from Systems. "I'd never do that."

Relief floods through me. I know we aren't in control, but hearing that Celdon is with me makes me feel a hundred times better.

We sit in silence for several minutes, both of us reluctant to return to our compartments and lie in the dark alone.

His breath comes in fits and starts, and I know he was probably kicked in the ribs until they cracked.

I feel so shitty that he was detained and hurt because of what I did. If I'd just accepted my bid like everybody else, Constance wouldn't be after me and Eli, and Celdon would still be his cocky, carefree self.

The boy in front of me isn't the same person I knew a few weeks ago. This Celdon is just a shell of my best friend.

Finally he gets up. At first, I think he's going to say something to me, but he just digs into his pocket and withdraws a florescent green pill bottle with a shaky hand. He pops a pill into his mouth and eyes me with an expression I've never seen before.

He won't say it, but I know he blames me for his imprisonment. Our friendship will survive it, but I can't ever take it back, and I can't keep him safe.

I sit alone on the dirty tile until my body temperature drops and my teeth start to chatter. When I finally get up and drag myself back to my compartment, I have this horrible sinking feeling that nobody I care about will ever be all right again.

twenty-nine

Harper

I'm so distracted the next day in training that it's affecting my fighting.

I block too slowly or not at all, and Lenny gets several good jabs in before Seamus huffs impatiently and sends us to lunch.

It's been a week since Eli returned from the Fringe, and I half expected him to be training us today. He isn't in the canteen, but Sawyer messaged me to say he'd been discharged that morning.

I feel irrationally nervous about his absence — thinking they must have sent him out to the Fringe again — but even Jayden couldn't send one of her best officers out into the field a week after his deployment without attracting attention.

Seamus puts me in the simulation room again after lunch, which makes the rest of the day go painfully slow.

When the bell rings to signal the end of the workday, I rush back to my compartment to shower. I want to get to dinner early to see if I can catch Eli.

I still don't know what I'm going to say to him. I'm furious that he lied to me, but we didn't even know each other then. It's not fair to hold it against him, but we need to talk — even if it's just to fight.

When I reach the canteen, a quick scan of the room tells me Eli isn't here. Celdon has also been conspicuously absent at mealtimes, and I wonder if he's even come up for air from Neverland since I last saw him.

I eat in silence with Lenny and Bear and wait over an empty plate until it's clear that Eli isn't going to show. I want to stay longer, but the tension and distrust have only escalated since the riot, and I know it isn't safe for Recon to hang out in the canteen.

As we walk to the megalift, I catch several angry stares from other tier-three workers. My fists clench automatically, and we head back to Recon as quickly as we can.

The others split off to go to their compartments, and when I finally reach my own, the first thing I notice is my interface blinking frantically from my nightstand. I should be wearing it to avoid rousing Constance's suspicion, but I can't stomach the idea of being watched twenty-four hours a day.

I grab it and pull up my message app. I hate the way my heart rate picks up when I see Eli's blank avatar. The message is short: *Meet me on the observation deck at 20:30.*

Without letting myself dwell on what Eli could want, I throw down my interface, yank my hair out of its ponytail, and brush it out around my shoulders. I don't really want to wear my uniform, but I don't have time to change.

I'm impatient as I ride the megalift all the way up to the top level of the compound. The lift doesn't even reach the observation deck; it can only be accessed from the emergency stairwell.

Drumming my fingers on the side of the lift, I marvel at Eli's genius meeting place. We can't talk freely in either one of our compartments, and nobody will be looking for us up here.

As I bound up the stairs, a horrible thought occurs to me: *What if it's a trap? What if Eli didn't send the message at all?*

Someone from Constance could be waiting to ambush me. I've been on edge all week, but looking for Eli distracted me. For all I know, they could have killed him already.

Now I'm in full panic mode. I should have told someone

where I was going.

I take the stairs slowly and drag in a deep breath. When I see the golden light spilling from the gap in the door, I square my shoulders, preparing to fight.

But when I emerge from the stairwell, I see Eli standing with his back to me, staring out at the open horizon. The setting sun is a blazing orange, burning itself out in the last few moments of daylight.

The observation deck is truly magnificent. It's the only place in the compound where you can find wide-open spaces. It's really just a glass box situated on top of the compound, designed to give the illusion of really being out there.

It's completely deserted this time of night. I think the emptiness unnerves some people. In the dark, it often feels as though you could walk right off the edge.

Eli turns when he hears me approaching. There's just enough light for me to catch the smile on his face when he sees me. If we were down below, I think he would hide it, but here it's easy to imagine it's just us.

I force myself to keep my expression neutral, but I'm relieved to see he looks better than he did in the medical ward. His sleeve hides his bandaged arm, he's standing upright, and his sunburn has faded to a golden tan.

"Hey," he calls. We're still too far apart to talk normally.

"Good to see you're alive," I say once I'm within earshot.

His grin goes a little lopsided, and I have a hard time controlling my breathing. "You could have seen for yourself if you'd visited me again."

That sends an odd mix of excitement and irritation through me. I don't know what to say, but the words come tumbling out before I can stop them. "Did you honestly think I would?"

His expression hardens, and in an instant, he drops the familiar Eli-the-asshole veil. "No. I guess not."

The silence hangs painfully between us, and I have the sudden urge to yell and cry at the same time.

"Did you think I would never find out?" I ask, my voice shaking a little.

"I really hoped you wouldn't."

His voice is dead serious, which causes something inside me to snap. "So you just planned to lie to me *forever*?"

"Yeah. I did, Harper. Okay? I'm not a saint. And what good would it have done to tell you? It wouldn't have changed anything."

I cross my arms over my chest, resisting the urge to hit him. "We wouldn't be having this conversation right now if you hadn't lied to me."

"Oh, that's bullshit. You would have *hated* me if you knew I was the one who recruited you. But guess what? That's my job. I have to help Jayden pick out the best kids that Recon can bid on. You're not the only one who's here because of me. If it wasn't you, it would have been someone else."

I wince. Up to this point, I'd only been focused on my anger. I hadn't considered the guilt that Eli must feel for his role in recruitment.

"And honestly, you have no idea what would have happened if I hadn't recruited you. You might have ended up in ExCon . . . or Jayden could have picked you anyway."

His voice is harsh, but when I meet his gaze, I see true remorse burning in Eli's eyes.

"I'm not perfect, Harper. But I didn't need you fighting me. You had to trust me so I could train you."

I can't argue with that, because he's right. I never would have listened to him if I'd known.

We've reached a stalemate, and I know I have to be the one to forgive. Eli has put up his guard, and he still thinks he made the best decision he could at the time. Maybe he's right.

"I understand why you lied," I say finally. "And it's not really fair for me to hold that against you. You were just . . . doing your job."

He nods and looks at me with wary eyes. "I'm sorry I got you involved in all of this, and I'm sorry I lied. I just didn't want you to hate me."

The sincerity in his voice is like a punch to the stomach. I avert my eyes, trying to control my pounding heart. The old Harper would have wanted to keep him swimming in guilt, but everything inside me is screaming to forgive him.

"I couldn't hate you," I whisper. "Believe me, I tried."

"Really?" His face brightens instantly, causing my stomach to do a little cartwheel.

"Yeah." I offer up a smile. "But I fucking hate Seamus."

Eli grins and shuffles his feet a little, which is strange for him. He's usually so confident. When he speaks next, I can tell it's taken every ounce of courage he has left. "I missed you, Harper."

Those four little words make me feel like I'm falling. My heart is beating frantically against my ribcage. I can't believe Eli is apologizing. I can't believe he said he *missed* me.

I want to act as though it's no big deal, but I can't control myself. He's completely thrown me for a loop and opened the floodgates to everything I'm feeling.

There's no one watching us — no reason for him to be pretending, if he was before. He can't possibly know the effect he has on me.

I take a step toward him, lifting my gaze. His eyes are startlingly blue, and his face is still illuminated by the dying light on the edges of the Fringe. The stars are just visible behind him. There's nobody else around, and he looks beautiful.

I'm close enough to see the faint lines around his eyes from a smile he doesn't show very often and the places where his cheeks are darker from sun and wind. His lips are tender from sunburn, falling into a slight, easy smile.

Deep in the pit of my stomach, I have an undeniable urge to do something reckless. I step forward until I'm dangerously close. I lift my chin and close my eyes.

The last thing I see is his amazed expression before I reach up and brush my lips against his. They're as warm and wonderful as I remember.

For the briefest moment, his lips curve around mine. I can smell him everywhere, and he makes a satisfied noise in the back of his throat.

I hear him drag in a deep breath, and then the reality hits me: I'm kissing Eli. We aren't putting on a show for Constance. I'm kissing him because I want to.

It feels insane and wonderful. I have no idea what's gotten into me. For a moment, I'm floating, and Eli is kissing me back.

But then the worst thing imaginable happens. Eli steps away from me, putting his hands on my shoulders. He pushes me away gently, and suddenly my lips are burning and exposed in the frigid compound air.

Horror floods through me. Eli opens his eyes and meets mine for a moment. He grimaces and then closes them again and shakes his head. He looks flustered and upset. "We can't."

I take a deep breath, struggling to find my voice. My heart starts beating erratically as panic sinks in. "God. I'm sorry," I choke. "I don't know why I did that."

The blood rushes to my face. What an idiot. Eli probably thinks I'm ridiculous now. *What the hell was I thinking?*

The horrible moment hangs there between us, and he drags a hand through his short hair and sighs. "No, it's all right," he says in a defeated voice. "I let this go too far. I shouldn't have let it happen."

He looks genuinely mad at himself, and for a second, I'm confused.

"We can't . . . *be* together, Riley. You're one of my cadets." He lowers his voice, and his next words are sincere and horrible. "I'm sorry."

I nod quickly, stung that he called me by my last name. He's scrambling to put up boundaries now. I can see it in his body language.

"I shouldn't have brought you up here." He gestures at the open deck, the vast expanse of nothingness around us. The stars are twinkling above us now, mocking me. "It probably gave you the wrong idea."

"Why did you call me up here?" I ask, willing my voice to sound normal. It doesn't. It sounds the way I feel — humiliated and on the verge of tears.

"I have to tell you something, and I wanted us to be able to talk without being overheard."

"Okay," I say with some effort.

"Can you look at me?" he asks gently.

I swallow. Leave it to Eli Parker to demand eye contact at a time like this. I meet his gaze, but the look in those eyes makes it too painful, so I focus instead on the bridge of his nose.

"I'm being sent out again," he says.

"What?"

"Soon."

Dread and panic flash through me. This is so wrong. "But you just got back! You were *attacked*! You're still injured."

Eli shakes his head. "That's exactly why Jayden is sending me out." He sighs. "She's trying to clean this up as quickly as possible."

Now there's a euphemism if I ever heard one.

"Won't that look suspicious?"

"Not at the rate she's deploying. The board has declared a state of emergency at the perimeter. Seamus goes out tomorrow, and Miles is being sent out again next week. We have to stop the drifters before they get too close to the compound."

I look out into the dark expanse of desert. It looks deadly still — peaceful, even. It's hard to imagine any humans alive out there.

"I'm sorry," I say. "This is all my fault."

He shakes his head. "Stop saying that. I wouldn't have let myself be dragged in if I didn't feel responsible. And if I didn't . . ." He stops and lets out an exasperated breath.

I don't even know what he was going to say.

"Please be careful," I whisper. "Don't give Constance the satisfaction of making this easy."

"Oh, I won't," he says bitterly. "But that's not what I came here to tell you, Riley."

"Stop calling me that!" I growl before I can stop myself. All the fear and disappointment have become too much for me. I hate that he makes me care despite everything and then rejects me.

Eli's gaze becomes serious. He doesn't address my outburst but speaks in a low, fast voice. "I came up here to tell you that Jayden's made a decision." He swallows, and I brace myself for the worst. "When I go out there, you're coming with me."

My stomach drops, and I feel suddenly dizzy. I'm sure he couldn't have said what I thought he said. "But . . . I haven't even . . ."

"In two weeks, you'll hit three months. You've already passed the minimum level of training, thanks to your pal *Seamus.*" He says Seamus's name as though it's left a bad taste in his mouth. "I'm sorry."

"But . . . she can't," I choke. "I was supposed to have a year!"

I'm torn between the urge to run and the urge to throw up. All my extremities have gone numb, and I feel as though I could blow over.

"I told you. Three months is the minimum when the compound's declared a state of emergency. She's rotating through her officers as fast as she can, but we're understaffed. She wants to get your entire class trained ahead of schedule, but you're the only one who's ready right now."

"But why is she sending me out with *you?*"

For a second, I swear he looks a little hurt, but that's probably wishful thinking.

"You have to go out with a higher-ranking officer for your first year," he says, a little too defensively.

"But why *you?*"

Now I'm sure Eli was hurt by the question, because his voice is angry when he answers. "I *requested* to go out for your first deployment, okay? If Constance is trying to get rid of you, I don't want you going out there with a moron like Seamus."

That tugs at my heart, but I push aside any temptation to see meaning in that gesture.

I still like Eli, but that doesn't mean I want to spend a week out on the Fringe with him in awkward silence. That's what we've got ahead of us now that I've screwed up everything by kissing him.

"Won't that make it easier for them to get rid of us?"

He shakes his head. "Jayden's going to send us into a hot zone no matter what. They're up to something, but we'll be ready."

I let out an angry little huff. "You couldn't have told me all of this before I — you know — *threw* myself at you?"

His expression turns sympathetic. "Hey, no. No, Harper. Listen. That wasn't your fault. It was mine. I let the lines get blurred between us. And I still would have requested you even if you had, you know . . . kissed me before I talked to Jayden."

I want to take solace in his words, but he looks incredibly uncomfortable, and all I can feel is blind panic. I can't even find it in my power to be annoyed that he won't own up to kissing me back.

I take a step toward the edge of the deck and lay my head against the cool glass. The stars are brightly visible in the inky, cloudless sky. The Fringe almost looks beautiful, but I know better.

In two weeks, I'll be out there. I'll be alone with Eli outside these glass walls. Constance will send us into danger, guaranteed. I'll be facing an army of rogue drifters, the radiation, and the endless stretch of desert wasteland.

In two weeks, I'll be as good as dead.

Author's Note

Thank you for reading *Recon*. I hope you enjoyed it. This was different from anything I've written before, due to the combination of research and speculation required to create Harper's and Eli's world within the compound.

I read up on closed ecosystems such as Biosphere 2, a three-acre research facility in the Arizona desert, to get a feel for the challenges the compound would face during its first three generations.

Biosphere 2 is a subject of controversy and fascination in the scientific community. In 1991, eight men and women went in as part of an experiment to see if humans could sustain themselves in a closed environment, growing their own food and recycling the air and water within the system. It was designed, in part, to test the application of such systems for space colonization.

The first experiment lasted for two years, during which time the subjects experienced starvation, problems with the ecosystem, and conflict.

Naturally, factions form when groups of humans are confined and isolated, which makes the compound's tier system very natural. With so many people living in close quarters, the threat of riots would be very real, making Control a necessary part of compound life. It also made sense to me that underground fights and a den of debauchery like Neverland would be natural byproducts of confinement and the strict caste system.

One of the big questions I faced when writing *Recon* was how big the compound would be. Obviously, the facility itself would need to be huge, but how many people would live inside?

Scientists don't seem to have reached a consensus on what a

minimum viable population would be for a self-sustaining society. Some estimate as few as 150 humans would allow for normal reproduction for generations, but I've seen estimates as high as 44,000. I knew I wanted the compound to be big enough that not everyone would know each other, which is why I wanted there to be at least a few thousand living in the compound.

With technological advancements, I believe a closed system will be possible in the future. My research led me to conclude that one of the biggest logistical issues would be growing enough food within the compound to sustain a population of thousands, which is why I provide a glimpse of the compound's advanced agricultural techniques and the types of food the characters eat. You'll notice Harper and the other cadets are always chowing down on very nutrient-dense foods like sweet potatoes, beets, and algae. Animal products like eggs are considered luxury items because the compound probably wouldn't raise very much livestock, though it's possible they would be eating cultured meat.

The compound's power source was another obvious question. Since the compound is located in the desert, fields of solar panels were a good source of renewable energy. However, the compound's energy demands would likely be met by a combination of solar energy, algae-based biofuel, and methane gas produced by compound waste. (The waste the compound's citizens generate would have to go somewhere, which is why Waste Management is its own industry.)

Finally, when creating technology for the characters to use, I wanted their devices to be more advanced versions of what we have today — not so futuristic that they would be impractical or difficult to imagine. This is why you still see souped-up versions of desktop computers and wearable devices. I don't believe keyboards or computer monitors will become completely redundant for work, but the interfaces as I imagined them also incorporate gesture-recognition technology.

I'm sure you still have unanswered questions about life inside the compound (and the events leading up to Death Storm), but more will be revealed as the series continues.

You can buy *Exposure* — book two of The Fringe — right now on Amazon. And don't forget to visit my website to stay up to date on the latest Fringe developments.

***

Did you enjoy this book? *Exposure* is now available on Amazon.

You can also connect with the author at www.tarahbenner.com or follow her on Twitter @tarahbenner.

Made in the USA
San Bernardino, CA
19 July 2015